Notes Without a Text and Other Writings

Roberto Bazlen

NOTES WITHOUT A TEXT
And Other Writings

Edited and with an introduction by Roberto Calasso

Translated from the Italian by Alex Andriesse

DALKEY ARCHIVE PRESS
McLean, IL / Dublin

Originally published in Italian by Adelphi Edizioni as *Scritti* in 1984.

© 1984 by Adelphi Edizioni, S.P.A. Milano
Introduction © 1984 by Roberto Calasso
Translation © 2019 by Alex Andriesse
First Dalkey Archive edition, 2019
All rights reserved.

Library of Congress Cataloging-in-Publication Data
LCCN: 2018027171

Dalkey Archive Press
McLean, IL / Dublin

Printed on permanent/durable acid-free paper.

www.dalkeyarchive.com

TABLE OF CONTENTS

Notes Without a Text and Other Writings

From an Empty Point

It is absurd to suppose that the point is empty.
—Aristotle, *Physics* iv, 214, a4

IT WOULD BE arbitrary, in speaking of Roberto Bazlen, to say what he thought; the fact remains that his presence forced others to think. Many phrases, judgments, aphorisms, and even lengthy arguments are attributable to him, including the ones published in this book. But nothing will authorize us to trace these data back to their premises: Bazlen's words were precise signs, and yet you could not tell where they were coming from or where they were going. Between an end and a beginning that were never articulated—and on which everything depended— assumptions rarely appeared: when it happened, it happened by accident. Bazlen silenced all the axioms; he disregarded the rules of the game of thought, and never claimed that he wanted to respect them. His rigor abided by other rules.

He was born in Habsburg Trieste, and he would always retain certain virtues of that mixed civilization's atmosphere. But it's best to close off the subject of Trieste right away, for the help it offers is misleading. Bazlen was a post-historical man, to whom no cultural framework or reconstruction of milieu would be able to do justice. As he got older, he became more and more the still-inexpert inhabitant of a world that, according to the logic of essences, would be the next world, once ours had gone extinct. Thanks to his powers of anticipation he perceived quite early, for example, the beginning of the Third World War. As he once recounted it: "1945, the war just ended. Via del Babuino empty, the shops shuttered. Out of a black car steps a dignified elderly couple who stop to gawk at the old furniture in the window of an antique shop."

Not only can a person be born, like Coleridge, a Platonist or an Aristotelian, he can also be born a Taoist—like Bazlen. Not that he ever said so outright: in his conversation, direct references could be completely lacking or at least very rare. But that's beside the point; Bazlen was a person extremely suspicious of his own arguments. In his notebooks, he wrote: "The worst enemy is the one who shares our arguments." What was Taoist in Bazlen was the immense agility, the fluidity—the "order in motion"—the covenant with emptiness, the casual circulation between opposites, and the attunement to germinal events. To achieve this, psychological knowledge, which Bazlen also possessed, is not enough; you also need the good sense of those who know how to lose their way, who know how to stir up further chaos and, the next day, can withdraw into an order made up of just a few elements, like the ones among which Bazlen lived in the second part of his life, both few and fitting, for elegance and the aesthetic sense perform an indispensable biological function: they keep appearances alive, they prevent the mirrors from shattering.

There are certain compulsory incompatibilities: the literary person doesn't want to hear about Eastern wisdom; the dissatisfied person chasing after Eastern wisdom doesn't want to hear about literature; the scholar doesn't want to hear about non-bookish experience; those who have non-bookish experience don't want to hear about philology; those who trust in the proofs of science don't trust in the proofs of mysticism; those who honor the mystical abhor experimental research; those who look to modernity see the barbarism of the past; those who look to antiquity see the degeneration of the present.

Corollaries: the literary person speaks in platitudes about last things; the reader of watered-down Eastern wisdom embraces every form of spiritual kitsch; the scholar doesn't know how to live; the man who knows how to live makes errors of syntax; the scientist explains the world by reducing it to an impoverished image; the enthusiast can't do math; the neophile doesn't see the antiquity of the present; the restorationist doesn't see the modernity of antiquity.

All of these incompatibilities are a fairly recent invention, one consequence among many of that fertile, schizoid principle that has governed us for some time now. Anyone who doesn't respect these maxims is suspect, an unserious character, an eclectic person, a man who sows confusion. Bazlen respected *none* of these incompatibilities—nor any others. In that sense, no one knew how to sow confusion like him.

Bazlen could be so centrifugal only because there was, at the center of him, an empty point that dominated everything. Seen from that point, the elements within him certainly didn't give the impression of being a jumble: if anything, they gave the impression of a form obtained each time for a moment, a form that expanded and contracted according to the breath in each of its parts. There was a composite totality, but, above all, there was the latent vigilance of that empty point. Today, it's easy to stipple yourself with all kinds of signs, the warehouses of culture have never been so well stocked and accessible; in the street we see people tattooed with letters they haven't even needed to read. Preparing for emptiness, on the other hand, is an abnormal occurrence—it always has been—and not only that: the modes of existence most prevalent at present teach us to forget even the possibility of emptiness. And this possibility was Bazlen's geometrical locus.

Friends and enemies alike have lamented Bazlen's continual elusion of his own work. But this variety of elusion was in fact

one of his most significant discoveries. By this I don't mean to
suggest that this book should be seen as belated reparations for
sin. There is no work here: only a bunch of notes organized by
others to form a book. Bazlen has been so successful at slipping
through the mesh, he has frustrated even this attempt to link
any writing to his name. In fact, I would say this is the most
persuasive reason for our having decided to publish these writings: the certainty that every effort to call this phantasmal work
the work of Roberto Bazlen will fail. The text of *Notes Without a
Text* is always elsewhere. I don't mean to suggest, either, that all
of this may be understood as the last appendix to the romantic
cult of the nonexistent opus, of the marvelous unfinished, of
life irreducible to the strictures of form. The role that romantic
nihilism played in Bazlen was much more radical, and allowed
him to corrode even this ultimate image of ambiguous salvation. Once this *destructio destructionis* was completed, there was
nothing left but to direct our gaze beyond the voluptuous tor-
tures of impossible literature.

In the ancient *querelle* between the man of the book and the
man of life, Bazlen represented the man of the book completely
immersed in life and the man of life completely immersed in
books. Among the numerous solutions offered him by the broken world, he had chosen this impossibility. "There is the age of
prologues, the age of the work, and the age of epilogues. (But
our moribund men were unable to invent epilogues.)" Bazlen
had indeed grown up among those who should have invented
epilogues and were not resigned to their lot; that was his terrain—the terrain of those born between 1860 and 1910 (he was
born in 1902). In those years, an irreversible and mysterious
transformation had taken place, which Bazlen has succinctly set
down in one of his notes: "Until Goethe: biography absorbed
by the work. Beginning with Rilke: life set against the work."
The process condensed in this passage has distant origins and
far-reaching consequences. The compulsion of the work, just at
the point when it reaches maximum intensity—at the precise

moment when the work throws off all dependency—also reveals the pettiness of its premises: to view the work under the rubric of results, and more particularly as the projection of a subject into an object. This marks the downfall of the work. Here, the shadow of Kitsch, hitherto cleverly concealed, is transformed into the body of art. The work loses its status, because, strictly speaking, it is not a result, it is not a projection, it is not attributable to an "I." Two opposing points of view, which had long lived together on ambiguous terms, are now broken irrevocably apart: the work as *transformation of a material* is the opposite of the work as *projection into an object.* In the alchemical tradition, the two concepts were still linked: the *opus alchymicum* was the accelerated maturation of metals and, at the same time, a projection, a demiurgic exercise. In the modern dispensation, however, these two possibilities—now dissociated—are each subject to a fatal contradiction: the work as transformation of material is never supposed to find a final and stable form; the work as projection, once the binding power of the rule of projection—namely, rhetoric—is no longer active, remains entrusted to the singular "I," emancipated and miserable, the most dreadful trap.

It is therefore a part—and a decisive part—of Bazlen's work *not to have produced any work.* What, on one side—for those who don't know how to see otherwise—bears the mark of sterility, is on the other side an astonishing affirmation, a perspective of what is possible. The paradoxes of the opus are serious and exhausting; even today, there are some very subtle scholars of these subjects who continue to approach them from every angle, making them more and more transparent, extreme, irresolvable. Naturally, Bazlen was aware of all of this and didn't fail to appreciate its seriousness, but, where he himself was concerned, with a move worthy of a Zen master, he turned his back and changed his course. "Once people were born alive and slowly they died. Now we are born dead—and some of us slowly manage to come to life." This must have seemed to Bazlen, then, the most urgent work: to come more and more to life. An endless transformation that required a divinatory capacity; not only the will to transform, but an *affinity* with what had undergone transformation: a shaman disguised in the clothes of a bourgeois, who had no desire to be recognized, intervening—with precision and a lightness of touch—in the network of chance.

Among the chief qualities of any work, Bazlen always included what he called "first-time-ness." Even a minuscule invention, a fleeting gesture, just by the simple fact of appearing for the first time, takes on another meaning, and this negligible addition to the world shuffles the order of things. After another moment has passed, though, this addition will already have lost its efficacy. This is why Bazlen had such a knack for pulling the rug out from under us and under himself, then rolling it away, such a gift for making it clear that there's no need to find your footing—that finding your footing may impede movement. (The empty point is, among other things, the place where there's no footing to be found.) And Bazlen's movement was constant, endless, with no fixed aim or direction: a process of self-transformation in which the slowly resuscitated elements followed a Poseidonic motion of ebb and flow between a pole of algebraic complexity, detached from substance, and a pole of motionless elementality, concealed within the substance. This process did not involve speaking or writing—and it almost might have left no trace.

—Roberto Calasso

THE SEA CAPTAIN

Prelude

THE SEA CAPTAIN'S house was old and comfortable. There were hydrangeas in the windows, a canary was singing in its cage, the captain's wife was sitting at her sewing machine, a dog was playing with a bone by the door.

The captain didn't spend much time at home. He was almost always at sea, and at sea he sat alone in his big cabin, he studied nautical charts, he fumbled with his precision instruments, he read little-known books whose trails he followed from port to port—otherwise, he stood on the deck and scanned the horizon, for hours on end, with his spyglass. If he arrived in a port where he'd never been before—but there were so few!—he immediately began wandering aimlessly about, on the steps he chatted up the fishwives, he tasted unfamiliar wines in tucked-away taverns, he went nosing about, through dark and twisting alleys, in the dusty shops of the junk dealers. By the time he went back aboard, he had seen everything, he had taken note of everything, he had formed an idea of everything, and in his cabin he opened the packages full of plants, stones, books, bottles of wine, and wooden statuettes. But, for one reason or another, these things were never the right things, and this made him more and more restless. He was sometimes overwhelmed by a sudden nostalgia for his wife and his life at home; when he returned, he would kiss his wife, he would pet his dog, and he would listen patiently to all the things that had happened in his absence; but his eyes wandered impatiently out the window, and his mouth hardened whenever ships, in the distance, passed by on the sea. And always he went back to his table by the globe, and set it slowly spinning.

Once, he had stayed at sea for longer than usual. When he came back home, his wife gave him a kiss and her breath was sweet. With a smile, she said:

"I've had to wait for you such a long time. While I was waiting, I sewed you a pair of red trousers. Let me show them to you."

And her voice was clear.

The captain was always very courteous. He thanked his wife and glanced at the trousers. But to himself he said: "My wife doesn't understand me. I'm a sea captain, the trunks in my cabin are crammed full of perfectly ironed uniforms—white for summer, blue for winter—and here, in the wardrobe, hangs my black suit, the one I wear to weddings and funerals. What am I supposed to do with red trousers?" He locked up the trousers in the black chest, but he sensed that something was wrong, and he set the globe slowly spinning. The next day he spoke a few ritual words to his wife, gave her a quick kiss goodbye, then fled. And he stayed at sea for even longer than he had the last time.

But this time his wife did not sit at the sewing machine.

"Why should I sew?" she asked herself. "He didn't even bother to look at the trousers; he just locked them up in the black chest, after I'd taken so much trouble with them. He doesn't understand me anymore."

She opened the chest, ran her hands over the trousers, and felt very sad. The day was empty, she began rummaging through the chest and found a box of cigars. And she thought disdainfully:

"If he doesn't want to wear my trousers, then I'll smoke his cigars."

And she lit a cigar, stared out the window, and blew reeking black smoke out toward the sea, which smelled of salt.

In those days, the One-Eyed Man had come to live in the city. Passing by the Captain's house, he looked up with his single eye at the woman in the window and said:

"Women who smoke cigars play cards, too!"

"Certainly," the woman answered. "Come up then and we'll play together."

And soon they were sitting down to play every day. The woman won and smoked her cigar, the One-Eyed Man lost and wore a look of contentment.

When, after a long absence, the Captain returned, he gave his wife a kiss, but her breath was no longer sweet, and her voice had grown hoarse. "My wife has become a stranger," the Captain thought, but he said nothing and continued to act as courteously as ever. Except he fled even sooner and stayed at sea even longer than he had the last time. One day, in the harbor tavern, the One-Eyed Man told the Craterface what he was doing with the Captain's wife. "You ought to bring her down here one of these days," said the Craterface. "Women who smoke cigars and play cards drink grappa, too." And soon the woman found herself sitting in the tavern every day, smoking cigars and playing cards. She went home late in the evenings, staggering drunkenly, and in the morning she lazed in bed.

By the time the Captain finally returned, the hydrangeas had withered in the windows. Nevertheless, he gave his wife a kiss, but her breath stank of tobacco and grappa and her voice had gone gravelly. He said to himself: "This time, not even for form's sake, there's no way I'm giving her a kiss goodbye." And he went away again at once, and he stayed at sea even longer than he had the last time.

One day a stranger sat down at a neighboring table in the tavern. He didn't smoke and he didn't play cards. He kept a bottle of mineral water on the table in front of him, and he'd delved into an illustrated magazine; from time to time, at long intervals, he turned the page, shot a glance at his three neighbors, cleared his throat, and took a sip of the mineral water. When he'd emptied the bottle, he cleared his throat and said:

"Women who smoke cigars, play cards, and drink grappa, also go to bed with men who have only one leg." "Certainly," said the woman, staring at him impatiently, without blinking, "exclusively with those who have only one leg." "Okay," said the

stranger. "Okay," said the woman. The stranger had already gotten up, slowly and ceremoniously, and his wooden leg did not
stop at the knee, but went all the way up to his belly. The woman couldn't tear herself away from the sight of it. Fascinated, she
leapt to her feet, took him by the hand like an automaton, and
dragged him avidly to the back room. The Peg-leg nearly fell on
the floor.

"And you're a clumsy one, too!" the woman barked out in
her huskiest tone, and already she'd slammed the door behind
them. The One-Eyed Man and the Craterface wanted to follow
them and started drumming on the door, but the Innkeeper
blocked their path, rolling his eyes about in the most terrifying
manner, and the two men retreated with whispered grumblings.
The illustrated magazine was still lying on the table. They
opened it, leafed through it for a bit, and immediately went
back to sitting side by side. They banged their fists on the table
and imperiously ordered a bottle of mineral water, then started
leisurely looking over the illustrations and giggling. Apart from
this, they remained very well behaved for the rest of the night.

Once more, the Captain came home after a long absence.
There was dust on the sewing machine, all the clocks and
watches in the house had stopped, the canary was dead, the
lamps were burnt out, and the dog on his chain was barking
with hunger. This time, when he arrived, the Captain did not
give his wife a kiss and he thought: "Kindness is out of the
question now, I really have to hit her. But she stopped understanding me a long time ago now, and I am a sea captain and I
have my nautical charts and my precision instruments and my
books, and all the seas of the world are open to me, so what do
I care about her stinking breath, her husky voice, the bruises all
over her body?" He decided never to come home again. For the
last time, he wound the clocks, then he took his black suit from
where it hung in the wardrobe and put it in his case. "As far as
I'm concerned, the rest of it can go to the devil," he thought.
And in fact he never gave another thought to anything else in
the house again.

By now his wife was living at the tavern day and night. The

One-Eyed Man passed out the menus, the Craterface filled up the glasses, and the Peg-leg sat contentedly beside her, not smoking, nor playing cards, but every once in a while taking a sip of mineral water and pinching the woman's thigh. The gas lamp poured out its thick smoke, the Innkeeper stood by and rolled his eyes about suspiciously; way off in the distance, the dog barked with hunger. But the woman no longer wanted to listen to that barking and was overcome with fury; the One-Eyed Man and the Craterface felt compelled to start singing Stille Nacht, heilige Nacht, the Peg-leg beat out the rhythm with his wooden leg, the Innkeeper rooted in his pockets and sang along in a whisper, lost in memory. He had tears in his eyes.

A long time later, the news spread through town that the Captain's ship had foundered and that the Captain had gone down with all his crew. At first it was nothing but a vague rumor. The sailors on a steamship that had arrived in the port had seen what remained of the vessel near an atoll and had salvaged a picture frame floating in a mess of empty cigar boxes. The woman recognized the frame: it was a gilded frame that the Captain had brought back from one of his voyages but that had later disappeared. Now, after its time in the water, it had lost its gilding.

The news did not make any impression on the woman. She continued to smoke and continued to play cards and continued to drink and let herself be pinched—if anything, her playing had become a bit more distracted, she laid down her cards absentmindedly, however they were dealt her, and the One-Eyed Man was almost always forced to win the game. He felt more and more ill at ease, and he looked at the woman more and more anxiously. As soon as the game was over and the woman, in the arms of the Peg-leg, went staggering off toward the back room, he heaved a sigh of relief.

And so they played cards less and less, and the woman no longer spent all day sitting in the tavern. At home she wandered around, empty and on edge, from one room to the other, she was bored, the rugs were piled up in disorder, her nerves were frayed, she couldn't take the dog's barking anymore. Once she really believed she was going crazy, she rushed outside, she bought some food for the dog, who finally shut up. But then, all of a sudden, the silence was so much worse, the rooms seemed dustier than ever, the windows emptier, the spider web on the birdcage grayer, she didn't even know what time it was, she was alone in the world, in the bathroom the leaky faucet was dripping, she bought another canary. But when the canary started to sing, she was more irritated than ever. She lit a cigar, she propped her elbows on the windowsill, she stared at the sea with empty eyes, a ship came into the harbor, and she said to herself: "Who knows if a ship will bring back his corpse or if the waves will throw him up on the beach, a castaway with a shredded shirt, he even brought his black suit with him, what a fine bit of foolishness, that would be the best fit, but he couldn't have worn it even once, he was crazy about his uniforms, only his red trousers are still here, if only I'd sewed him a red jacket to match—my God, there's so much dust on the sewing machine—when he was alive, he didn't want to put on his red trousers, now that he's dead he'll have to wear them, after all it's never too late; and so he'll end up being buried all in red, that will really suit him well." And she whistled. "Why didn't I sew him a red jacket that time"—the question popped into her head—"but only the trousers? It was too much to ask of him, that he should want to wear red trousers with his uniforms," she smiled to herself, "or with a black jacket. He wasn't altogether wrong. In fact, it was really my fault."

She sat down at the sewing machine and began to sew the red jacket, and the canary sang in its cage, and she saw herself before the Captain laid out on the bier, dressed in red, the organ rumbling, the sailors' widows sobbing as though he'd been their husband. The sun was setting, she had to work fast, what would they think down at the tavern if she turned up so late? But at bottom it was his fault, because he didn't even need to say a word, it would have been enough for him simply to open his mouth.

In the tavern things weren't going as they were supposed

to. Of course, everyone was acting casual, the Innkeeper stood there with furrowed brow, the One-Eyed Man had a cadaverous pallor, he'd never managed to win so many games in a row. Something had to happen, and so the Peg-leg gave her a big, very special pinch. But she shot him a mean look and said in a cutting tone: "You messed up my dress!" Everybody was embarrassed. Some time went by. At a certain point the Peg-leg said, out of the blue, by way of an excuse: "You know, I was born with only one leg, you shouldn't think that I had an accident. I'm a bona fide monster." The woman smiled sweetly. Then, without warning, she let out a shrill scream that pierced everyone to their marrow, she threw down her cards and jumped up on the table. Clutching her skirt around her legs, which she held tight together, she pointed her finger at a mouse that had stuck its head in the spittoon. The Innkeeper disappeared in a flash and came back with a broom. Everybody had gotten up and started running around helter-skelter, primed and ready to lend a hand. But the mouse scurried off to the back room, and no matter how they pushed at the furniture, this way and that, he seemed to vanish. The four of them came out in a state of great excitement, there'd been a major event, of the sort that doesn't come along too often, the ice was broken, now things could get back to normal. But to their surprise, they saw that the woman was already getting ready to leave. The Peg-leg winked at her and shot a quick glance at the back room, but she said simply, "The mouse . . ." and was already at the door. The Craterface showed himself to be particularly pushy and tried to hold her back. "No, trust me, today the best thing for everybody would be to let me go. Tomorrow everything will be all right again," the woman said, in such a tone that no one dared reply. And so she went away. But a moment later she returned: "Lucky for me, I've just remembered the umbrella I forgot here last week. Otherwise, who knows how long it would have sat here." She took the umbrella and left.

The next evening everything really had gone back to normal as she'd promised. Only the Innkeeper found the woman's calmness suspicious, and behind his counter he followed her every move with a fearful, leery eye. But for a whole week she went on as calm as could be. Every day she continued to sew, slowly, the red jacket; it wasn't easy, she didn't have the measurements, and besides, the corpse must surely have bloated by now. So she made it bigger, but it was a pity she'd never made a close study of a drowned man's corpse. And in the evening she felt strangely light and satisfied, and with her foursome in the tavern she was chipper and relaxed.

When the jacket was properly sewn and ironed, she opened the black chest to put it away next to the red trousers. She picked up the trousers and suddenly turned very pale: "Even a corpse couldn't wear trousers such as these! Lucky for me he didn't even look at them!" One leg was longer than the other; the distance between the buttonholes was uneven, and besides, the buttons hadn't been placed in line with the buttonholes; she'd forgotten the fob pocket under the belt, and when she'd exhausted her stock of red thread, she'd gone on sewing with black thread as though nothing had happened, it hadn't even crossed her mind to go out and buy another bobbin of red thread, she was so absorbed in her work, so in love with it. It was lucky he'd drowned. So he'd never know.

It was as if she'd received a blow to the head. For a long time, she stayed stock-still before the chest, the trousers in her right hand dangling on the ground, she stared straight ahead, and her face became more and more somber and hard. Suddenly, with real hatred, she threw the trousers in the chest, slammed the lid, lit a cigar, and started pacing like a beast in a cage. She boiled over with rage. The cigar wasn't drawing well. And at that exact moment, the canary started to sing. She would have liked to strangle it. She lit a match with such vehemence that the match split in two. Then she threw the cigar out the window, a ship was coming into the harbor, never had she hated her husband so much. This was all his fault, all her life she'd made sacrifices for him, her body was on fire and meanwhile he'd gone on leafing through his stupid nautical charts, ah, yes, if only she knew then what she knows now . . . and stupid as she was, she'd darned his socks, and ended up spending her days at the sewing machine, and meanwhile he was going around the world, having a gay old time, and that's how it was, until in the end he'd driven her to the tavern. Just at that moment, the dog barked. That mutt could go straight to hell too, she wouldn't bring him anything, the thought didn't even cross her mind. And she stood before the mirror, she made up her face slowly and carefully, he'll have to pay for this, it was lucky, all things considered, that she had the Peg-leg, at least if you compared him to the others. With ruthless eyes, she looked herself over for a long time in the mirror, she cinched her dress at the waist and gave a good smack to the globe, which went on spinning long after she'd shut the door behind her. As for the light, she had forgotten to turn it off.

She went directly to the Innkeeper's counter, she poured herself a glass of grappa, she left the bottle open and threw back her head, she emptied the glass in one swallow; a moment later, she poured herself another and drank it in one swallow again. The trio at the table looked on with curiosity and asked her what was going on with her. "Nothing," she replied, "I'll be with you shortly." And the One-Eyed Man began to shuffle the cards. When she'd emptied a fourth glass, she went over to the table and picked up her hand even before she sat down. Not even in the best of times had the One-Eyed Man had such persistent bad luck. He was flushed with enthusiasm and dealt the cards in flying tosses. And at the end of every hand they emptied their glasses. Even the Craterface was off his head with happiness: only his nurse had been capable of knocking them back like this, all his life he'd been waiting for this moment. And he refilled the glasses by pouring from way up high so that they foamed over. The Peg-leg neither smoked nor played, but the atmosphere of the tavern had infected him, too: with half-closed eyes, with a private little smile, he pinched the woman, but not right on her thigh; he'd begun lower down this time, near her foot, his hand mounting gradually higher and higher, so that he covered her all over with blue marks. The tavern had never been so cheerful, the gas lamp poured out its smoke like a locomotive, the Innkeeper stood by and chewed on a toothpick.

He didn't know quite what to do, and he felt more and more uneasy, and little by little the noise in the tavern increased, and the woman laughed and squealed at the top of her lungs. Out of nowhere she tapped on the Peg-leg's hand: in reality, this hand had been thrusting menacingly high, but the woman wasn't sore in the least, she writhed with laughter and started pinching the One-Eyed Man and the Craterface with both hands. "You should get something out of life, too. Men ought to be blue even under their blue uniforms." And the two of them laughed a shamefaced laugh. But a moment later they'd stopped, they were pale with horror, the woman was really hurting them, and they tried to get away. But she jumped up like a savage and ran after them, they turned frantically in circles around the table, they bumped against the wooden legs, they fell down face-first on the ground. The woman grabbed the broom that had been there since the night of the mouse and said: "And now I'm going to ride to that place where we all belong." She rode the broom in whirling circles like a lunatic through the dingy tavern. And the two men followed her, hopping on all fours and howling: "Hop, hop, hop, little horsey, gallop away!"

But in the meantime the Peg-leg had gotten up and placed himself in front of the back-room door. When the woman went past him, he grabbed her with a vise-like grip by the arm, threw her into the back room, and, pivoting around on his wooden leg, went in and slammed the door in the others' faces. Gone were the days when the two of them would have liked to break the door down. Now they writhed with laughter and shouted back obscenities. When they saw that the Innkeeper was unconcerned with them—he went on resignedly chewing his toothpick, it was clear he knew that this would be the end—they started taking turns peeping through the keyhole into the back room, they giggled and nudged each other. Today they really had no need for the illustrated magazine.

The woman woke up at the crack of dawn. The Peg-leg snored with his mouth wide open and clutched a pillow tightly to his stomach. On the floor lay the wooden leg and the broom, which together formed a cross; nearby, like a holy water font, stood the bidet. The blankets and clothes of the woman and the Peg-leg were all tangled in a pile. The woman reached out with mechanical gestures to gather her things together, then slowly got dressed. Her head was empty, and touching it made her hurt all over. One stocking had fallen into the chamber pot, and she had to put this stocking on. Cautiously, she opened the door to the Innkeeper's counter, and a sticky, heavy smell rose up to meet her. The Innkeeper stood hunched behind his counter, his head slumped on his chest, he was pretending to sleep. She crept past him on tiptoe, holding her breath, and as soon as she was out the door she realized how scared she was of the Innkeeper, which was something that had never come home to her before. She slipped her shoes on her bare feet, the leather hot and slimy. Wearily, she limped through deserted alleys, with the feeling that something was eating away at her stomach. Back at the house, the light had been on since the night before, and it blended with the brightness of the dawn, everything was unreal, as if it were drowned, she thought. She stripped naked then and stood before the mirror; her hair fell in clumps to her shoulders, her cheeks were sunken with greenish shadows, her conjunctiva was inflamed, she had a bruise under her breasts, a bite mark from the Peg-leg. She threw herself on the bed, her palate bitter-tasting and dry, her skull like a cave of stalagmites, her stomach in pain.

She couldn't sleep, she couldn't get up, she couldn't go on lying down. Everything was pointless, if only she had had something to do, a faucet dripped in the bathroom, it was all over, better to kill herself. She ended up in the bathroom, the water ran steaming into the tub, she didn't know when she'd gotten out of bed. The water was boiling hot, the woman nearly passed out, sweat beaded on her brow, she rubbed herself with soap like an automaton until her pores opened up, but the blue mark beneath her breasts would not go away. She combed her hair neatly with a comb that was missing two teeth. She took two pills, the bottle no longer had a cap, the toothpaste no longer had a cap either, God, everything was falling into total disorder. One of her husband's rusty razor blades was still lying by the sink.

The woman lay down on the bed again, her lightheadedness had passed, now she was finally going to be able to sleep, she thought. But she was still awake, she stared with wide-open eyes at the ceiling of the room, but in fact he, too, with his pedantic sense of order, he, too, thoughtlessly left used razors lying around. Her clothes and underwear were piled up in a corner on the floor, just as they were last night in the back room, tumbled together with the Peg-leg's. She jumped to her feet again in a state of lucid panic, quick, quick, quick, like a lunatic she rubbed the soap into her linen, which she rinsed until the water was so clear it could be drunk. When everything had been hung on the line, out in the bright sun, she felt herself growing calmer, now I can finally sleep, a siren sounded in the harbor. But she was scared of the bed, something sent her skittering from one room to the other, her life was empty, like the picture frame above the chest, oh, if only the dog would bark, she walked past the chest, the end of one of the red trouser legs was sticking out from under its lid, dangling on the floor. Maybe I'll be able to sleep, she thought, and she lifted the lid, she took out the trousers, the scissors were on the sewing machine, she sat at the machine to take the trousers apart: no ships were coming into the harbor, no ships were leaving the harbor, and she stared out the window, at the empty sea. Night had fallen, but there was still a glimmer in the sky, she lit a cigar, and then she went on unstitching the trousers, piece by piece, ripping out thread. The municipal orchestra played the funeral march, the sailors' widows sobbed into their enormous handkerchiefs, but she, the only captain's widow, was wearing long black flowing veils, the coffin was lowered into the grave, a huge crown of hydrangeas was placed on top of it, the woman swooned into the mayor's arms.

That night the One-Eyed Man played solitaire, the Craterface was drunk and stared straight ahead with a lost look in his eyes, the Peg-leg gave visible signs of disquiet, he had already emptied two bottles of mineral water and he was scratching himself nonstop. The Innkeeper had seen him coming and stayed hunched behind his counter. Never again would there be a morning when he found the back room in such wild disorder, never again would he have to empty the glasses slow and solemn, never again would he hesitate at the window, breathing in the odors of the night one last time before cracking it open. Outside, the rooster crowed for the third time and the Innkeeper's eyes rolled slowly about. The tavern had never been so quiet.

It was quiet in the city, too. Maybe the sailors' widows were weeping in their darkened rooms, but there was nothing to be heard outside. And the children were sleeping, as if they'd never had a father. Only the Helmsman's wife wandered, adrift in the empty streets. The bats rustled around her. She wore a black dress and a black cloth over her head. Her eyes were fixed darkly on the distance. Her lips were bitten. She had a pustule on her chin. Otherwise, her face seemed made of stone. She walked by the Captain's house and the dog burst into a fit of barking. The Captain's wife was torn from her reveries. It was the dead of night. She had the pair of scissors in her lap. As she worked, her period had begun. She hadn't noticed before. Her stomach was still giving her trouble, but otherwise she felt pleasantly calm. Until then she'd been going to the tavern every night. Now it was too late. Pieces of red cloth were scattered around her. The cigar had left a black burn on the shelf of the sewing machine.

Voyage

IN THE CAPTAIN'S cabin, a crazy chaos reigned. He was homeless now, and forced to drag everything he happened to acquire
with him on his never-ending voyage. And therefore tall piles
of books were stacked up along the walls, and in a corner there
were two rolled-up rugs, one big and one little. There were
empty cigar boxes, silver foil, letters in need of reply everywhere—even on the desk, stuck in among the barometer, the
old Chinese teapot, the new Italian coffeemaker, the measuring
instruments; and under the table he preferred not to look. A
yatagan, an umbrella, and a mandolin were stuffed into the
wastepaper basket, the skeleton of a large bird sat atop a trunk,
in the left-hand drawer was a pile of holey socks, on the wall
the calendar indicated one December 31 or another. The picture
of his wife in its gilded frame also still hung there, and she was
always before the Captain's eyes, with her vacuous, affianced
smile, her fixed gaze, her stiff neck, her well-lacquered curls. He
didn't even see it, it was so much a part of the chaos of the cabin.
But from time to time, he did see it, and then immediately he
picked up a book and read.

The Captain seemed impassive. He'd kept on going from
harbor to harbor, never showing himself shaken, always impenetrable, all the seas in the world were open to him. Yet from
harbor to harbor his uneasiness increased, and the greater it
became, the more rigid and laconic the Captain became—he no
longer exchanged a word with the fishwives, basically he knew
everything already. He'd tasted every wine in the world—and so

16

he sat, in one alehouse or another, and after a certain number of mugs of beer his legs grew heavy, he felt as though he were tied fast to his chair, and too lazy to get up and go nosing about the junk shops, he stared straight ahead, benumbed, until it was time to buy some chocolate and go aboard.

He went back to feeling genuinely well only when the ship left the harbor again and headed for the open sea. After a while he managed to organize things in such a way that everything he had to do in the ports could be attended to in a single day, so that the ship would come into the harbor in the morning and by evening it could cast off again, even when he had a long voyage behind him and a long voyage ahead of him. The crew grumbled and the Helmsman in particular was furious. For months he'd lived far from his wife, and every day his brow sunk lower. The Captain couldn't stand the mere sight of the nape of his neck, he could have almost screamed with rage. But he controlled himself, he could understand human weakness, nothing human was alien to him, he might well say—and so he wanted to console them with the stopover in the next port; they would surely have to spend a few nights there; he himself was intending to wait for a ship commanded by another captain, his friend. This man was an Oriental, and it had been a long time since the Captain had spent a whole night chatting with him. "And the Gypsy Woman still lives there, doesn't she?" said the Cabin Boy, looking at the Helmsman with bright eyes. The Helmsman grinned, the sailors grinned, and the Captain, impenetrable as ever, returned to his cabin.

The voyage lasted a long time, the Captain bustled about and made calculations, outside the door the Cabin Boy was playing his accordion, the Captain opened a book then laid it down, the ship rolled, the piles of books threatened to topple, the Captain ate a piece of chocolate, and the portrait of his wife smiled in its frame. So it was that a book fell into his hand, a book he'd bought from a stall just because it had an old binding, he hadn't really looked into it until this moment, and now he began to leaf through it without any special curiosity, but as he went along he began to read more carefully.

It was the history of the reckoning of the years, the Sacred Book that kings used to read, compiled by
during his exile in   ,[1] with the list of dynasties and kings and nobles, with all their undertakings and their real names, inscribed in the year of their birth, rubbed out in the year of their death. And the Captain read of the creation of the earth and the heavens with all their stars; of how the fathers and the fathers' fathers had come from the far side of the sea, where the sun rises; of the subjugation of the indigenous peoples, the emigration to the north, the stops made during the emigration and the defense of the moats; of the delimitation of the city, the oak struck by lightning, the building of the temple, the construction of the palaces, the dykes, and the aqueducts; of the wars with their victories and defeats, the conquests and triumphal marches; the great misfortunes, the floods, the epidemics, the fires, the famines, the havoc wreaked by the locusts—the Captain stumbled like a sleepwalker to the chest of drawers, his mouth was tasteless, he opened the chest with the key, he put an enormous piece of chocolate in his mouth, then he locked up the chest again—of the infiltration of the neighboring tribes and how they were routed by wild dogs; of the repression of the plebeian revolt and the killing of the first horse; of the first men entrusted with the books of laws, punishments, places, and hours pertaining to torture; of marriage, and of the rights of the principal wives, and the duties of the secondary wives, the courtesans, the slaves, the untouchables, and the lepers; of the offices, the occupations, and the limits of the arts—the hips of the gypsy shuddered supplely in his grip, the woman defended herself tooth and nail and bit him savagely, struggling in a blind range with all her strength, but naturally, in the end, the Captain won out, and with a last exhausted groan her eyes rolled upward and, her mouth agape, her head went down upon the pillows. Now the Captain's mouth had a sweet chocolate taste, he sat with the book in his lap and stared into the void. Abruptly, in a single bound, he got up, carefully smoothed out a piece of silver foil, folded it lengthwise, and used it as a bookmark

1 The two blanks correspond to lacunae in the manuscript.

between the pages of the Sacred Book. Then he went over to his measuring instruments. It was the first time in a long while he felt eager to arrive in a port. There, he'd finally see his friend again, the Oriental.

It was still light when the ship docked, but the landing formalities were endless and when finally the Captain was able to set foot on dry land it was the dead of night. A waiter informed him at once where he could find the gypsy—and now he was nearly there. The neon lights befuddled him, the headlights of the cars with their reflections on the asphalt as polished as a mirror rushed over him, and he didn't dare cross the street. It was even harder finding the right person to ask directions without immediately becoming involved in humiliating complicity; the whole city swarmed with potential confidants, already with the waiter it hadn't been easy.

But in the end he found himself in a brothel, as silent as a church, in the middle there was a fake palm tree, the sofas were red, there was a great commotion on the walls: fauns chasing nymphs, sailors chasing naiads, mermen chasing sirens. The Captain carefully inspected the whores, but none of them appeared to be the gypsy. Suddenly, the fat blonde next to him cawed, "Hey, handsome devil," and gave him a resounding slap on the thigh. A widower winced and, with an intimidated expression, began wiping his glasses with a black-trimmed handkerchief. The Captain made up his mind to ask if there was a gypsy in the house. The blonde laughed, mockingly:

"That one's been upstairs a good long time with the Helmsman, and if I know him, that bed will be creaking until tomorrow morning. Go hang around in the hallway and you'll hear it all . . ."

The Captain didn't bat an eyelash: he stood up, courteously took his leave, and made for the door. But the blonde didn't give up so easily: she grabbed him that instant, plucked the cigar from his mouth, and whispered something in his ear.

"No, thank you," the Captain said courteously, "I'm sorry, but I must be going, it's already late."

"Then you should have come earlier . . ." said the blonde.

She puffed on the cigar, the tobacco was strong, and she started coughing in a frightening manner. The Captain delicately freed himself from her arms and went for the door. The fat woman went on coughing and threw the cigar on the ground; and then the widower stood too, picked up the butt, and set it in an ashtray.

"It's so easy to start a fire . . ."

"With your butt, there's no great risk," said the angry blonde.

Everyone burst out laughing, the widower even louder than the rest.

"Now they're laughing at me too," the Captain thought, "in fact, I deserve it," but he felt very ill at ease. He wandered aimlessly through the streets with an inscrutable expression, he was careful to keep away from the neighborhood near the docks, it would be painful to run into the waiter now. The streets were almost empty, dark clouds covered the moon, the scent of linden trees wafted from the gardens, an old man was waiting for a dog to finish pissing in a corner. The Captain went on aimlessly walking, faster and faster, he'd already passed this spot before, the mark of Cain was starting to burn on his forehead, he passed the brothel again, and that, that was much too much. Of course he could understand it all, he was reasonable and unprejudiced, and he'd never entertained certain illusions, thank God, but the Peg-leg, well, that is much too much; and then a One-Eyed Man and a Scarface. And when one considers that she'd hardly tasted his wines, showed no interest, sipped them out of pure politeness, and he'd brought home certain wines men dream about, while now she reeked of rotgut grappa. And once he'd brought her back a complicated jigsaw puzzle from Japan, you had to have a special combinatorial talent to do it, it was really exciting, certainly more enjoyable than those idiotic card games, and how many other things had he done for her? His heart beat more and more furiously, his face was on fire, he was walking faster and faster. And how many times had he wanted to embrace her and she'd refused him, with quiet firmness: "Leave me be today, please, I'm really incredibly tired . . ." —but she couldn't have been so incredibly tired, since she didn't even sleep, since she went on staring and staring at the ceiling, and just when he was on the verge of falling asleep himself, she suddenly said, if he ever happened to be in America again, he ought to bring her back a dozen nylon stockings, they were much better made there, whereas the ones she'd bought just the other day already had a run . . . and now she had run off with this Peg-leg . . . run off? —at a hobble!!! And so he continued to turn furiously around and around, making a big circle around the brothel, and he continued to tell himself his own story, more and more furiously. Of course he could understand it all, but it was still an injustice, after he'd always wanted the best for her, after he'd held her in the highest regard—his ears whistled, his sympathetic system buzzed gloomily as a gong, his brain was hot and bigger than his cranium—but soon it was only a perfectly abstract fury, an objectless despair, his wife could do it, the gypsy could do it, it was only the mark of Cain burning on his forehead, what he would have liked to do was strangle the Helmsman. And now it began raining, too, all the pastry shops were closed, he found himself in front of a café not knowing what to do. If the first person who came out was a woman, he would go in, and then here came a couple. Really it would have been better to have considered this; however, just at that moment, a woman also came out, but now his heart wasn't in it, so he started wandering the streets around the café and landed, soaked to the bone, in a beer hall. With the second glass of beer he felt calmer, with the fourth he was sagacious in the extreme. He was jinxed, when something's not right it's wrong, his conscience was clear, he'd really borne everything from his wife, up to the end, it couldn't be denied. Outside, the rain was beating down, he ordered another beer. It wasn't even her fault, periods of transition are always confused, systems break down, Europe's in danger, the problem weighs on everyone. Well, at least it was dry in here, in here it was protected, in here it was warm, everything else was basically of no importance, he would not go back aboard. Letting himself go gradually, a stranger to everyone, his mind observes clinically the stages of progressive decay, his teeth loosening, then falling out. There was a swamp inside him, the bar was a swamp, in the end there was just a thin wall between swamp and swamp, he ordered one last glass. The more beer you drink, the warmer your feet get in their wet shoes, the thinner the dividing wall, and in the end everything is just a hot swamp, the amoebae swim around, the pain of the world has ceased, Christ is superfluous. The rain had stopped, but the sky continued to loom dark and forlorn. He was afraid of the cold wet air, contending with the chill was a hopeless enterprise, he ordered one last glass, for real this time. They'd already stacked the chairs on the tables around him, now it wasn't a swamp anymore, it was a bare forest, sixteen miserable trunks rose from every table, eternally desiccated in an eternal winter, the leaves no longer whispered, and only now did it become clear how filthy the floor was, an old witch was sweeping up between her legs.

When he finally found himself out in the open, it wasn't as cold as all that, but the sky was still dark and forlorn, and the fact that he'd given such a big tip to the waiter, even this, in a certain sense, boded ill. As luck would have it, the grate on a pastry shop was already half raised, he stuffed himself with countless sweets, sweets absorb beer—but the light of the streetlamps in the dawn was dim and spectral, the gray clouds were oppressive, the city was inhospitable . . . ah, Europe!

The atmosphere aboard the ship was no less forlorn. The rain had washed the deck from stem to stern—and yet . . . When he thought of his first voyage—his father had brought him along with him once—the deck shone then, iridescent, in those days it gleamed like a mirror, back then they still scrubbed it well, with a soap solution, now they make it easy on themselves, with lye . . . and he got into bed and fell straight asleep.

He woke up in the early afternoon, the Oriental's ship had been sighted. His head was empty, but the sun shone as it shines only after a good rain, and he shaved himself with pleasure; his wife was far away, as never before, without a real crisis you could never be free of anything, and then it's only little by little, by stages, that you get over something—last night's crisis was a part of this, he couldn't completely understand it anymore. And soon he'll go right back out to ply the sea, and even distance plays its part. And so it was right that the Oriental's ship should arrive at just that moment, yesterday would have been too soon. Now he felt calm inside, and now he was hailed by his friend's calm wisdom—tonight he would help him settle up the last accounts, and then, washed clean and grown mature, the next morning he'd go out to meet a new and purified life.

It took a little while for the ship to arrive, and so the Captain opened his chest with the key and sat with his supply of chocolate, at noon he hadn't even eaten. Then—the offices, the occupations, and the limits of the arts; the preparation of dyes; the divination surrounding building sites, the use of the dowsing rod, the means of preparing and killing the boar; dreams, premonitions, invocations, and superstitions; the interpretation of the flight of birds and the viscera of animals; propitious and unpropitious times, days of sowing and days of harvest, clean and unclean animals, the properties of plants and the preparation of draughts and poisons; talismans, surgery, trepanation of the skull, bloodlettings, dental hygiene; the occult forces of the magnet—but his mind was elsewhere, he'd kept playing with his keys, outside the sun was shining, he would have liked to walk a while on deck, he felt really liberated, he started whistling, as quiet as could be . . . Then he heard a louder, more casual whistling, a satisfied, cheerful, placid whistling. It was the Helmsman, loose-limbed and beaming, his hands in his pockets, his cap backward on his head, calmly returning from his rounds. The Captain had never seen such insolence! He felt suddenly woozy with rage, everything boiled over within him, his heart hammered in his chest, it was much too much, the fellow must be fired on the spot. He slammed the cabin door loudly behind him, paced furiously as though in a cage, this was crossing the line . . . Of course he didn't want to make excuses, many things were certainly his fault, he had to admit it, absolutely, and the fact that he hadn't put on his red trousers at once, that showed a real lack of tact . . . but a One-Eyed Man and a Craterface, that was really below her, after everything he'd done for her, but it had all been pointless . . . And he told his story to himself again . . . Spending another night in the port was more than he could bear—and he gave the order to head straight for the open sea. The Oriental Captain's tranquility had already put his nerves on edge, for him it was easy, his upbringing was so different, he who even had a bona fide Oriental Helmsman—he would have liked to see how it was if he had his worries!

The ship pulled away from the dock and the Captain felt calmer at once. He stood on the deck and stared at the port, the houses were getting smaller and smaller, they looked like toys, but their outlines remained discernible, painted and polished by the night's rain. Back there, somewhere, to the right of that ungainly tower, there was the brothel, yes, it was right over there, a tiny little toy brothel, shiny as could be, seen from this point of view the port looked like a veritable garden city, when you were walking in its streets you didn't notice how green it really was. The city grew smaller and smaller, her mouth became softer and softer, the fat blonde yielded softly and mechanically to his embraces, she panted rhythmically and without imagination, she had little bubbles all around her mouth. When she came back to herself, she warbled blissfully, "You almost crushed me . . ." and when the Captain came back to himself, the city was only a gray stripe in the distance. He gave a few orders in an incisive voice, walked energetically toward his cabin, and turned the key in the lock.

It was absolutely impossible to go on this way, something had to happen! At last now he would finally give an order without any regard for himself, he'd permitted himself too much, setting off at a moment's notice on a simple whim, it was the purest anarchy, worse than infantile, no child behaved like this. From here on out, a new life begins, the crisis over his wife is behind him now, now he would make a real plan, without a firm plan everything falls apart! He threw his cigar out the window and wrote:

(1) get rid of the portrait of my wife

(2) make list of all neglected tasks (correspondence, letter of explanation to the Oriental, etc.) . . .

as long as the past isn't put in order, it's not advisable to think of the future, and starting today the past must be put in order—today: at the top right, the date! . . . What day was it, anyway? In a rage, he rushed over to the old calendar, tore it off the wall, and threw it straight into the sea—and now for his wife's portrait!—at which point, he abruptly interrupted his fit of rage, went over to the table, and noted in a clear fine hand:

(3)   buy new calendar,

then he resumed his fit of rage at the point he'd interrupted it, and now he really took his wife's portrait in hand and the little scraps of paper fluttered out into the wind. Then without thinking he hung the empty frame back in its old place on the wall, one couldn't just leave it lying around, the cabin should be shipshape, and at that moment he felt slightly befuddled but no less in control, standing before the empty frame now hanging on the wall, and he began to reflect on all the things that he still had to make a note of . . . Of course:

(4)   soap solution instead of lye (Cabin Boy!).

(5)   finally sit down and make a systematic study of modern physics, two hours a day, whatever's going on, without modern physics nothing more can be accomplished, that's where the new thinking begins . . . And

(6)   it suddenly occurred to him: marry a Siren and stop! — It was an idea, and he understood then, suddenly, what he'd always been searching for, a Siren! He was after all a sea captain, how could he have been so stupid to think he could be happy with a woman who lived on land, everything followed solely from this solitary fact, a really deep understanding was ruled out a priori, the women of the sea are there specially for the men who live on the sea, the women on land were forbidden to him, his wife had blue marks on her body, he was quite excited, those women, for God's sake, wouldn't sew him red trousers, lucky for him he'd brought along his black suit. Excited, he paced back and forth in the cabin, left leg, right leg, imagining that he walked with one leg, and a Peg-leg—she went to bed with such a thing, whereas he, with his well-developed, well-toned legs, with his hard, flexible thighs—that fellow can't even bend over—and the Captain found himself standing in the middle of the cabin,

before the empty frame, and he started doing bends: me-
two-legs, he-one-leg—he had gone completely mad. And in
the empty frame there will be the portrait of the Siren, but
in the meantime he had to get that frame out of here. And
he wrote:

(7)   But first of all: clean up the cabin. It was obvious, he
needed to start here, and to begin with his socks, nothing in
the cabin bothered him more (even if he couldn't see them),
he'd buy himself all the socks he wanted in the next port,
and, for God's sake, this time he wouldn't put it off until
later, his demon opened up the left-hand drawer, which was
full of holey socks, his demon threw them all into the sea.

At that point, the Captain felt quite relieved. The great liberation wasn't far away now, it was enough to start off well. For
today, this was enough, enough to do this much every day, and
before you know it everything will be in the best possible order.
And now he'd go back to reading the sacred books, not that he
really wanted to go back to them, but even the fact that he was
finishing reading something had its place in the general order,
books that aren't read to the end are chains that bind us to the
past, so let us return to the occult forces of magnets. And he read
of the four days of fasting and the hundred days of abstinence,
the days of yogurt, the days of stuffed capons, the prohibition
against hulling rice; new book: of the names of children and the
expulsion of the spirit of evil mothers, education, circumcision,
and the initiation of the young; he stood up and made a note:

(8) Buy socks in the next port (*instead of nylon stockings*,
popped into his head);

of relations with ghosts and with menstruating women; of
funeral ceremonies, specifications for funeral lamentations, the
adventures of the soul after death; of cock fights, savings banks,
and the blessing of boats; of dances, orgies in the sacred enclo-
sure, the emasculation of intruders, ablutions and penances; of
the seven ways of liberation, this is particularly important, he
wouldn't read it until tomorrow morning, today he didn't have
enough concentration. He was almost happy again, he picked
up his spyglass and felt like going on deck, but he thought it

over, he turned around, he crossed out point number 1, it was already taken care of. Carefully, he crossed out the words until it was no longer possible to make out a single letter, until all he saw was a pitch-black line on a white background, which meant: the new order had truly begun. And he looked solemnly at the transformed cabin, every superfluous thing had been eliminated, every essential thing sparkled in its proper place— and now he felt quite happy, happy with his own interior cleanliness, and so he went out. The Cabin Boy was sitting lazily, legs dangling off the side of the ship, he was eating cherries and spitting the pits in the sea, making long arcs. When the Captain passed him, the Cabin Boy said:

"Wasn't that strange?"

"Wasn't what strange?" asked the Captain.

"Just now, all those socks that drifted by . . ."

"Socks?" the Captain said, his brain going cold. "Very strange, I didn't notice anything, I've just been sitting in my cabin, making calculations."

The Cabin Boy looked at him with bright eyes, spit a pit into the sea in a majestic arc, and played a little trill on his accordion. And the Captain, instead of proceeding to the upper deck, retreated at once, and locked himself up again in his cabin. Once more he'd thought he stood on the threshold of a new life, but the past persecuted him mercilessly, he would never be free, because of his wife everything would go wrong for him, he'd have to give up on Sirens, that had just been a moment of exaltation; now he'd received the cold shower he deserved, he picked up the Sacred Book with a mechanical gesture, but immediately he put it down and turned his attention instead to his calculations.

The next morning he felt very uneasy when he slunk out of his cabin. He approached the sailors with extreme mistrust, but this mistrust was uncalled for. There were no suspicious intonations, no suspicious looks. And the Cabin Boy was sitting on a coil of rope, he was reading a detective novel and didn't even notice his presence. The only surprising thing was the appearance of the Helmsman. He walked around in a deep funk, preoccupied, on strangely stiff legs, his brow hardly visible at all now. There was something wrong, and the Captain called to him. The Helmsman approached him gingerly on his stiff legs, as if on stilts, and said, plaintively:

"I have to be very careful how I move . . . "

"But what's wrong?" asked the Captain.

"I'm afraid I've caught . . . the gypsy . . . and on top of everything else, she had the gall to ask me to buy her some ointment in Arabia, if I ever get there, something that can only be found there, I forget what it's called . . ."

The Captain was exultant, God was just, God was with him, the past had really dissolved, it had been an attack of pure persecution mania, somewhere there was a Siren awaiting him. He was quite affable when he said:

"I'm really very sorry, come to my cabin in a little while, I'll get you some hypermanganate and give you an injection, I hope that will help you feel better soon. I need you more than ever now, I have plans for a long journey, on which many things depend . . . "

And in his enthusiasm he held out his hand and the Helmsman gripped it tightly.

"Ah!" said the Captain, then went back to his cabin and washed his hands.

God was with him and from this everything followed: this was just a cramp between one phase and the next, these were only the labor pains of a new life. His wife belonged to an outmoded stage of development, now that everything was in the past he could in fact be grateful to her, in fact she'd opened up all the seas in the world. How true it is that one matures only day by day, the Captain thought, and then it's absolutely out of the question that the Cabin Boy should have noticed anything, he was sitting on the other side of the ship, all he had seen were some socks in the wake.

Everything was sparkling, he summoned the crew, it was the first time he'd made a speech to his men: he said that he was planning a long voyage, that it would be the most decisive voyage that they had ever made together, that he recognized that he had sometimes been gruff with them, for which he asked them all to forgive him, in the end he was just a man like other men, but in the last few days he'd really come to understand so many things, and now he had in mind a very different destination, more than that he couldn't say . . . the world itself was on the threshold of a new era, soon all the nations would unite, and then a new phase, so to speak, in the history of the world would begin. And once he'd reached his destination, they would all have double pay, in the meantime the Cook should bring the Helmsman six cans of milk, the Helmsman, as they knew perhaps already, had unfortunately fallen ill, he had had an accident, but it was to be hoped that soon he'd be as healthy as the next man, the Captain continued to put his faith in the loyalty of his crew. In moments such as these, the sailors didn't know how to behave, and they stared at the deck in embarrassment. Only the Cabin Boy looked at the Captain, with his bright eyes. Then he pulled a banana from his pocket.

The Captain had the flags hoisted, it was a real voyage in search of a wife. The sky was blue, a cool breeze drifted in off the land, wispy springtime clouds scudded on the wind, the dolphins leapt with pleasure around the ship, the Cabin Boy played along with them on his accordion, the Captain was rejuvenated, to be alive was a joy.

Now he was taking action, the time to read in the Sacred Book had passed, the seven ways of liberation, that was only a theory. Now he was putting his cabin in order in earnest, it was almost spooky even to think how he could have stood all that disorder before. Order in here meant order in his life, it meant order out there in the vast world, the small transformed the large, he continued to work relentlessly, the cabin was swept and the macrocosm started to shine, he organized his books according to language. —The problem was the empty cigar boxes: to throw them away or not to throw them away, that was the question. To keep butterflies and beetles in them, that would be, as it were, ideal, but it was unclear whether he would ever collect butterflies and beetles, at sea it was difficult, and these boxes would never do for fish. Pity! And so, after a moment's hesitation, he organized them according to size. But even after his death, order ought to reign, life went on, and he wrote:

(9) last will and testament.

The sky was blue, the Captain sat at his table and went on calculating ever-new routes, he consulted old books, he stood on the deck and looked all around with his telescope: no Sirens in sight. But that was to be expected, it couldn't happen so soon, for how long had it been since a Siren had appeared before human eyes, patience was called for, no endeavor was ever accomplished except by patience, patience, patience. Tenacity he had in spades, he could thank God for being made that way, it was even preordained, and so he remained fearless and calm. The most perfect order would soon reign in his cabin, there was not much left to do, and then the new life would *have* to begin, the books were already organized by language, now he classified them by subject: philosophy, maritime law, medicine, theology, classical and modern physics. By which point all that remained was the left-hand drawer, where he'd crowded all the things he hadn't yet decided whether to get rid of or not: and then his correspondence still needed seeing to, but the letters themselves were already all together in a folder, all he had to do was answer them; then again there was still the lingering problem of the cigar boxes, and besides that the two rolled-up rugs. But this was easily solved: the small rug goes under the table in the hall, the big rug stays rolled up and gets stowed in the hold, that would be best, he calls for the Cabin Boy that instant and has the two rugs taken away at once.

Serene and determined, he stepped out of his cabin, in perfect harmony with the clear sky—and the deck shone and gleamed and sparkled like a mirror. Soap solution, thought the Captain, these are the miracles of a good, thick, rich, old-fashioned soap solution . . . and at that very moment he found himself flat on his back with his legs in the air. In a bound, the Helmsman was beside him, helping him to his feet. The Captain gave him a tight-lipped smile, no, he wasn't hurt, it was nothing, but he, the Helmsman, had to be careful how he moved, a leap like that could really be dangerous.

"No," grinned the Helmsman, "I think I'm clear of it, I haven't seen anything for seven days now, I can do all the gymnastics I want . . ."

And to give him a demonstration, he immediately did a deep knee bend.

"I've been better for ages now!"

"You never know . . ." said the Captain, and in that instant God gave him a revelation. "Silver nitrate! The stuff burns terribly, I'm sorry, but I have to tell you, if you don't use it you can never be sure whether you're cured or still sick. Five or six times, to be completely certain, in the next five or six ports."

The Helmsman again took on that sniveling look of his, which inspired confidence.

"I'm telling you for your own good. You'll start in the next port. And until we get there, it's milk, milk, and more milk for you."

And the Cabin Boy studied him closely with his bright eyes. Then began peeling a banana.

"There's never one day of peace," the Captain thought, things were already getting dangerous again. But perhaps destiny would be diverted once more, except it had to happen soon, five or six ports, if you make good time, there's still some leeway, and first you have to find the Siren. Nevertheless, he started fretting again about his cabin. And had the Cabin Boy made the soap solution so greasy on purpose . . .? The possibility that he'd noticed something this time couldn't be completely ruled out, and yet the Captain had emerged from his cabin long after, and in the meantime the Cabin Boy had probably moved from the other side of the deck, to avoid any suspicion. All of this confused and troubled him; not that the mark of Cain had begun to burn on his brow, but still he was cautious; and the two rugs were leaning in a corner, rolled up.

The ship continued on its way, the sky was summery and cloudless, but the Captain still went on hiding in his cabin; he was leery; he went on and on doggedly calculating new routes; he had to drain time to the dregs. But finally their provisions began to dwindle, soon they wouldn't have any more water on board, he was obliged to set course for the nearest port. "After all, it's just the first of six ports," he said to himself, but it was no real consolation, and in fact he would have preferred not to set foot on land at all. But he could not betray himself in front of the crew, and so, having bought a rich stock of socks and a calendar, he spent all his free time at the movie theater.

When the movie was over, the Captain went back aboard to give the order to depart. The Helmsman wasn't there. But that was understandable. At these doctors' offices, the waiting rooms are always chock full, the waits are endless, and you couldn't really expect him to come running back on the double with all that burning he'd be feeling. And so the Captain walked patiently back and forth upon the deck. Anyway, he still had four or five ports ahead of him, and this was only the worst-case scenario: it wasn't written in stone that the Helmsman wouldn't be cured before then. But really it was dragging on too long, something else must have happened, he's not the type to make a fuss because it burns a bit. Finally, a carriage stopped in front of the ship, the Helmsman jumped out, he paid the coachman, he embraced a negress in a red dress who was leaning out of the carriage, he was aboard in four bounds, gave the negress a farewell nod, and the negress replied with a nod of her own; he presented himself to the Captain and announced to him with a giggle and a beaming look:

"Silver nitrate is an old-fashioned idiocy, that's what the doctor told me, nowadays there's something more sensible, sul-fonamides, you swallow a couple of pills and never think of it again . . ."

He gave a salute, ran whistling toward the mast, climbed it like a monkey, and from up there he gave a few more salutes.

Contain yourself, thought the Captain, no other words managed to come to mind, and he said, mechanically:

"Now we can finally depart!"

This was not a well-formed phrase, and the Captain chewed his lips. He gave the orders for departure like an automaton, and like an automaton he went back to his cabin, on the deck banana peels were lying everywhere, he felt stunned. Stunned, he opened the left-hand drawer, then closed it again, stunned, he opened the Sacred Book, the silver foil was wedged in before the seven ways of liberation, he closed the book again, stunned, he opened the introduction to modern physics, a letter still awaiting his reply had been slipped like a bookmark into the middle of the introduction, he closed the book, he had to put the Cabin Boy in his place now, if things continued this way the deck would be a veritable garbage heap, but he had to be very careful not to betray how worked up he was. To express himself clearly and calmly, every phrase like a crack of the whip, respect and discipline. And, stunned, he sat at his table and began again, like an automaton, calculating routes, just to do something, he didn't really believe in any of this stuff anymore, in a certain sense he'd already abandoned the whole business, he had given it up. And soon he lay down on his bed and fell asleep. The next morning the Cabin Boy asked him if he'd enjoyed the movie.

This was the coup de grâce, the Captain locked himself in his cabin, there at least he was safe. He lay on the bed, in the end a man finds himself really exhausted, when he's tried everything and nothing succeeds, he feels more and more isolated. My God, my God, why have you forsaken me? It had been pointless, destiny had no use for him, he was condemned with no chance of salvation, and now everyone really was against him, he knew it with the utmost precision, he hadn't just been imagining it, unfortunately it was objective enough, it must be conceded. Soon enough now not even the crew would obey him anymore, and in everyone's mind, as usual, would be the Helmsman with his huge neck, God how he hated him, the ship wasn't big enough for the two of them—but the actress was blond and beautiful, with what tenderness, with what abandon she'd offered up her lips at the end for a kiss from that imbecile . . . —and now, somehow, like a specter, he felt like doing something, clearing out the left-hand drawer, reading of the seven ways of liberation, going back to calculating the route . . . but he simply didn't have the strength to do it today, he was really exhausted, when in fact nothing had been accomplished, even the simplest thing became an insurmountable task, you lose your self-confidence, if at least there were someone to exchange a few words with, but this isolation . . . And after all you can afford to do nothing for a day, tomorrow, after a good night's sleep, you'll put everything in its place, all these difficulties can be overcome, and then, if nothing else, there's always modern physics, and the new thinking. His mouth was tasteless, but there was no more chocolate—because of that stupid movie yesterday he'd forgotten to buy any, he rolled himself up into a ball on the bed and thought of the actress in the film.

And so another day passed, and the Captain was obliged to go up on deck and give orders in which he no longer believed.

There were no suspicious intonations among the crew, no suspicious looks. The Helmsman was sitting at his helm, the Cabin Boy was sitting by himself with his detective novel. But the Captain knew it was only pretend, maybe they were still clinging to the hope of double pay. They tried to go on believing in him, but with each passing day their doubts grew stronger, he'd spoken with such euphoria and assurance of his destination, he simply wouldn't survive a humiliation of this kind. And he headed back to his cabin, on the deck they were dropping banana peels all over again. He glanced around, no one could see him, and with his foot he cautiously moved the peels to the edge of the deck. Then he looked around again and sent them flying with a kick into the water. "You have to do everything yourself . . ." he grumbled, and once again he started to tell himself his story, which, in the meantime, had become much longer and sadder. The big package of socks still lay there unopened, the frame was empty, no course led to the Sirens, somewhere around here was the new calendar, which read: January 1. But perhaps he had gone at things from the wrong direction, with his stupid, ankylosed European mentality, whereas everything was loose and limber with his friend, the Captain who came from the East—all of Europe went at things from the wrong direction, it's not a question of will, it's not a question of planning, it's not a question of calculated routes, the more calculations you make, the farther you get from the Sirens, the

Sirens are the daughters of chance, this time he would put his trust in the sea, the sea perhaps would push him in the right direction. And tomorrow he would finally organize the left-hand drawer, today he felt too groggy to do it, he simply didn't have the strength, and meanwhile he got in bed and rolled up into a ball, one of these days perhaps he would hear the Sirens singing.

But the next day the Captain was even groggier, he had a headache, he granted himself another day of anarchy, after all he couldn't let himself be devoured by his duties, one does and does and does and does, and if the others simply do nothing for him, in the end, when he'd had enough—he would roll up into an even tighter ball, outside it was a working day, outside it was autumn, outside the crew was becoming more disillusioned and contemptuous by the hour—you swallow a couple of pills and never think of it again, and so the reign of the Helmsman begins. For Europe, there's no salvation, in the sea the sharks are prowling, here in bed he was warm, here he could finally get some serious rest, by God he really needed it—and the actress was beautiful, maybe the Siren was like the actress, he strained his eyes to see, as if she were in front of him, with what tenderness with what abandon had she offered him her lips for a kiss.

And the sun set, and the sun rose over the sea, and over the sea a ship wandered with no destination, and in the cabin there were two rolled-up rugs and a bed, and on the bed lay a sea captain who'd curled up into a ball, he had stopped shaving, he had stopped washing, his saliva dribbled on the blankets, his ears pricked up to hear the Siren's song. Perhaps it wasn't a song, it was a feeling of being carried, a refuge, a joy, it was the assuagement of a strange hunger, it was too beautiful, perhaps it was death, he couldn't go back anymore, it was the only way to be delivered from the Helmsman.

And the Siren sang:

The Song of the Siren

Tenderly and with abandon I offer up my lips to you for the first kiss, and between us there are no misunderstandings, and from this day forward we will live together forever, in a light-filled apartment with central heating;

and I am a gypsy, and I am wild and wicked, and you are afraid of me, and in the end you think you've tamed me, but my hair is untamable;

(*the negress*)[2]

and I am beautiful and noble and sweet, and I am the last of my bloodline, and I have weary hands with long fingers, and I ask you, hesitating, if you will come on Friday and take tea;

and I am a *fausse-maigre*[3] and sweet and maternal, but I am so many things, and so I am also ironical; now you have uncovered my hormones, sleep, little baby, sleep;

and I am a very practical *bricoleuse*,[4] and if there's a short circuit, I will fix the lights, you don't understand anything, whereas I even know how to write in shorthand, I just need you to dictate to me;

and I am inexorable and just and regal, and I scorn what is not up to my own level, and I leave the sewing of trousers to tailors;

and I am a girl, and you lead me by the hand, and you explain the world to me, and then we eat vanilla ice cream with whipped cream together on the sun-soaked terrace of the Esplanade;

and I have a cigarette in the corner of my mouth and my hands in the pockets of my *tailleur*[5] and a tennis racket under my arm,

---

2 At this point there was supposed to be, apparently, the song of the "negress."

3 The phrase refers to a woman who appears rail-thin but who is, on closer inspection, shapely. [AA]

4 A handywoman. [AA]

5 A suit. [AA]

and I pass by you laughing with a girlfriend of mine;

and I am all immediacy and I paint from my unconscious, and I'm hoping that soon you'll send me some money, then I can go pick up my sweater from the dry cleaner, and perhaps I'll stage an exhibition of my paintings in Paris;

and I am eighty years old, and in my day people still knew what beauty was, my chinaware was beautiful, my lace was beautiful, but the most beautiful thing of all was the first time I went to Italy;

and my mother is a cow, and my father is a pig, and you, help me, I have no one in the world except you, but be careful, a mere nothing is enough to compromise you, and then there will be a great scandal;

and I am the communist girl with her folder under her arm, and as soon as the signs of any sort of sexual anxiety appear in me, we take care of the matter, as a courtesy, in the cleanest and most practical way possible;

and I am sixteen years old and vicious, and at the door of the house everything breaks loose at once, God how stupid I was even just two years ago, but it takes too long to get to the door, in the meantime buy me another martini;

and I am fat and vulgar and I am the biggest whore in the world and I'm looking for fleas in the hairs of my pubis, and I offer up my ass for you to kiss, and I sing along with you in my sepulchral voice—and while I sing, the others peel away from you and turn toward each other, you no longer have any need of them, they no longer have any need of you, they bite at each other, they roll up into balls side by side, they make love to each other and they suck at each other, they forget you and they forget themselves, one panting moaning tangle of bodies, no one can be told apart there, where is Greta Garbo, where is Lili Marlene?—women, salamanders, harpies?—they are Sirens of the mud, and their moaning is my song, listen to how the knot of bodies resounds, covering the noise of the crew out there, sink down deeper and deeper into me, tomorrow's another day, the new life, today my song rocks you, rocks you more gently than the pitch of the ship out there, out there is the Helmsman, out there it's cold, the piles of books have toppled, the shards of the Chinese teapot are scattered everywhere, and the chaos in the cabin is more terrible than ever—my song is warm warm warm swamp, there is no more sea, there is no more sky, another moment, another moment, listen to the song, I am singing your life to you, for where is the border between song and life. . . ?

But apparently there was a border, and apparently the Captain had arrived at the border, the ringing of the ship's siren pierced his flesh, out of nowhere came a crash, and the Captain found himself in the water.

Whale

DRUNK AS A skunk, the Captain tells about the Sirens. Everybody starts laughing. He stares at them bewildered, at a loss for words, then launches on:

"Waiter, another grappa! And if you don't even believe me when I tell you I was engaged to a Siren; ah, for a long time, there was nothing—you don't believe me, you lack imagination, but I, I could tell you how I traveled around in the belly of a whale," and everybody roared with laughter, "for how did I get to this island?—In the belly of a whale—you lack imagination, I have enough to go around, and I swear to you, as surely as two and two make four, that's how I was borne across the ocean— you lack imagination," he mumbled with the utmost sadness, he seemed to give up the game, and then, suddenly, "Grappa, grappa for everyone!" and he threw his watch on the table.

"Well then, tell us, once and for all, how it was down there in the belly of the whale . . ."

But the Captain was wary:

"You've all lost your imagination, you stopped believing in voyages in the bellies of whales a long time ago—and if by some chance you do believe, you probably imagine that you sit down there comfortably, snug as a bug, and that there's electricity, and that the door on the left leads directly to the bathroom, right? and that you'll be let off at the proper stop, and the manager of the whale will say the honor was all his," he added sneeringly (the whole thing had been said with ironical intent), "but I, I," and at this point he pounded his chest, "I saw it, I know how things are in the belly of the whale, but if you smirk at me, if you smirk at me and don't believe I was in the belly of the whale . . ." he spoke in an ominous voice—and then he collapsed: "but you lack imagination."

Pause. In a tone of contempt:

"No imagination at all."

And he fell silent, mulling things over and staring straight ahead.

"Well then, tell us, once and for all, how it was . . ."

"How it was?" he winced. "How it was? How it was? It was dark . . . dark . . . dark . . ."

He furrowed his brow as though he were about to sum up:

"Dark! And you are so alone, so alone, so alone, and you only have one woman, who then has blue marks on her body . . ."

At this point, his voice turned plaintive.

"And everything that has been, and everything that will be, turns and stirs around you, and everything stinks, and you know why everything stinks? Because it's so dark you can't see it."

And he began blubbering miserably, and someone interrupted:

"Take it easy now, at least you got out . . ."

"Got out?" he screamed. "Got out? I slipped out, smooth as could be," he said, mockingly, "slipped right out on my soapy ass . . . Got out?" he mumbled, appalled and offended, he felt no one understood him . . . Then he shouted in everyone's face, with immense disgust: "You're spit out! You have to slither out, you're spit out and then you have to slither outside . . ."

He seemed to be tallying up all the humiliations of his life—then he added, in a gloomy voice, staring straight ahead:

"You're spit out only if you slither out, you can't slither out unless you're spit out," he looked around him sternly, "and if you don't slither out when you're spit out, and if you're not spit out when you slither," he looked around him with an expression of demonic impatience, "if you miss the moment, you understand, this single moment . . ." his shoulders slumped, "you go on sitting in the dark, and you don't know whether you'll be spit out again, if you'll be able to slither out again . . . The most desperate thing, the worst, is that you actually don't want to get out of the belly of the whale at all, for where is it going to spit you out?" he said in a sappy, sermonizing tone, with his arms outspread, "you'll be spit back out into this world, but what is this world really?" in a tone of revelation: "Nothing but a grain of sand in the belly of an even bigger whale . . . you have no imagination," he said, resigned, but suddenly he held out his hand, index aloft: "It's warm down there, down there you're safe, and you can't just slip out when you're spit out, but you have a guilty conscience, and you know that it must be done, you're pushed, you're irresistibly pushed, and you're sitting there, paralyzed with fear, and you pray to the good Lord, you pray that it won't spit again, that it won't spit again, and now you're keeping a watch on its rumbling, in the morning it's going to spit, it's not going to spit," and he started weeping bitterly . . .

"And yet there was something pleasant in all that stench . . ."

The Captain was seized by a fit of rage:

"It's obvious you understand absolutely nothing, the stench down there, it's not that it was nice . . . it's the stench of *everything* . . . ages and ages have to pass before nice smells come into existence, but then it will be the smell of the individual—one smell rules out another—but the stench down there is the world before the idea of needing to be redeemed has come to be, everything stinks in perfect harmony, down there *everything* still exists . . . and outside is the sea and iodine, and these are healthy things, whoever wants to have clean lungs . . ."

Another thought struck him like a bolt from the blue:

"Why, where are you spit out, after all?" he asked in a sappy, sermonizing tone, with his arms outspread, "you'll be spit out into this world . . . But what is this world really?" in a tone of revelation: "Nothing but a grain of sand in the belly of an even bigger whale . . . You lack imagination," he said, resigned. But suddenly he held out his hand, index aloft: "But I tell you that one day this world will be spit out, one day this world will slither out, no, it won't slither out, it will be spit out," he shouted, "spit out!"—and here he let go, his head dropped down on the table, and he fell asleep.

When he woke up the next morning his head hurt, his ragged uniform was stained with the grappa that he'd vomited up. He'd completely forgotten what he'd said, he had to move on, he didn't drink even the tiniest drop of alcohol, he had only one coin left in his pocket, he set off, and off and off he went, and he came to a forest.

"Bah," he said with disdain, "those fellows can't even imagine how it is in the belly of a whale." He was quite worked up. "A whale is a ship, only everything's mixed up down there, the engine room and the hall and the cabins are heaped up higgledy-piggledy—perhaps others find it out for themselves—but a sea captain has experienced these things firsthand, and now all he can smell is the stench."

[Shipwreck]

Some time later, the news spread through the city that the Captain's ship had wrecked, and that he had drowned together with all his crew. A steamboat, which had just arrived in the port, had spotted the wreckage drifting off a coral island and had recovered the bodies of some of the sailors.

The news made no impression on the Captain's wife, she continued to smoke, drink, and play cards; only she'd become more distracted in her playing, she threw down the first card dealt her more carelessly than ever, and the One-Eyed Man began to get bored, why should he go on playing if he could never manage to lose? And so the woman went to the tavern less often during the day, and since she spent less time with the trio, she was no longer so constantly drunk. But at home she was bored, and so she bought herself some new oleanders and began watering them regularly. "What a pity," she thought, "that my husband's corpse hasn't been found, I would have liked to bury him in his red trousers. But perhaps someday he will be found, perhaps one day a ship will carry the corpse into the harbor, the corpses of shipwrecked men always have ragged shirts, in any case I should absolutely start sewing a red jacket." And so she sat down again at the sewing machine, and she was so immersed in her work on the red jacket that she didn't even notice that night had fallen, and night, up to then, had pushed her irresistibly toward the tavern. That night, the One-Eyed Man played solitaire, while the Craterface stared relentlessly straight ahead, the Peg-leg gave visible signs of disquiet, he didn't play cards, he didn't drink, and there was no one around to pinch.

But the Captain hadn't drowned. Calmly, for a long time now, he had steered his ship from port to port, he had seen the coasts of foreign lands, he had studied the maps, he had looked out into the distance with his telescope. Once, however, the ship had ended up in a current that wasn't marked even on the most recent maps, and the Captain had just barely realized what was happening when a tremendous tempest broke loose, the ship crashed into a coral reef, the crew was swallowed by the waves. The Captain was many times lifted on the crest of the waves and many times sucked down into the depths of the vortex, and it was only by swimming desperately that he managed to stay afloat. Gradually the tempest died down, the waves grew calmer, but the Captain felt more and more exhausted and incapable of resisting, and when the sea was almost smooth again, he was so tired that he stopped swimming altogether. He was so tired he didn't feel like swimming anymore, his weariness was lovely, the sea was lovely, he didn't feel like swimming anymore, he didn't feel like piloting a ship anymore, but like dissolving into his weariness, dissolving into the sea . . . "You fish, you jellyfish, you kelp." But at that moment, one last, ponderous wave appeared out of nowhere, lifted the Captain, and threw him up on a round coral island. His left leg banged against the coral, he tried to stop the bleeding with his hand, and when he brought it to his lips, the blood of his veins was salty, like the water of the sea.

"I can't even dissolve into you, oh weariness, oh sea, up to now I looked into the distance and didn't see the sea, up to now I studied maps and didn't know my own blood, now I know the fish and the jellyfish and the kelp, oh salt of the sea, oh salt of the blood, and now, in the middle of the blue sea, I'm forced to pace around a red disc, continually around and around, until I die of hunger and thirst."

And so, tortured by hunger, tormented by thirst, he continued to go around and around in circles, hopeless, until he fainted dead away on the hard ground of the atoll.

After exactly seven days, a naturalist alighted on the coral

island, which he had never seen before. He dipped his ther-
mometer in the water, he chipped off the tips of the rarest coral
with his hammer and immediately glued labels to them with
his saliva. Just then, as he was returning quite satisfied to his
ship, he happened on the Captain's lifeless body, he supposed
he must be an aboriginal, and had him carried onto the boat,
and from there to the ship. He locked the Captain in a cage
and, cautiously, succeeded in dripping some cod-liver oil and
hormones into his mouth. The Captain gradually came to, only
the cod-liver oil and hormones made him feel so terrible that he
couldn't even manage to speak. And it was only when dry land
was in sight that he felt able to utter the first word. But when
the naturalist learned he was dealing with a shipwrecked captain, he no longer felt inclined to take care of him and ordered
that the door of his cage be unlocked.

And so the Captain found himself alone in a port that was
utterly unknown to him, he looked out at the sea, into the distance, he no longer had binoculars, and he lamented:

"And now here I am, a poor sea captain, my ship is smashed
to pieces, my crew, who used to obey me, are all drowned, the
trunks in my cabin, with my beautiful uniforms, white for summer, blue for winter, have been swallowed up by the sea, along
with my black suit, now I can't go to weddings or funerals anymore, my leg is injured, my shirt is torn, my jacket is ragged, oh
if I only had my red trousers, but they're at home, in the black
chest. I want to go home, my wife has bruises on her body, and
her breath reeks, and her voice is hoarse. But I'll close my eyes,
I'll plug my nose, I'll stop up my ears, but I want my trousers, I
want my red trousers."

And so he wandered over bridges and springs, and in the
days of summer the sun blazed and he didn't have his white
uniform, and in the nights of winter the north wind blew and
he didn't have his blue uniform, and summer and winter he
wandered with torn trousers, and so he got to know that in
summer the sun blazes, that in winter the north wind whistles,
and in his wanderings he saw the animals and the plants and
the stones of the earth, until then he hadn't ever seen them, he

was a sea captain, he had lived on the sea. And after summer and winter, he finally arrived at the port that was his homeland, alone, coming from the highway, on foot, indeed his feet were bloody, up to then he'd always come by sea, on his ship, with a crew that obeyed him. Already, from a long way off, he saw the dog playing with a bone by the door of his house, and he decided then not to close his eyes, he approached the house and the scent of the oleanders wafted from the windows, in his direction, and he decided not to plug his nose, and a canary sang, and he decided not to stop up his ears.

Finally he had found it, the new life—the shock of the cold water was very strong, and this was the only thing that crossed his mind—what didn't cross his mind, but what he did, was to start swimming vigorously—after lying down so long, it was almost an athletic pleasure to see how he managed to make better and better progress with each stroke—suddenly, he felt happy; now it was here: what he'd been searching for all his life was the shipwreck, this was the great liberation . . . His wife could do what she would to him, and the Helmsman could do what he would to him, too—alone, all alone on the infinite sea—but he looked cautiously around him, to see if there was some trace of the Helmsman—strange that the ship had completely disappeared—where was he now, really: latitude and longitude? and the sea was calm and mild, but damn it, there was no land in sight anywhere—how had he imagined that they were shipwrecks?—the sea swallowed and the women looked on from afar—this would be just fine with her—and he swam and swam— this would be just fine with her—that in the end the sea should toss up his corpse on the shore, then finally she could be sure that he'd never be coming back again—and if she saw his corpse, perhaps she'd realize what she was missing, and what he had really meant to her, and what she had been doing with him—now he lies there, white and pale—goddamn it, a corpse in the water, don't give it a thought, don't give it a thought— and he swam furiously, with all his strength, toward who knows where—let's say toward the sun—the important thing is to keep on in one direction, not to swim in circles, otherwise the last chance is lost—maybe it's land, maybe it's death, he wasn't afraid, he had a strange sense of security, or maybe his sense of security was so great just because the fear, below, was so great, and strangely the ship had disappeared, it wasn't even bubbling up from the deep—they were all drowned, so it seemed—if the Helmsman hadn't drowned, and here he looked around him again, everything had been pointless—and he swam, and there

were those who said that your whole life passed before your eyes
in such moments—strange, what a bureaucratic thing, nothing
passed before his eyes, not even a thought of his wife, if that
beast hadn't driven him out of the house, it's because of her that
he's about to die, it's fine with her, this is what's happening—

swimming eastward, to meet the Oriental—after swimming
toward the sun, socialism—but over there is the night, and in
the end, in spite of everything, he was swimming toward the
sun—the aptness of the symbol, swimming toward the night,
acceptance of death, consciously in the night—

The fish and the jellyfish and the kelp of the sea.

a red point in the distance—and he swam and swam and swam,
and the red point grew no bigger—

enough, the sea, melting away into the sea, there's no goal, no
salvation—now he had to forgive everyone, forgive everything,
everything in death—he had to be solemn—to leave off swimming, and a moment later he started swimming still more furiously—*coquetterie* with death, he was conscious of his immor-
tality.
     Memories of youth, every stratum had to be set free—at the
last moment before death you understood the complex—but
he wasn't facing death, and the dead no longer know anything
about their complexes—he would never have recognized the
complex—

Dying—the thing left him cold—but at the thought that
a shark might tear off one of his legs, he felt appalled, paralyzed—a one-legged man, God knows if he can swim—you
don't believe it but that's how it is—he tried keeping one leg
stiff—he was in the middle of the sea, it was a question of life
or death, and he had a red point before his eyes, and that might
be his only salvation, because it had grown a bit bigger, the fool
was performing experiments—

groggy, continuing to swim, becoming more and more just a jumble of pains, mechanically, unconsciously—in the middle of the sea, there was a pain in physical form that went on swimming toward a red spot,

oblivious among jellyfish and corals

Huge reversals could now be expected in his consciousness, but there was no trace of them—perhaps the great metamorphosis only consisted in the fact that he was just a pain in physical form pierced by splinters of consciousness: the unreturned book, lent and recalled, and the nylon stockings, somewhere—death, and a one-legged man only needs a single stocking—an artificial palm tree, and the sole sign of metamorphosis, if he should ever take a seat at a bar again, wine, wine, no beer . . . before him, he saw the castle, the part exposed to the sun, and he knew the vintage—it was a good idea, a stroke of luck, he had a fountain pen on him, you could feel the sun, not like here, in the water, idiot smile, *l'inconnue de la Seine*,[6] too simple, too simple, too simple, the suspect poet—what a coquette he'd been with death, and when death had really announced itself: *noblesse oblige, littérature oblige aussi et on dirait que sa littérature a été honnête*[7] (?)—his death provided proof of it: death absorbs ambiguity, or else ambiguity speaks out against death—ambition must take its toll—and in the end, it's nothing but coquetterie, I know it, if I didn't escape I'd never get over the lie of life . . . in life, *and*

---

6 Allusion to the unknown woman drowned in the Seine whose face was so beautiful a death mask was made of it. Rainer Maria Rilke's Malte Laurids Brigge records seeing one of the many copies of this macabre creation: "The mask-maker I pass by every day has two masks hanging outside beside his door. The face of the young drowned girl molded in the morgue because it was beautiful, because it was smiling, so deceptively smiling, as if it knew" (*The Notebooks of Malte Laurids Brigge*, trans. Burton Pike, Dalkey Archive Press, 2008, p. 56). [AA]

7 "*noblesse oblige, littérature oblige* too, and it looks as though his writing is honest." [AA]

what is it really: life: death by the thorn of a rose[8]—and so one
keeps on going down the spiral of lies—

writing about me, my watch is waterproof—a sharp pain
shot through his arm while he held it before his eyes, it was 3:55
p.m., somewhere, below, kelp, with roses it's too simple, and
what does 3:55 p.m. mean?

that he had lent out the sixth volume of correspondence,
and he swam more and more furiously: order after death, one
shouldn't leave works unfinished: a stroke of luck that his muscles were so solid, they could even indulge in the song of the
Sirens—a pain, a pain, and the fact that I'm still alive I owe
simply to a justifiable feeling that I am immortal: accordingly,
up to what limit: eternally a priori—and tomorrow you'll take
a hit, a slightly stupid thing to say in the water—more and
more minutes, he looks at his watch, it is 4:12. They were only
splinters of consciousness: the red spot was already very big,
a coral island—clear before his eyes, *a red globe—death of the
suspect poet*—the smaller the splinters became, the bigger the
island became—the island was already very big, it was strange,
he couldn't manage to think anymore—there were supposed to
be great myths, Poseidon strangely of human stature, and the
man was quite small and called Ulysses; and the gods were small
and the smallest of them all was called Pallas Athena; and there
was the cycle of high tide and low tide, and sometimes the small
ones win: how could this be, if they never won—and the smallest had the most cunning weapon, and he won—somewhere,
the even smaller ones await him, and that's why now, in the sea,
I'm not so small then, better death, but I have chosen death and
Poseidon has helped me—and out of the ever more choppy sea,
a high wave that tosses him up on the beach—

"Ahi!" shouts the Captain, struggling to find his legs, on the
atoll, one of his feet was wounded by a prong of coral—he was
losing blood, he put his hand to the wound and then to his
mouth, and the blood of his veins was salty like seawater—

toward the end: more and more exhausted and unable to resist,

8 The "suspect poet" killed "by the thorn of a rose" is Rilke.

so tired that he left off swimming altogether—he didn't feel like swimming anymore, weariness was lovely, the sea was lovely, just not to swim anymore, just not to pilot ships, TO LET HIMSELF BE CARRIED (that damned Oriental, it was all his fault), to dissolve away into weariness, to dissolve into the sea— and the calmer he became, the more the sea convulsed, and when he stopped swimming, the wave; "ahi!" said the captain—

why go down, why wasn't it in the cards—it was night and it was day, and the red point is just as far away as ever, the sea becomes green, and the sea becomes yellow, and the red point comes closer and closer—

continually picked up and thrown aloft by the waves, continually sucked down by the vortex—

night on the sea, the red island and the red of the sea—the moment of confession: edifying; literature through and through— thoughts turn in circles, *his body no*—

the smallest; it was really the moment of the smallest, high tide and low tide, it is no longer the moment of the great, what does great mean, and what small

the Captain was close to death, but he was awfully cultured—

but the suspect poets are great because they recognize greatness, is it not perhaps a question of dominating what is great? Ulysses, in whom domination ends and triumph by cunning begins—solutions, death is not a solution, it's only the end of our deplorable art, it's a liberation into a trivial sort of calm, but that's not why the Captain kept swimming, it was only because his muscles kept swimming—liberations are not always solutions . . .

Here, the first difficulty for the narrator—because there's a man

swimming in the water, and what has to be said in such circumstances—that he becomes more and more tired, and what
thoughts he has, and at what point his lovely plasticity is going to arrive at its end—and his thoughts are only fragments,
splinters. And between the awkwardness of *monologue intérieur*
which is not at all suited to the tone and the awkwardness of
an intervention on the part of the narrator, he chooses the lat-
ter, what else could be done?—and the narrator's intervention
remains somewhat foreign to the story, but the tone can be resumed, it's only a parenthesis, whereas the *monologue intérieur,*
with all its undercutting of the music of the language, set down
in the middle of a genuine narration—and in the end, we find
ourselves in the sea, and even the pounding of the sea inserts
itself among the voices, and the whole thing is only a parenthesis—one can also skip this—but between the shipwreck
and the island, there must be a certain number of pages . . .
There has to be *distance* and the sea used to be distance—and
accordingly, the trick of the author who is telling the story—
THE PARENTHESIS A SINGLE SENTENCE—which ends
quickly, then Poseidon intervenes—because the author (as yet)
has never actually fallen into the water, but as an old *routinier*
of shipwrecks—and things he's experienced cross his mind . .
. the incomplete Schopenhauer (the pigment shop) . . . and
in the end, there are borders and barriers between books and
you—but better the suspect poet, because the sea is here and
the thoughts are my own—

swimming on his back letting himself be carried—

swimming, swimming, swimming, all night, all day . . .

. . . all this because he heeded the Oriental . . . the struggle with
the great sea monster: the great sea monster used to be the sea
itself . . .

The dead of night when he falls into the sea . . .

the point at which
he is no more

Alone at last, this thought crossed the Captain's mind, he
smiled. Apart from this, impassive as always, he began swimming with all his strength. How he had hated the ship, how
wonderful that all the books had dissolved into the sea. It was
all so obvious and inevitable, he had known it always, always,
and he had even wanted it, that time when he'd refused the red
trousers—that had been the first step on the road to being shipwrecked—how far back you have to go, half a lifetime of pain
and hate and dreams and work and pride, how many things you
had to go through, just to arrive at a nice plausible shipwreck,
well devised and neat, the internal logic set in motion by a pair
of red trousers, dry, had to lead, finally, to a pair of blue trousers, soaked through—when he was a child, they would always
take off his wet underpants—now his were soaked, an infant's
dream come true.

Now everything was in order, his tumble into the water was
a part of the plan, and even if he didn't know it, he could say
where he was, he was at the end of the prologue. And now, no
more sirens, the only ones, the only real ones in the paintings
in the room at the brothel. —Now just Tiamat, Tiamat, finally
creating a cosmos, he was swimming, and he felt good, finally his muscles were moving after long stasis—what a disgrace
the ship and the port and the house were, now he had the sea,
and he even had a plan, and then the happy ending, the *happy
end*[9]—unknown on an unknown coast, the hero who emerges
from the sea, the aboriginals bring him fruits from the fields
(and where should fruits come from, the asphalt?) and from
somewhere, in the interior, there were gold mines and fields of
diamonds (and washerwomen)

Silence, no radio around

so long as he is not exhausted, he will not be tossed up on the

9 In English in the original. [AA]

shore—he knows this, and mechanically he continues to swim

Let us, slowly, unroll the big rug

FROM NOTEBOOK B

Island

HE LIVES THROUGH death by water . . . then carried away by the current.

Oblivious among jellyfish and corals.

He's irritated with the Oriental, that's what happens when you let yourself be driven along to—

Men are small, where in the world today is there an Alexander whom you can ask not to stand in the way of your sun— how are you supposed to overcompensate for your inferiority? Hence the mass, he grows furious with the mass, and suddenly discovers that he is alone—

How many things would have to be set right—but on an uncharted atoll, it's not easy to set everything right

He hurts his right foot, red blood in the blue sea (as blood simply dissolves in the sea, in no time everything turns blue— where his blood had been)

Songs of the Sirens: *Auprès de ma blonde—Long is the way to Tipperary*—Lili Marlene—Santa Lucia

And mashed potatoes, tender, soft, smooth, heaps and heaps of them—the mistake is that they always serve too little of them—

heaps, and hot, steaming but not scalding, so the belly is all
filled up.
Yes, said the Siren, and she began to peel a mountain of potatoes.

(The water always recedes whenever he looks the other way—
only when he manages to stop in the middle does he make out
the spit of land.)

The inventory of an atoll is swiftly made:
coral, the ends of broken oars, faded labels—
the desiccated tree (= the artificial palm tree)
stone
spider webs
old junk, a barrel, a broken ladder, an old nightstand, a stove
(broken)
broken champagne flutes
A couple of lovers had engraved their initials on a piece of coral,
encircled by a heart—and obscene symbols.
The coral is dusty, gray, even the relentless wind doesn't succeed
in cleaning it

The wind had piled up a mass of objects of every kind in a pit
Objects from his past (almost unrecognizable) (a shredded book
of pictures, indestructible) (the *auction*)
butterflies (strange, what do they live on?)—but tragically not
one cigar box
ancient temple of friendship

All surroundings nothing but decoration

The despair of not being able to smoke (he finds a cigarette
butt—he makes fire, a page from a newspaper—with wood
from the desiccated tree)

Famished and with knees trembling—

He trembles constantly on the island (but it need not be said: he trembles—he felt himself trembling constantly)—then acceptance

CRUSOE—How far we are from the days of Crusoe! Today one washes up only on eternally barren islands, the future is on the sea (the Navy song), the red coral pricks, the garbage of the past

He gets more calloused and colder, and sits down on the empty barrel

Hunger—he feels weaker and weaker and at the same time stronger—irritation becomes strength and the urge to act—but Saturday morning is decisive, loneliness, certainly, loneliness *à deux*—he would like a cat, but a human being . . .

Gastric juices were a springboard

Now he had to let himself be driven along aimlessly again, but it was another thing, before the destination had always been smuggled in (the Sirens), but now it was a matter of letting himself be genuinely adrift—life or death

There is even an Aboriginal who belongs to the darkest prehistory. That's why he's called: Thursday afternoon.

The Captain thinks refined thoughts.
Ho-eh! says the Aboriginal—

The Aboriginal broke off a snake-shaped branch of coral and showed it to the Captain: "Croissant," he said, beaming. Then he slowly started tearing it apart and chewing it. When he'd finished, he slapped himself on the belly, he lay down in the shadow of the coral, stretched out his legs, and began to digest, beaming with happiness—(The blessed days when humanity experienced prayer in this way.)

There are no skeletons. So the tourists have either been saved by passing ships or attempted, one way or another, to get back to dry land, and perhaps they succeeded, or perhaps they drowned. Until now always dominated the current, now being carried away by the current. The land can't be far (the driftwood of Columbus), the current knows it, he sets off on the barrel—either death or land.

He entombs himself in the song of the Sirens and grows more and more depraved, until his hunger overwhelms him—the third day he sets off . . .

In a pit, he curls up into a ball like a fetus and tries repeating the song of the Sirens to himself: and I cook so well, and I set the table and in the morning I bring you tea with bitter orange marmalade in a white room with gauzy curtains—and at noon, to begin with, a turtle soup—no, the Siren corrected herself, for lunch we begin with appetizers, with a slice of San Daniele prosciutto, with a light fluffy mayonnaise and some strong dark beer—no, the Siren clarified, to begin with caviar on toast and butter and lemon and vodka—yes, and let's not forget, to end with strawberries, herring, and Liptauer

The strictly necessary—away with everything that's not essential between God and him—

The Land of the Fishermen

THE CAPTAIN REGAINED consciousness in the tavern of an inn, in the land of the fishermen. Two of them were staring at him and smoking their pipes.

"Oh, he's regained consciousness," said A to B.

"Yes," said B.

The Captain opened his eyes and looked quizzically around him.

"Oh, he has opened one eye and looked quizzically around him."

"Yes," said B.

The Captain heaved a sigh.

"Oh."

The Captain said:

"Who are you?"

"Oh, he's asked who we are."

The Captain received no reply and closed his eyes again.

"Oh, he received no reply."

The Captain turned over restlessly . . . The Captain moaned:

"Oh, you see he's moaning and crying out for water."

But B. had an idea of his own, it was original, and this time his idea was terribly witty:

"As if he hadn't had enough water already."

It was too funny. The two of them started howling with laughter and then together they left. Down below, they reported that the Captain had regained consciousness . . . as if he hadn't had enough water already . . . The news swept through the whole village, a strong gust of humor . . . (There's one boy who doesn't understand the story, it's explained to him, he still doesn't understand, he really was a rather stupid child . . .).

The Captain was lying in bed with a powerful thirst and didn't have the strength to get up . . .
(This is just how fishermen live, slow, solid, very close to nature . . . they have roots, they aren't so swift-witted, the others die of thirst, but we have the breath of eternity . . .)

Nothing changes in the fishermen's village, they have the breath of eternity, and their life and their nets—aren't they the same as they were in the days of Homer?—and their laughter is Homeric when a beam of genuine humor, loyal to the roots, bursts in from between the clouds of their preoccupations (unexpectedly) and sheds its light on the dispassionate seriousness of their existence. For us, for our corrupted stomachs, maybe all this is a little uncouth, oh, the misery of our niceties, and even their rhythm, for us, children of a hurried age, corrupted by our degenerate intellectualism—what they say is eternal, they repeat everything always, it's a way of dropping anchor . . . into the germ of all that is . . . they know the laws and the roots and the course of the seasons.
Events are scarce in a fishermen's village, but they are profound . . . Even the Captain was an intellectual, he knew only—to the extent he was attached to his ego—that he was thirsty and yearned for a drop of water . . .

Around the hut a little garden, for foreigners. Lampshade of colored paper. Chinese lanterns swaying in the wind. An advertisement for toothpaste. A kiosk with sweets covered in powdered sugar, picture postcards, matches, illustrated magazines, drinks, shaving razors, fishing rods, pipes.

The dirty tables.
Cod-liver oil—exportation

one of the two men asks the Captain where exactly the Sirens are. "The Sirens are always in the left-hand drawer—and that's why my right foot hurts."—he took off at a run, there was no salvation.

How to capture the Sirens—it was absolutely necessary to jettison the half-Siren—it's not as though we're cannibals—

the two fishermen, who later evaluate the watch

Homeric terminology

the fat boy who approaches him

first of all he buys cigars, then he drinks a lot, in the end all he has left is his watch—

You are fishermen, and the sea serves only to provide you with food, and you are familiar with the fish near the coasts, but you know nothing about the Sirens

Here it is, the new life

After the fishermen's huts, sand—crossing the desert

The inhabitants of this place are simple and cheerful, only foreigners are sad and double—the villagers walk around with thermometers and sweaters of three different shades

The Girl of the Woods

THE VOICE AND the breath of the Girl of the Woods were more limpid than those of his wife. Not only was her breath limpid, everything was limpid in the woods.

"Come and get me, you're limping," in a single bound he'd nabbed her. "Oh you're pinching me, you're incapable of playing," he wants to embrace her and console her "and your beard is too long and you stink and your body is covered with red marks."

She looks at him with all the ruthlessness of innocence. She demands too much, she demands too much.

Maybe I'll find a way out, but there are only ways and no ways out.

"Yes," said the Girl, as though revealing an important secret, "you have to go to the city of the Gray Men."
There must be other ways, but I'm in the hands of the Girl of the Woods and she doesn't know any other way, she has never heard of topography (otherwise she wouldn't be the Girl of the Woods).

When the Girl of the Woods saw him in his gray clothes, she was excited. "But now you're going to give me a kiss!" "That I can't do," said the Girl of the Woods, "you don't understand, I'm tired, and besides a man has just now lost his way in the woods,

64

a man much grayer than you, someone who, so to speak, is completely gray inside. I'm sure you've never seen anything like it before!" exclaimed the Girl of the Woods, with sincere excitement. The Captain was disappointed.

"Oh," said the Girl of the Woods, "your trousers are really nicely ironed. "The Hermit up there told me once that men with nicely ironed trousers go far."
"Yes," said the Captain, "but does the Hermit wear nicely ironed trousers?"
"No," said the Girl of the Woods, "just yesterday he threw away his last iron . . . But *I* iron, I iron, I iron . . ."

"The Hermit up there told me that real money only grows on trees."
"Why doesn't he go pick it then?" asked the Captain.
"He searched for it for a long time, but he never found it, and so he stayed in the woods and became a hermit . . ."
"I don't have any more money, my uniform is torn from top to toe and it's covered with red marks, but you can only get clothes in the city, I simply must buy myself a new uniform."
She gives him a green suit: "So at least we have some common ground."

"Just as long as you follow the direction of the comet. There's a new comet in the sky. It's a very strange comet and everyone in the city says that it's an omen, that its time will come."
"What makes it strange, this comet?" asked the Captain.
"It has a long tail and no head. I'm sure you've never seen anything so beautiful before."

The Captain was blissful. He knew now that what he'd searched for all his life was the Girl of the Woods.

A gray young man passed them and in one hand he had a horrible machine, in the other a big empty flagon. The Girl winced.
"He wanted to change my blood into water—he pricked me

and it hurt way too much. You pinched me, he only pricked me. I never want to have anything to do with a man again for the rest of my life. Now I've got a lot of experience. But I've got this huge sense of guilt about him saying that lukewarm water is nobler than blood."

He colors the water with aniline," the Girl says, "isn't that a splendid word? And just think of it, later I can drink it." (Anyway, it was progress.)

"You understand, I'm really afraid of men who change wine into water—but he promised me that afterward he'd color the water with aniline, and now I feel calm and I love him.

"Now I have grown up."

He can't do knee bends.

"Come, I want to show you everything I have." And with a mysterious look she led him to a rock, she rolled back a stone and down below, hidden in a hole, there were glass beads, a department store catalogue, a red comb, ("You see, it was missing two teeth, so I ripped out every second tooth, and now doesn't it look new?), the stump of a candle, pieces of colorful fabric, a mandrake root.
"My gift to you, people say that it brings happiness. You see, if you look at it from this side it's a man, if you turn it slowly around, it's a woman. And now I'll show you something else," she said—and she started delicately unrolling a tiny piece of blue glass from a cloth.
"If you look through it, the world is completely blue. But you have to close one eye, because it's so small."
The Captain was quite touched. If only he had all the things he'd collected on his ship, or if he had some money, he would have bought her more beautiful things, but he didn't have even the smallest coin.
A record album. "Obviously, it isn't a whole record album," said

the Girl, laughing, "but who knows, maybe I will find one, someday, a whole record album."

The box of seashells. She has sticky hands. "But you mustn't tell anyone. It's my own idea."

"Yes, you know, once upon a time there was someone I liked so much, and he gave me a bit of wine to drink, and then I laughed so much I couldn't stop. Then the wine turned into water. Naturally the water also tasted quite good," she anxiously hastened to add: "but I stopped laughing."

She put her hand under his nose to kiss
"Two years ago, when I was even smaller . . ."

In defense of the Gray Young Man: "You know what he said: it's very difficult, but I repeated it to myself until I'd learned it, he said that it's sublimated anal eroticism.

"You know, he explained to me that he projected his unconscious side on me—and you understand, I'm very proud—but now I have to be very careful and be a good girl, because he said that if I'm not a good girl, he will take back his projection right away."

The Gray Young Man goes around the woods with a gas mask and a radio under his arm.

"After all, I can tell you everything . . . you know, I am so pure . . . you know, when at night everything outside is dark, and he is stretched out beside me, and he is so gray, and he keeps the gas mask within arm's reach, and the radio announces that there's nothing new about time—oh, it's so beautiful, there's no way anything so beautiful has ever happened to you . . ."

She defends the First Gray Man: "Look, he really did change wine into water" (she is extremely angry)

The Second Gray Man: "In the service of the idea."

"Just imagine, someone else told him no, and then right away he ran to me, but right away, just imagine it, isn't it beautiful? And you know what he did after that?" . . . She stared at him, beaming. The Captain didn't know how to reply. She, still beaming:
"He seduced me!"
"How did he do that?" inquired the Captain.
"Oh, he said to me that he'd loved me since forever, just imagine! . . . and then he promised me that, if I was really a good girl, maybe one day he'd give me a uniform . . ."

On the First Gray Man: "He ran straightaway to another Girl of the Woods and told her that he'd loved her since forever. And so we are so happy, all four of us."

(The Gray Young Man: he was always running around the woods with a big bundle of newspapers and magazines under his arm.)
"He loves me so much because I remind him of one of his sisters whom he was very fond of and who died of cancer, just imagine . . .
     "But what do you want, I've always dreamed of getting married and I always imagined everything down to the smallest details and it was always a big party with the groom in tails and me in a white wedding gown with a long train, but the dream always ends when I go into the bedroom with my husband, at most there's a kiss, and then it's all over."

"He wrote it for me—only I read so badly—here is the sheet— she took out a little wadded-up piece of paper and deciphered it with effort: he is an au-to-di-dact. Yes," said the Girl, with a dreamy look, "an autodidact—that's why I love him so much . . . and I, I'm an illiterate, I learned the word straight off, but he told me that he'll pull me out of it in a snap."

"He practices birth control with me—you can't imagine how handsome he is . . ."

The Gray Young Man: "Really, I should love a miner's daughter, but around here there are no mines."

The Gray Young Man: long neck, stooped

In the Gray City the Captain pounces on the first woman who comes his way. Then he feels offended because the Girl of the Woods hasn't even been able to wait for him a couple of weeks—he's done it too, but he is a man, for a man it's a completely different thing.

"He absolutely had to vaccinate me."
"Against what?"
"I don't know, I don't care, to get vaccinated is just so beautiful—I would so much like to be vaccinated . . ."

the paper flowers in the vase:
"But in the woods you have real flowers . . ."
"But these are made of paper . . ." explained the Girl of the Woods with bleak excitement . . . Then she looked at him with an uncomprehending expression: why is he simply unable to understand that these flowers are made of paper. (Yes, he didn't understand. He didn't understand and it was discouraging. Everything's unpleasant: *the artificial palm tree*).

She wanted to darn his socks . . .

(anal eroticism): "What on earth doesn't he know, this man"— she shakes her head in admiration—"where on earth do you have to go to learn all these things . . . ?

What on earth doesn't he know, this man:
with the Renaissance a new feeling for the world comes into flower

Freud's eternal merit was

The Gray Young Man: after the scene with the Girl of the Woods he has a bandage on his neck.

To marry a lady centaur.

"Don't smile, act natural," says the photographer. "Your hair is too neat—it isn't natural."
In the end, her hair is disheveled and her face is distraught.
"What a pity that you can see the woods. But later it can be erased . . ."
"What would you have preferred . . . ?"
"The walls of a prison," says the Photographer.
She was beaming.
"Don't beam, act natural—that isn't natural—put on a more serious expression."
She ruffled her hair.

"What a pity that we're in the woods, the most natural thing would be the walls of a prison."
She was quite desperate—around here, there are no prisons: "I know how terrible it is to live in the woods," she said, *conscious of her own guilt.*

In the end she weeps . . .
"Like that, don't move, that's it . . ."

The Captain sees the photograph of the Cabin Boy . . .

"Something happened in my life . . . you will never know . . ." She becomes capricious . . . "But this I won't tell you . . ." (later: after all, a person can tell you anything) . . . "I have a right to my . . . hold on a minute . . . pri . . . privacy . . ."
Something begins to move in him . . . paradise lost . . . You shouldn't get mixed up in it . . . She's half naked . . . "This isn't going to arouse you, I hope . . ."

"You know what he is . . . homosexual . . . isn't that beautiful?"

He's wound up, wants to know what she's done in bed with the other. Everything becomes contradictory . . .

He finds her with red-lacquered nails

"He says it's a feeling of inferiority."

The psychiatrist rolled his eyes around with a terrifying expression . . .

She has written beautiful letters, wants to become a writer . . .

He still doesn't have a watch . . .

He tries to organize the Girl of the Woods's place . . .

He grows distant—but feels guilty because he can't manage to get rid of this tense pain.

"Strange, you know, I've never lost anything."

He offers her a pipette (and a monocle).

This is the difference in methodology . . .
(He is naked, shivering with cold, in a lonely, frozen world—yes, he blubbers, meth-o-dol-og-y. . .).

Polyphilus: (he is washed clean) (WOODS SOUND SPRING WOLF SLEEP)[10]

"To me, the wolf does nothing" (in the end, she runs off)

"Basically it's a psychological thing . . ."

---

10 Reference to the *Hypnerotomachia Poliphili.*

Gray City

THE INHABITANTS
THE population was not cheerful or simple. And the foreigners
were sad and double.
There were:
the man who spits on everything in the street
the man who shuts the window before clobbering his children
the frail woman who drags two suitcases to the bus stop . . .
the man who's afraid of catching cold
the philosopher with hemorrhoids
the grandfather who makes dates with his niece's daughter
and someone stands at the window and stares at a street where
nothing ever happens . . .
the woman who buys sleeping pills in the night pharmacy

and on Sunday they yawned

the fat man never stopped making sacrifices

At the ship-owner's house—how can he find another ship?

He asked to leave, he had to run off immediately to wallow in
the misery she inspired

The impossible child, who devours cigarettes

In the city of the Gray Men, gray progress proceeds along its unstoppable course: the slaves had been set free and the slaves finally became waiters. The first breath of the new age could already be felt in the air (it was an age of utmost splendor).

The city of the Gray Men had its usages and customs. The universally human—the eternal values. One part of the population spent its time in front of, another part behind, a till.

Once in a while somebody got crucified, only out of fear of the Savior.

He always had to do the same work.
"But I've already learned."
"Here, one isn't supposed to learn, here one is supposed to work—(all the better, here one learns only in order to work better)."
"But I am a Sea Captain . . ."
"No, you're just a shipwrecked Captain."

And so he tried to become a Gray Man—he discovers that he finds mechanical work satisfying, and with the money he's earned he buys himself a gray suit, and with the gray suit he goes to see the Girl of the Woods.

I have been so wrongheaded, this is what life on land is.
Perhaps I haven't been completely wrongheaded, but anyway there are lots of things wrongheaded about life on land.
I've never been wrongheaded about anything at all, but all life on land is wrongheaded. (On three occasions, he sees the same vulgar happiness.)

Now I understand the city of the Gray Men who work during the week and on Sunday have their pleasures and their parties: then they embrace and wish each other countless more identical weeks of work and Sundays of cheer, and countless more parties for embracing and weeks for working—now I no longer need to have a guilty conscience—I've lived their life, I really must have had a guilty conscience and so I've lived their life, now I can scorn them in good conscience.

And out of despair he spent all his nights in a tavern. And he'd never learned to play cards, and he didn't even read newspapers, and he stared, broodingly, straight ahead. In his inebriation (blood and sea and wine) images of Sirens—I'm not a shipwrecked Captain, I am a captain who's been shipwrecked and who washed up on a beach, the beach was part of the story—and I slithered out of the belly of the whale, and here, too, I slither out, and with my gray suit I go out into a clear world—

"And what are you making?"
"Shoes!"
"And what did you make yesterday?"
"Shoes!"
"And what will you make tomorrow?"
"Shoes!"
"So your life is made up of nothing but making shoes?"
"If I didn't make shoes, you would have to go around barefoot . . ."
"That's just want we need, for you to stop making me shoes!"

The Captain was very disappointed: no renunciation he had made previously was ever so difficult. He no longer had a wife, the sea was off limits to him, he lived in the Gray City and felt nostalgic for the woods, in the woods he would have been able to discover his innocence, but innocent in the woods he was nostalgic for the Gray City. —He took it out on God and continued talking to himself . . .

The Burgomaster's wife. She doesn't go anywhere, but if sometime by chance he gets a ticket . . .

With effort, he earned a little money, but in the city there were no uniforms to buy, only gray suits—

The Captain dreams of making big deals, by making deals he

thinks he'll be able to buy a big new ship, but the deals fall through his fingers. Once I'm rich, I'll buy myself thousands of new uniforms—but the money was hardly enough to get his shoes resoled.

He tried to make deals—and while he waited for a way out, he felt tormented—it was not a matter of seeing if he knew how to do it skillfully or not—but business operated according to the gray law and, no matter how sincere his efforts, he couldn't manage to make any money following the gray law—he followed his own law, he had nothing to do with the gray law, and it was, it could almost be said, quite random if at any time, on any point, the gray law coincided with his law—it was a veritable roulette wheel—but his law didn't coincide with the gray law and it was his fault, he would have had to know both laws, but he didn't even know his own, and it was fitting that the two didn't work together, he had to serve two masters, but it wasn't simple. Where is my mistake—he thought—and he drank up in wine the little money he made.

Here you're lost forever—See you in the next culture.

And finally will come the splendid day on which he'd fulfilled none of his duties: sometimes we have the duty to do our duty, sometimes we have the duty not to do our duty—it isn't simple.

Difficult, difficult, difficult . . . one blow after another . . . and they have no external logic connecting them, nor internal logic, only a common denominator: You mustn't do it—maybe I'm damned—damned to save myself. Once I was scared, maybe for the blasphemy these words represent—but now I'm not scared anymore—and until it becomes a blessing, it's a curse.

Somebody gets crucified: an absolutely unconvincing face: "But Christ was crucified after his Father had forsaken him, and these people are crucified so that, for the love of God, Papa Christ doesn't forsake them . . ."

"But things aren't really like this, this is pure fantasy—what matters is that blood flows from the cross . . . we just want to change it into water . . ." (Christ and Pontius Pilate—feet and hands . . . whereas we take a shower.)

The miracle that would liberate him never occurred, the miracles that kept him alive occurred constantly

With effort, he managed to get away, by taking a path he'd refused

In worlds that for a long time he'd abandoned

The Captain thought: "After all, anyway, I'm still alive, and after all, anyway, the others are dead."

"If I don't do this deal, I don't do my duty. The deal can't come through, because it doesn't belong to my way of doing deals. People think it's a question posed in an infernal and insoluble way. But it isn't so—because, due to the fact that I do my duty, and due to the fact that the deal doesn't come through, the solution appears to me, which otherwise would never appear to me."

"Whose golden bottom is this?"
"Whose golden clavicle is this?"

The stench of cars: the stench is a consequence of speed, and if you're going fast the stench stays behind you.

They walk around like halves of a couple of lovers.

They don't know what they're afraid of

Black were the chimneysweeps, the gravediggers, the priests. White the nurses, white the psychiatrists, the dentists, and the bakers.

They often light huge fires. Strange that they love fire so much, they who are gray. They don't love fire, it's a necessary evil—they love ashes, ashes, the painters and writers. (The artists are recognizable by their flabby bottoms.)

Someone had heard of the bird Phoenix and he was very ambitious, so he wanted to make a big fire and on it he put a nightstand, and the nightstand rose from the ashes and soared into the sky and became the constellation of the Nightstand. But the poet created a great work, under the sign of the Nightstand, and . . .

The old were venerated because they preserved the memory of days when everything was less expensive. An operation: the old man shakes his head: "In my day, with that kind of money, you could have gotten your stomach sliced open a dozen times at least."

The Burgomaster: fat with skinny legs.

The Burgomaster had had a neurosis about Sundays until the construction of the Eiffel Tower got underway.

"Life is getting more and more expensive, I am getting more and more fat."

He admires the strong. When he runs out of arguments, he becomes infuriated and calls in the Strong Man . . .

He hikes up his trousers and starts scratching his varicose veins.

"I'm happy to talk with you because you're 'a complete man,' you are a 'brilliant conversationalist,' you have experience and intelligence."

The Gray Young Man is ambivalent:

"She's a dear child, but she's disorderly.

I've been telling her that forever, and I repeat it to you.

she doesn't want to understand

intellectually she's disorganized."

He pulls out the most disparate things from his folder

Scandal because the Captain talks with the Burgomaster's Daughter. They have to meet each other in secret. Still, they are found out. The mother attacks him, the father is cowardly and avoids the subject.

The Burgomaster's wife's only problem is with the servants.

The relationship with the Morphine Addict. She'd bought an old pre-dieu. She let down her hair and said that it dated from the Renaissance. (She's the Gypsy.)

At the house, he opens letters: "What's this! A girl should have secrets from her parents?" When they meet, they are seen by the Washerwoman and the Washerwoman tells the Burgomaster's second cousin by marriage.

Scene: "He doesn't go to bed with me . . . he goes to bed with the maid—and I can't say a word, and then if she leaves me it's difficult for me to find another, just imagine that one of my friends told me that one of hers asked her if she could go out twice a week."

The Captain has to leave the girl alone because the Burgomaster's Daughter has to marry the Apprentice, who is cultured, and just seeing how he weighs half a kilo of sugar makes it obvious that he is a man to be trusted.

The flagellants: "We outlawed it, but then crime rose so sharply we had to make it legal again." (For fear of cancer.)

Purification: public enema.

Girl of the Woods

The Girl of the Woods tells him filled with admiration about the splendid things the Gray Young Man has told her. (It's something that the Captain had once said to the Gray Young Man, who had taken it in the stupidest way possible.) "Yes, you know why I love him so much? He told me . . . that no one has ever really understood him so well . . ." "Oh, yes, no one has ever really understood you so well," said the Captain, and he was furious.

The tree: "He told me that it's a masculine and feminine symbol, but it's not an indecent thing, because it's natural."

The scientist: excited because with female hormones the mice become three times bigger. The mice multiply at a worrisome rate. Then they escape from their cages—and the epidemic comes to pass.

Some produce, others consume.
To consume it's necessary to produce, and producers A consume the products of consumers A.
"As you see, the circle is closed . . ."
"Then everything could be eliminated immediately . . ."
"But then life would come to an end."
But hasn't it come to an end already, once the circle is closed?"
The Burgomaster is horrified and ducks into the washroom.

A Sunday stroll with the financial situation in order and hormones in order—suddenly he goes insane: it's the end of life. "Lord, don't give us our daily bread every day!"

The Captain has a relationship with the woman next door. "Do you love me?" The Captain retreats—the woman reminds him of the fat blonde in the brothel.

The hydra: continually sprouting new heads!

Cold—end of the year: December 21
Christmas: compromise with the Christmas housewarming party at the Burgomaster's. "He begs for heat."

March 21 already the positive side predominates
"the days are longer than the nights"

He tried to be alone: nothing binds me to her—phenomena
conquered—strategy—duty—but he can't hack it, he tries to
get into his good graces—parasite—
(everything becomes diplomacy)
So long as he wanted to have the ship, it didn't happen—the
ship is always a gift—the problem is bread, water, a bed, and a
coat—everything else is a gift.

He's an heir, he can only inherit ships.

The great fear of cancer.
Everyone's afraid of cancer.
Everyone feels it, here it hurts, here it must be cancer

Fantasy about the end of the world (someone alleged that the
world had already ended and that from now on everything
would only be reflections, schema, the way the light continues
to reach us long after a star has disappeared).

The Burgomaster: protector
      pissing duel
      stomach ulcer
      "She's stubborn—
      and now she's no longer a child . . ."

The Burgomaster's wife: she searches for a long time in the dirt-
iest corner, she sits down on the floor and cries

Burgomaster's Daughter: Nausicaa with a tennis ball . . .

The Captain hadn't shown the Burgomaster's Daughter any love
(love is a bad word, let's say that he'd been irresponsible), a dilettante, he had to save her, he couldn't have her on his conscience,

I am her last and final disappointment—he had to save her, the four men in the inn come to blows, why didn't he ever do it when he was with his wife?

but they shouldn't be disturbed . . . Yes, he said, they're together day and night, and they work uninterruptedly . . . "But what can they can they be doing?" asked the Captain . . . "They're saving human-ism," said the other . . . "Then they really shouldn't be disturbed," said the Captain . . .

The mute. —The paralyzed . . .

The Burgomaster: "Then you're the new foreigner. The police alerted me of your arrival. But people who come back from the Castle of the Grail have good prospects. There's only one alter-native: it's the Castle of the Grail or here—the modern. "But there's also the eternal," thought the Captain.

The Persecution of Destiny

A world war erupted.

Lassitude, apathy, resignation. Toothaches.

And the specter of the great uprising (of the internal eruption) when liberation begins.

Famished, he eats too much and is overtaken by sleepiness, while happiness passed him by—bewitched

(prostitutes himself, and tells stories to eat?)

He walks around spasmodically, stumbles, crossing the street is now a perilous adventure, at night at the intersections suddenly the big lights loom, he can't calculate the distance, the distance of the ships that pass, that girl knew how to calculate it with precision, he was in the middle of the road, noise and stench, the nervous tension was too great, he was afraid.

The worm on the table (primitive culture)

Anonymous letter

Taxes

The telephone always busy (he is thrown into a persecution mania and believes someone has picked up the receiver.)

Chitchat—he smokes too much

He thinks he's found peace when, one day, a gray young man tells him that he and the Girl of the Woods are in love, and this stirs him up. It's the Apprentice who knows how to measure sugar so well (she is surprised and excited, and then she falls in love with him).

He waits for the mail: letters that aren't for him arrive, a catalogue of books that he can't buy, a postcard with greetings and an illegible signature (WHO THINKS OF ME?)

Now the Captain is almost on the verge of shipwreck—because the real shipwreck is when everything dissolves into the water, there isn't enough land here to drop anchor—and yet there must be an anchorage—

Where was the error? He had to become a sailor, but with the intention of becoming a captain again—and suddenly this was magic, and therefore black magic, because he had an intention . . .

He knows he ought to love the Girl of the Woods—but the

Sirens always come between them . . .

and in the end he hears the song of the Sirens again—and again he falls into the water—the *same thing* has to *be repeated* always at the most varied layers before it's overcome (but are the layers finite in number?)

As the persecution dissolves, more and more colors return— when he leaves the city everything glistens

A lonely Christmas

The Captain hopes that a woman will help him but they always want something from him, the Captain removes the stuffing from the pillows (plunged into his thoughts), etc.

Hamlet had nice legs, and he showed them off, and he showed them off . . . and then: for God's sake, even the cinema has its possibilities of expression, for example monologues . . . he kept his mouth shut and yet he could be heard, and what could be heard was exactly what he thought . . . it was almost as beautiful as a ventriloquist . . .

Then some country or other calls its people to arms against some other country . . . the temples are destroyed, the villages burn . . . somewhere on the battlefield a clavicle . . .
"Whose golden clavicle is this?" . . .

out for a stroll with holey socks. The hole was always rising up out of his shoe. He thrust his hands into his pockets . . . so that the trousers went down and covered his heels . . . But the pockets of his trousers were also a bit holey, and the heels of his shoes weren't quite right either. . . yes, so that's how things stood . . . (Achilles's heel) . . .

Too expensive: that one may not have enough money to buy something, this the Captain learns quickly and painlessly, although here it's a matter of not having enough money for what is *almost* of vital importance—but that something should be too expensive (the ugliness of what is too expensive), this was more than he could take . . . he erupted . . .

The trams transport surplus meat . . .

The fat old women on the tram wobbled and he laughed. Generally he laughed in an amiable and commiserating way, but sometimes it was impossible to stop himself and he concentrated on the principle that governed the wobbling.

Cleaning his own shoes: he had to arrive at simple joy, destiny teaches him humility—but the only thing that comes of it is that finally he knows why he never wanted to clean his own shoes . . .

The complications of money: give me a loan until the day after tomorrow—it will come no later than the day after tomorrow . . . but the day after tomorrow everything will be sorted out, certainly, otherwise I'll die of hunger.
Money makes the rounds . . . In the end, the blonde has the other blonde's dough, he has lent it to him, but if she can't give it back until tomorrow, I can give it to you tomorrow, but first he has to make a call . . .

In a magazine, he sees a photograph of the actress . . . it's all unleashed again . . .
The photograph of the actress in the Bible.

The next day he already had a relationship with the seamstress next door.
She sews him trousers . . .

He is euphoric—the master of the house reproaches him for banging on the door—the Captain doesn't buckle, but a vague memory of the mark of Cain.

Problem of the watch . . . (repaired when everything is put in order)

when he goes back, the shop is closed due to "grave family bereavement"

Burgomaster: "Please, touch me a little here on my stomach, it's swollen, it must be an ulcer"—he goes to the pharmacy and points to a jar with his umbrella

the picture by the modern painter: *Seated woman without a cat.*

The Burgomaster: the newspaper folded into the prayer book.

I found myself with annoying work to do—and I couldn't write letters because first I had to finish it, and I went to sleep so as not to begin it—
money already spent—money not received—
my work (with a guilty conscience because the others' work needs to be done)
wintertime lethargy (rhythms of life)
Rome mud
that in order to write I need to drink, but in order to drink to eat, but eating makes me heavy, and therefore melancholy, therefore I drink without eating, but drinking without eating the wine goes to my head and the next morning I feel it, and then I can't write, and guilty conscience because I'm not writing, and therefore no letters, in order to work, but the work is annoying, therefore sleep, but too much sleep, and by now not sleeping is a triumph, and therefore to the cinema

The two lighted buildings. On one side , they were continually in session to battle against cancer, on the other they were continually in session to save humanism. They don't want cancer, no, they want humanism, yes—they ask too much, they ask too much.

The abbot-like ways of the Captain: "She's my new love . . . "
"But I, alas, always used to stop at that." Later: the Captain's crisis
over his dilettantism.

In the Gray City, too, problems with order: take care, so that
disorder doesn't set in . . . Shopping, he barely has any money,
brand-new, he begins the new life . . .
but he sits around for hours with a shoe in his hand, reflecting.
When everything is really put in order, he remains there, and
he's empty, and he doesn't know what he should do.

Shopping in the drugstore: half a kilo of sugar . . . he stands at
the counter, old women shoulder past him and are served before
him . . . when finally it should be his turn, an energetic woman
comes in and is already shouting at the door: two kilos of sugar.
He would like to flee . . . when he sees how the half kilo of sugar
is weighed he decides to emigrate . . .

The tomb of the Unknown Employee.
Loyalty to duty, it's on this that the life of the city is founded.
Hidden heroism: in spite of the rain, punctual to work—and
even when his mother dies, the day after the funeral he goes
punctually to the office, eyes bloodshot from weeping.

The ooze that is approaching from every side.

(Hells, Charon—the obol)
The Burgomaster's Daughter—Persephone—Eurydice—goes
away without turning back

(What Karma must the Captain overcome in the Gray City)

But it would seem the Captain exercises some sort of attraction
over the Burgomaster—he's always rubbing against his legs, like
a cat, until he's converted him, he'll have no peace—

The Persecution of Destiny Dissolves

meets the Oriental Captain: "What a pity that last time you didn't wait for me. I know that you weren't happy with your helmsman, and my helmsman's brother was out of work, and I would have been happy to recommend him to you. . . they're splendid helmsmen . . . I searched for you for a long time and then they told me that you set off again after just one day . . .

(Oriental helmsman on the new ship?)

"I brought you a rug, then I found out you were dead and I left it to your wife."

he has work to do, he is bogged down, he has a guilty conscience. —His employer calls him on the phone with a guilty conscience, he would like to pay, because there's no more need for his work—he hasn't gotten rid of the manuscript—guilty conscience between the call and the message—

(Heracles): he gets stung by the scorpion

the old captain a curmudgeon . . .
he sailed past all the sirens, but they were only hallucinations, optical or auricular illusions . . . from then on, he became curmudgeonly, his ship sits motionless in a distant port, decommissioned . . .
When he dies, he leaves the ship to the Captain . . .

Before setting off, he offers the Girl of the Woods a gramophone (?), a pair of golden shoes . . .

Just when he comes to understand, the bond between the Girl of the Woods and the Gray Young Man is loosened. But he draws back, the Captain can be fulfilled only with the Girl of the Woods—he is slightly piqué. He makes a present of the golden shoes and leaves. —He wakes up to the Burgomaster's Daughter's charms. He decides to set sail for his port to find her (he figures this out through the ship on which she sets sail) and she gives him the courage to face his wife and the widows.

Guilty conscious for having driven her to the tavern—his cowardice (posing as courtesy) in avoiding a confrontation with the three of them: he defeats them internally, visionarily

His head is clear, the cloud dissolves, the Gray City is gone . . .

The Burgomaster's Daughter

THE GRAY MEN whispered that she was hysterical. She was very confused. Sometimes my contempt is greater than my anxiety, sometimes my anxiety is greater than my contempt.

The Captain tells the story of the port and the tavern. "I don't want to be saved," she said morosely, "those who are born in the Gray City can never ever do anything good—but as I can't do good, I prefer to do evil, they deserve it."
the next day the girl disappeared

and this was the Burgomaster's Daughter. "How clear are the voices that are singing." Then she said: "And perhaps these voices will remain clear forever and won't have to grow hoarse."
"That I don't believe," said the Captain, "they still have their whole lives ahead of them, complete with heavens, hells, and purgatories. And so their voices will also grow hoarse, and then clear again, life never stops moving, and so they'll be both happy and unhappy!"
"Happy and unhappy, yes, but happy with great happiness, unhappy with great unhappiness. They play together in the garden, and they've been spared their parents' gloomy room, with its solemn angst and anemic joy. Their father could never have beat them, their mother would have given them the bread from her own mouth. And the beatings would have shaped their lives, the bread would have poisoned their lives. It's a lucky thing their parents are dead, a lucky thing that you'd want to marry

89

the Siren" (and they would have had to beat their children).

"Yes," said the Captain, "a free child is better than a living father. And I went around, in a certain sense, with a guilty conscience, and this all depended on pots of geraniums and the canary in its cage. It's true that near the vineyard I grew roses and went hunting with my hawk, but in my house there were always the geraniums and the canary constantly scurrying in his cage. I think that geraniums and canaries belong in the tavern . . ."

"And I was just on my way to the tavern," said the girl, and she started to laugh.

The Captain said to his wife:

"Let's take the cage and the potted geraniums to the tavern. Let's grow roses and get a falcon instead!"

At first the wife was very surprised, then something flashed across her mind, and finally she grew excited:

"Don't you think dogs with their wretched bones would be much better off on the doorstep of the tavern? Let's get a cat instead."

"You're quite right, but ever since we starved him, the dog is so much meeker, so much meeker that he'll surely die soon. I think we ought to let him die in peace. Then we can get a cat. Of course, it would be better to have a lion . . ."

"That would be grand," said the woman, still enthusiastic, "but everything has its limits, perhaps we should be content with your cat."

The Gray Men had even found a name to describe her behavior: they said that she was "hysterical"—and with that, for the Gray Men, the problem was solved (whispered contemptuously).

"I should tell you that you're still very young and that major unhappiness is minor unhappiness, and major happiness is minor happiness. But perhaps I'm as young as you are, and I believe in a time when, happy or unhappy, voices will remain equally clear."

with his descents into hell and his ascensions to heaven, yes, but without the eternal purgatory of his parents

"Yes, their place is in the tavern, and I'll put them there. But it's not a simple thing. When I came back this time and saw the colorful pots and their smell wafted toward me . . ."
"Hydrangeas don't have a smell!" the Burgomaster's daughter bluntly observed.

He went to his wife's house with the news. "Listen, hydrangeas don't have a smell, what made me think that the hydrangeas smelled—and that's why they're the symbol of eternal love. 'Eternal love has no smell.' The place of eternal love is in the tavern. Perhaps they used to smell, once upon a time, perhaps precisely when my grandfather was swallowed by the whale—perhaps he had to be swallowed by the whale precisely because he knew the smell of hydrangeas—but I felt enticed to come back home only to discover that hydrangeas don't have a smell anymore—and now their place is in the tavern. Roses still have a smell—I think as long as they go on smelling, we should go on growing roses . . ."

"They belonged to the days of my grandfather—the hydrangeas in the window—but my grandfather was swallowed by the whale, and when he came back out those days were over, and I came into the world to see hydrangeas in the tavern."

Do you have any news from your country? (Life is getting more and more expensive.) "Yes, a lot, but everything that happens is always and eternally the same. Once, I received an unnecessary letter of excuses from my father: he's so gray that he forgives even—but what could have happened there? Gray progress continues. —THE END

"I spoke to you of the vast world, you gave me the courage to return from the vast world."

"You don't believe that I, too, may be a siren?" "Probably, but you have these doubts, and so you're harmless, and getting better." "Yes, but anyway . . ."

The Cabin Boy

THE CABIN BOY comes in a car and marries the Burgomaster's Daughter (the Burgomaster's wife is slightly nervous: she inquires about the Cabin Boy, whom she liked, she admits).

"No, I went on swimming in circles and I was sure everyone had drowned."—he forced the Helmsman's head underwater— (he'd grown sentimental and might have bragged about how difficult this had been) "I left you alone, you were in enough trouble already."

"I will do everything possible to forget you" (pointless pain). Discussion with the Captain: "It would be unfair not to take you adequately into account—and besides I'm indebted to you for a couple of pesos (and a flask of wine too).

"Don't be afraid. All the others drowned. For the sailors, this is of no importance . . . but the Helmsman . . . seamen dead or alive—it's all the same . . .

(The children bite their lips, they understood!) You see, fifteen years ago, everyone would have wept and that's how their lives would end.
(But let's take them with us.)

On that day, the Innkeeper's wife entered a convent, grew moldy there, and by and by ascended to heaven.

93

The Cabin Boy became a detective, redskin, and boxing champion. "You only saw your battle with us two, and not my battle with the Helmsman—but one of the two of us was superfluous—and I held his head underwater until I was sure he wasn't going to celebrate any kind of resurrection . . .

The Helmsman's Wife

THE EPIDEMIC CARRIED off many widows, epidemics provoked by mice serve expressly to carry off widows. The others have already gotten remarried and have in any case rediscovered a place for themselves in life, life goes on, they have all forgotten their husbands. Only the Helmsman's wife remains, she has no husband, she has no children, she wanders around pale and hungry, her lips are bitten, and her empty eyes stare into the distance, her face is covered with pimples. The orphans have already been taken care of, an orphanage has been established. But the choice of the first directress was not a very happy one: they would like to give the post to the Helmsman's wife.

"You mentioned the Helmsman's wife. You don't want to sew, and there's no question you shouldn't, but I need new uniforms—give her some work, just a little at first, perhaps we'll manage to make her work on a regular basis and then she'll get over her rigidity. I don't feel comfortable around her and I'd prefer to have another seamstress, but the Helmsman's uniforms were very well sewed and after all he is dead because of me, I want to make sure she doesn't die because of me too, it's my responsibility—it would be wrong to say too much, and I know everything that's happened, and everything I've thought, and I know it's worth a thousand times more than her life, and the life of the Helmsman, and the lives of all the sailors, but in a certain sense my conscience isn't clear, I want to fix everything that can be fixed. I don't feel comfortable around her, the best thing to do is to put the sewing machine up in the attic. (So that she, too, will be able to earn her living.)

The wife relayed this to the widow and thought she'd answer her with some obscenity. But she said in a toneless voice, "Okay," and on the first day she came for an hour, then two, and finally she stayed sitting all day in the attic, at the sewing machine, like a stone—black, silent, unbending, and she sewed with a resentful, bullied-looking expression.

One day the wife said: "I think that instead of working at your uniforms she should work for herself. Earlier, when I opened the attic door, she rushed to hide something. I saw it was a colorful fabric, with flowers. And when she turned back to face me, her eyes were no longer fixed on the void, in fact I'd almost say she looked at me with something like insolence." "You see," said the Captain, "it was good to give her something to work at, now she's gradually waking up to a new life."

One day the seamstress appeared suddenly transformed: she continued to wear her black dress, but her voice was less hollow, her body more limber, and overnight all the pimples had vanished from her face.

"She is really flourishing," said the Captain, "I managed to put things back in order, now she has a purpose in life again, she's felt protected by us, her work has done her good, I don't need to have her on my conscience anymore. The Helmsman always told me she was quite a good woman."

she asks herself if the Helmsman's last thoughts were for her. Always healthy, nimble-footed, with his sailor's stride—our happy nights of love, she has always been faithful to him—

the dog starts sitting next to the sewing machine.

Tavern

The Innkeeper got old and became more and more chatty

The stockings were kept as a devotional souvenir.

Advertisements for Coca-Cola (as a surrogate for pornographic photos) (Peg-leg no longer takes out the photographs, but stares at women in bathing suits) (the decadence of the Sirens)

"Ah-ha! I was helmless, I was the widow of the Helmsman— now, I have another helmsman . . ."

When the Captain sees the advertisements, he recognized in them the Sirens degenerated and trivialized

Radio—television (they sat quietly in front of these images).

The dogma of the immaculate abortion of Mary

So many illustrated magazines.

The Captain fraternizes with the trio, drinking with them.

1. He pinches men
2. Gratitude for the hydrangeas
3. He finds the Helmsman's wife
4. Betrothal

5. Vision of the new man

6. The entanglement (*Death of the innkeeper*)

1. But the four in the tavern had been spared by the epidemic. The gas lamp poured out its thick smoke, the One-Eyed Man had taught the Craterface to play cards, the Craterface had taught the One-Eyed Man to get drunk. Once in a while they fought and swapped insults. The Peg-leg sat there very quietly, he didn't play cards, he didn't smoke, he pinched the other two on the thighs. At first he'd done it for lack of women, but then he'd had to admit it was just as nice with men.

2. The four of them never managed to explain to themselves why they'd received a gift of hydrangeas and a canary. They sat there all night and puzzled over it. Finally they thought that they'd figured it out, there was no other possibility: the woman was nostalgic for the fine hours they'd spent together in the tavern and sent them as a sign of her gratitude. Now they knew what they needed to know and planned to pay her back in kind. And so a box wrapped in a light blue tissue paper was delivered to the woman's house. And with it a pink letter. In the letter it was written: an unforgettable gift in return, from those who retain a memory of eternal friendship, of unstinting fidelity, and of eternal cordial memory. Followed by signatures . . . Even if you had to forget us, we will never forget you . . . The woman unrolled the paper and opened the box: inside, wrapped in tissue paper and protected by confetti, there was a slate with sticks of chalk, a corkscrew, and some sugar tongs (what can be done with them: put them away in the black chest!)

(In the language of flowers, hydrangeas signify: I want. In the language of fidelity, canaries signify: if possible, always apart.)

They'd kept the socks—but there were holes in the heel . . .

3. The Captain would gladly have gone down to the tavern more often, but the smoke was too much for him, and so one

day he brought an oil lamp that he'd bought on one of his voyages. It was night and, to his horror, he spotted the Helmsman's widow sitting there, her floral dress was open.

"Now finally it's like it was in the good old days!" the One-Eyed Man shouted at him, coming up to him full of enthusiasm. "All women are the same—and he goes to bed with her, too—as they have been since the Assumption of Mary!"

"What is he blathering on about?" the Helmsman's widow groaned, and she powdered her chest prudishly.

"But even if she wants to look refined, ha, ha!" the Craterface squealed, "now we have some experience . . . We know it's possible to get by very well even without women!"

"With you there's no danger!" said the Peg-leg.

"Unfortunately, that doesn't always hold true!" observed the Innkeeper. "His eyes rolled slowly around. He thought of his wife, who'd run off with a sailor who played the accordion.

The oil lamp was admired at length and swiftly set on the counter, under a bell jar.

("God, how indiscreet . . ." and she prudishly powdered her nipples, her breasts wobbling like gelatin.)

The next morning, the Helmsman's widow was again sitting punctually at her sewing machine.

4. The Peg-leg gets married: "Even I will grow old and weak and die. But my line mustn't come to an end. It's an important line. I am one of the pillars of human society. But then I must get married soon, because when I'm old my son must already be grown up and be able to carry on my activity. Not only must my line not come to an end, but it must also never be inactive. What I have inherited from my fathers must be my son's inheritance too. He'll have to work to get it and he'll do it, no doubt. I'll love my wife forever"—and he pinched her to seal what he'd said—(and the Captain had even laid the groundwork for this marriage.) The Captain saw that the Peg-leg went on sitting there with his face all covered with grease, the Craterface struggled to keep his eyes closed, and the Peg-leg

hopped in circles around the tavern. "What do you want?" said
the Innkeeper, they've experienced unity, they've found out that
they're too specialized, and faced with the experience of unity
there's nothing to be done. It's in the air, the times are chang-
ing, they want unity, in my day they wanted synthesis, and my
father, God bless his soul, wanted only Alsace and Lorraine. The
times demand the creation of a new unity."

(*ne voulait que la revanche*,[11] wanted only Trento and Trieste.)

5. They were sitting around again, as usual: "We want to do our
duty, we haven't been allowed to do it, it was really too boring
and wearisome. At first we thought the task would be passed
down to the next generation, but then we found an easy way to
make sure of it. The Craterface and the One-Eyed Man must
get married, too, God willing the next shipwreck will furnish
fresh young sailors' widows and our children will always inter-
marry (grandsons and sons of grandsons), we want to make
cross-breedings according to the laws of selection, and one day
the age will bear fruit and the new man will appear, with a single leg, and somewhere on his face a single eye, and his face will
be one big crater."

The gas lamp poured out a thick smoke, the canary sang, on the
bar the hiss of a rattlesnake could be heard (we are becoming prim-
itives), and with his face transfigured the Innkeeper sniffs the hydrangeas. When the Peg-leg seduced the Helmsman's widow, the
world was in flower . . . it was his Indian summer. Later: the Helmsman's widow is "happy," there's only one thing missing, that the Peg-leg
has a tattoo . . . He proposes . . . a big beautiful flower with a lifeline .
. . "It would be beautiful, but I'm not to used to that kind of thing
(it embarrasses me) . . . "What would you want?" He reflected: " . .
. A cannon." "That, too, would be beautiful, but it would scare me
a little." "So what would you want?" She turned red all over, she
threw herself into his arms, and she whispered something in his
ear . . . "Splendid," said the Helmsman, and he puffs out his

11 "wanted only revenge." (AA)

chest and rushes away that instant to get a tattoo.

BUT: the Innkeeper had been standing at the bar the whole time, and he'd listened in on the conversation with great satisfaction . . . When he'd heard the cannon mentioned, he'd given a nod of approval . . . but, as he hadn't understand what the woman had proposed, his heart was heavy . . . he wanted very much to ask, but he didn't dare, his Indian summer was over, and this is where the slow death of the Innkeeper begins . . .

(He tries again on various occasions to find out what the tattoo is of.)

Death of the Innkeeper

THE INNKEEPER WAS old and tired. He said: "Life has dealt me some low blows and the perfect number is four, and now that you have a wife at home I'm superfluous. I've slaved away for you, with sweat on my brow, and you're ungrateful, you haven't had faith in me, but when you're old like I am, then you'll understand me. Now I'm old and I'm transfigured by age, now I want to make one last sacrifice, but the last sacrifice, this last time, will be a rooster. Bring me a rooster, I want to kill it, my ancestor did it before me, roosters have become really expensive, during the last epidemic they sacrificed all the roosters, there was a real boom, but anyway it isn't a bad business: I sacrifice the rooster and in compensation, after death I'll find myself in a much bigger tavern,[12] at every table a Innkeeper dozes, and every table has its gas lamp and exhales a thick celestial smoke. And if it turns out I don't have to die right away, you could still make me a rooster soup, and if it's still possible for me to do it, I would drink the rooster soup, and in this last rooster soup I would drink all the rooster soups of my life (I'll let them pass before my eyes, before my eyes that are already growing cloudy). You could make me a rooster soup right now. Already I welcome death, and besides, you'll shed bitter tears over me, you haven't understood who I am, while I was alive, you will see it when I'm dead, but then it will be too late. I

12 The German word for "tavern" is *Spelunke*, which also means "cave." There is an obvious play on words here, in keeping with the various Socratic and Platonic allusions in the story of the Innkeeper.

have no torch to pass, in compensation I have a gas lamp, and I bequeath it to my wife, she'll become a good innkeeper, the gas lamp is under the bar, the matches in the right-hand drawer, I'm leaving everything in order, as you can see, despite my old age, I'm not forgetting even the smallest particular. Because I'm transfigured, and I welcome death. And I breathe in once more, with all of my senses open, the scent of the hydrangeas, my eyes wander around and see flowers and gas lamps, I die in beauty, the great tavern awaits me."

The three others looked for the rooster, but they couldn't find it. The rooster had vanished. The Innkeeper started screaming like a man possessed, he was in a state of spasmodic tension, he followed their doings with anxious eyes.

"Find the rooster, you damned fools, find the rooster; otherwise I won't reach the tavern, for the love of God, I'm dying."

They searched every nook and cranny. The Craterface said, thoughtfully:

"Maybe we could sacrifice the canary instead."

And for this he got a kick from the Innkeeper, who was still screaming like a man possessed. Suddenly the rooster sang out beside the sewing machine, they found him beneath the woman's skirts. The woman was quite surprised and assured them that she absolutely had not noticed him, but the Peg-leg's face darkened. The Innkeeper continued to scream:

"But what's with him, looking down there . . ."

But then he screamed again:

"Quick, a bucket!"

The bucket was brought, the Innkeeper killed the cock quickly then lay down on the sofa, his face was transfigured, he closed his eyes.

"Now, he's sure to say something very wise, in valediction," said the Craterface.

But the Innkeeper said nothing. The Craterface said to the Peg-leg:

"Give him a pinch, maybe he really will say something very wise."

The Peg-leg pinched the Innkeeper; the Innkeeper moaned

"Ow!," his eyes opened and rolled around questioningly.

"The soup is ready?"

"Ready in a tick," the Peg-leg shouted in his ear. "In valediction, you must say something very wise to us."

The Innkeeper reflected for a moment:

" . . . Everything is relative . . ." he whispered, and his eyes closed.

"These words were not only very proper," said the Craterface, "they were also beautiful and solemn; pinch him again, maybe he'll say something else very wise."

"Life is kind of funny. Men are puppets."

This was even more beautiful and articulate, and just as solemn and distinguished.

The Craterface said:

"I think it might be good to give him one more pinch."

"Ow!" moaned the Innkeeper, and his eyes rolled still more wearily around in his head . . . "But now, I'd like my soup . . ."

"No," shouted the Craterface, "you're running out of time, I really think that your last hour has come, soon you'll breathe your last breath, now you're going to mumble something else very wise to me!"

The Innkeeper whispered almost inaudibly:

"To understand everything means to lose . . ."

At this point he broke off, his eyes closed, his face irradiated the beatitude of a superior life.

"How far away he is now . . ." said the Craterface. "I think that now he really is in the great tavern."

"Yes," said the One-Eyed Man, "*mourir c'est partir beaucoup*; but unfortunately he took his wisdom with him to the tomb and we'll never know what it means, to understand everything . . ." and he started pinching the dead Innkeeper.

"Completely useless," said the Peg-leg. "I knew it, he'll never say another word . . ."

"No," said the One-Eyed Man, "that's not why I'm pinching him, it's because the city is crawling with sailors' widows, I'm going to marry soon, and in the meantime I'm practicing on an inanimate object. Only when a man has perfectly mastered the technique can he take on living objects, anything else would be irresponsible, a mishap can always occur, it can occur quite easily, one can never be too careful, thank God for the empirical tradition."

With these words the Craterface had approached and started pinching him too, cautiously, but he didn't look convinced.

The One-Eyed Man consoled him:

"You'll see, with a living woman it's probably better."

And they went on pinching the dead man, one out of sincere conviction, the other probably out of a sense of duty and altruism.

The Innkeeper: "All my life has been nothing but a preparation for death."

"You don't have faith in me, I've been your father and nothing should be hidden from a father."

The Innkeeper: "Soon I'll die—ultimately, I'll be spared nothing. Instead of hanging around me like a bunch of idiots, my dear friends, jot down my last words . . . At the top right, put the date . . . (he dies)."

"The beauty of death, that soon the body crumbles into dust. *Vanitas, vanitas vanitatum.*"
His lungs rattled.

The woman had started to pluck the rooster. "Just think," she said, "an hour ago he was still alive, and already he's dead and his eyes are closed forever. But life goes on, and our sadness mustn't make us forget our daily duties, and the day's events have shaken us up and we feel exhausted, and we deserve a good rooster soup, unfortunately he wasn't granted the right to taste it, thanks to God."

The Peg-leg gazed at her with a satisfied expression: it was the rooster that had sung three times when the Captain's wife had gone away. "He's sung his last song now!" thought the Peg-leg, and he stared affectionately at the mother of his future children. The Innkeeper lay there, his face was transfigured by death, there were no blue marks on his body. They had placed the hydrangeas all around him, and in the meantime the soup was ready. "The Innkeeper is dead, long live the Innkeeper's wife." The four of them wiped the sweat from their brows, slurped the soup, and right away regained their strength.

"It's beautiful, the peace of death," said the Peg-leg, "but there is an even more beautiful peace, long is the road that leads there, we've only traveled the first stretch and haven't reached the end, and our only consolation is that the road is strewn with flowers" (at this point he winked flirtatiously at his wife) "and when at last, in the lower heavens, all the stars are in a bad sign, and the moon is in the sign of the Shark, and the sun is in the sign of the Cow, then a time of great peace will come for the new man: gracefully rolled up in a ball, he will suck with his single mouth on his solitary foot, his one eye closed, the meaning of time fulfilled, the circle closed . . ."

"Ow!" the woman cried, "but that hurts!"

The Craterface had given her an awful pinch. In light of his previous experiments, he thought that marriage wouldn't suit him, but he wanted to make sure it was in fact nicer doing it with a living woman. The Peg-leg jumped up and threw a tuft of hydrangea at his head. The Innkeeper was dead and now they could finally let loose. The canary sang, the dog barked, the age of eternal quiet was still a long ways away. It turns out that the tattoo depicted a vase of forget-me-nots . . .

"I look back on my hardworking life with pride."

It's the maternal second cousin of the Unknown Soldier.

"There won't be any need to say of me that . . ."
"Let's clean up. The corpse shouldn't lie around here in all this chaos, if someone comes in he mustn't get the impression we don't know how to live."

The new innkeeper also kept canaries and hydrangeas under bell jars, where they grew splendidly. For a long time they had ceased to be alive. Perhaps the canary had scampered off and continued to sing, even though he'd been stuffed for quite a while now, and perhaps the hydrangeas had continued to flourish, even though they were made of fabric and iron wire. But as it happened that the first canary died of hunger, because the woman hadn't given him anything to eat, and as it happened that the hydrangeas withered, because they hadn't been watered, this will remain a secret for the ages.

Return

FOR A LONG time the Captain had forgotten about his wife.
News of the epidemic in his native port gave him hope that she,
too, was dead (though she wasn't a widow)—the discomfort of
remembering her (I will plug my nose, etc.)—but he still sees
the red trousers before him, he discovers he's deeply nostalgic
for the trousers—he had only looked at them a moment—oh, if
only the Burgomaster's Daughter had sewed me a pair of trousers.

"It's my fault," he said, "I should have understood her, and I
should have put on my red trousers—I should never have disappointed her."

"And perhaps even the kiss of the Sirens . . ."

She wears a white dress—she's fixing him something to eat ("I
haven't forgotten what you like")—caviar with vodka—and San
Daniele prosciutto and mayonnaise and strong beer and turtle
soup—and strawberries and herring and Liptauer . . .

The Captain eats too much, and what's more he no longer likes
the taste of Sauternes, etc.

Discomfort seeing the widows and orphans, he didn't exactly
have a guilty conscience, but he didn't like to look them in the
eyes. After all they didn't even know that the ship had foun-

dered because he wanted to marry a Siren, it could just as well have been a tempest, a new current not marked on the maps.

But after his return the widows are anxious, they think that their husbands might come back too. Nearly every day one of the widows came to inquire if he was really sure that her husband had drowned. The Captain obviously couldn't assure her, he could only explain that the chances were very good it had happened, and the widows went away not at all consoled.

Only captains are granted resurrection from the waters, but who knows, perhaps there was a captain concealed among the crew.

And so he went back into the house and his wife came up to him. Her arms and her neck and the tops of her breasts were white and bore no trace of bruises. Her voice was clear. And he gave her a kiss as he entered, and her breath was even purer than when they had given each other their first kiss in a long-ago spring. "This is the kiss of the Girl of the Woods," the Captain thought.

She said: "Your gray suit is all in tatters."

He thought: "Perhaps it's actually the kiss of the Siren."

She took him by the hand, she led him to the black chest and opened it: inside were his red jacket and his red trousers, freshly ironed, just like his uniforms used to be.

"Until you get some new clothes, you'll have to make do with the red suit."

She spoke these words in a rather courteous tone, with not so much as a trace of triumph in her voice.

"Red's better than gray anyway."

"Anything's better than gray," said the Captain. He said it in a courteous tone, but the phrase was still somewhat tactless. He wanted to make things better and said how nostalgic he had felt for these trousers. "I could see every last stitch of these trousers as clear as day. I think I'd be able to recognize every last stitch."

Even from a long way off he saw the dog, by the door of the

house, was playing with his bones, and he decided not to close his eyes, and the scent of the oleanders in the windows wafted toward him, and he decided not to plug up his nose, and a canary sang, and he decided not to stop up his ears. And even from a long way off he saw the dense smoke from the tavern rising into the sky . . .

They drank tea in the bright room (and there was the small rug, which now he had to unroll), but despite everything the DEEP DEPRESSION AFTER THE RETURN: the ceilings too high, the sounds rang out in the emptiness, he couldn't manage to fill the rooms, the emptiness between one object and another—everything almost alien (repetition of the woman's emptiness).

The woman, laughing: "In the meantime I sewed the red jacket, I want to show it to you." The Captain said: "This time, I'm going to put it on right away."

The Captain is thin, the jacket is too big for him, and the trousers aren't finished.

Conversations After the Return

"THERE'S SOMETHING STRANGE, though," said the Captain, "I can remember everything exactly, you know I have a good memory, but there's something that I'm not quite sure about: was I or wasn't I in the belly of the whale? I have no memory of how I ended up there, only how it was in there and how I managed to get out, that I can see as clear as day, I must have been a little stupider back then, but all the same, back then I must have known where I came from, and now I really can't say . . ."

"It wouldn't be the first time," said the wife, "and after all it runs in the family . . ."

"What do you mean?" asked the Captain in surprise. "What does it have to do with my family?"

"You yourself once told me that your grandfather had fallen into the sea during a whale hunt and been swallowed by a whale . . ."

"Oh, that . . ." said the Captain scornfully. "But he never managed to get out again."

He smiled: "If you sew me another pair of trousers . . ."

"No," she said, in a strange, serious tone, "maybe that was my mistake. That is why seamstresses exist, to do these things—perhaps I'll never pick up a needle again . . ."

"Yes," the Captain said a bit anxiously, "but if I should lose a button . . ."

"I'm not sure about that either," she replied, still serious, "the best thing would be to discuss it when and if we need to. (It will be best to decide case by case.) And let's not make plans."

Long voyages, but equally long periods at home. Sometimes he brings her with him on his voyages, he'd never gone anywhere with her since their honeymoon:

"I should have always brought you with me, even back then."

"No," she said, "that wouldn't have been right, then I wouldn't have sewn you the red trousers. And I wouldn't have gone to bed with the Peg-leg either. You know, I've always loved you, from the start, but now, if I think back on it, I feel that my life only really began with the Peg-leg."

"Yes," he replied a little while later, "and my life only began when I started chasing after the song of the Sirens."

(But his wife seemed not to have heard these words.)

She told him everything—there was only one thing she didn't mention, which was that the red trousers were poorly sewn. "He has faith in me again, I have a right to my privacy, it's the only way to save our relationship."

The Captain: "These last few years I've been picturing the red trousers constantly, I can recognize every last stitch."

She didn't smile, she thought: "This is my secret. It's good he's said this to me. I wanted to tell him everything, but I'd make him look like a fool, now it all has to be left the way it is. Besides, there's nothing I can tell him, he has to really have faith in me—and I'm not betraying him if I insist on my right to a secret. That the trousers were poorly sewn will remain my secret forever—and this secret only makes our relationship stronger."

"We'll hire a seamstress . . ." (She sits all day at the sewing machine and gets paler and paler.)

"No, it was my mistake, I should have smoked bad cigars (the fact that I haven't been smoking black cigars)."

The Captain wears his red suit *pro forma*—the trousers are perfect, the jacket cuts into his armpits.

The Captain was shocked: "It's one thing to restore things to order: if a seamstress works all day in the attic, she'll need to spend her nights in the tavern. But I have been so stupid that for whatever reason I had to believe it was possible for someone to thrive while spending all her days at the sewing machine. I'm afraid it's all down to the dog, I thought that he'd die soon, but now I see that the meeker he becomes, the more eternally he lives. I think my wife will take him to the tavern, and then we'll get ourselves a cat right away . . . But there must be something seriously wrong with us, otherwise we could get a lion right away . . . Who knows, everything has its limits, I've said it once, but you haven't seen how the limits shift, who knows . . . Anyway, it's a good thing if the dog is finally going away . . . He would have liked a turtle, but he agreed to get a cat . . . "But now even the sewing machine is going to end up in the tavern," the wife explained with unexpected vehemence, "now we're beginning to figure out where the error was, I think the sewing machine drives you to go to the tavern even if you don't sit up there sewing in the attic, even if, like me, you sew on the ground floor. And the seamstress has to stay up there, with the sewing machine, they have to stay together, perhaps in fact the one is only a part of the other, and even the most important part, and up there she'll sew for us, and she'll come here only to do her work, and to hand over the work she does to us, and then she'll receive her pay—and she'll be able to spend it immediately, in the tavern, playing cards and drinking. And if you go away again, I won't want a seamstress at home anymore, and I'll look after the red roses . . ."

That night they put the sewing machine on a cart, and they put the dog on top of the sewing machine. The seamstress will go away with the cart. The dog had no bones to play with—but to make up for it he wagged his tail . . .

But the seamstress had finished her first new uniform, the house was clean, the Captain could go on another voyage.

"Yes," said the seamstress, "the dog is mine. When I used to work in the dead of night, he was always barking, now I go away to the tavern with the sewing machine and, would you look, he's wagging his tail."

When I'm alone, I still can't manage to walk around like one half of a couple of lovers.

"The hydrangeas are a symbol of eternal love. And they have no smell. I think that eternal love has lost its smell. The one thing that's certain is that I don't love you and you don't love me. We're too mature to feel that way, and too free. Love means freedom, and freedom absorbs love. It might even be said that the more one loves, the less one loves. What people call love is obsession, anxiety, seduction, inversion, clinging to what they read in elementary-school textbooks. One could hold out hope that humanity has matured by now, another few world wars, another few crises of puberty, and all this chatter about love will be over and done with. Don't you think?"

"This would be just the right moment to tell him about the red trousers," the woman thought. But she reflected on it another moment and all she said was: "I think you're right."

They agreed and began kissing each other passionately.

The black scar: he wants to remove it with his finger and then realizes it's a burn mark. "You have to be careful," the Captain said. His wife's face darkens, then a moment later brightens again.

She says something in a somewhat bitter tone: "For once I want to think of myself, too. Away with the sewing machine."

"And why not? All you had to do was say the word."

After this the wife's fit of rage, because she has to resew the trousers—moralism doesn't suit him.

The Captain is very embarrassed to be walking around in his

red suit—

He often thinks about the fit of rage, when in the Gray City he had regulated hormones.

At his house the photograph in the frame that has been regilded, he stands before it and it affects his liver, like the Burgomaster.

The Captain is happy with his wife, and because of this he's very irritated—that was all he needed. And then he went back for the Burgomaster's Daughter, holding out hope that he wouldn't find her again, women don't understand that a man also cares for other women.

The suit stank of naphthalene: "Get this stench out at once, it's giving me a headache"—and his wife hung it on the same line where the wash from her last night in the tavern had been hung.

The port was at first just a fine gray line, then a real toy city— then larger and larger: my house—a tiny little toy house.

" . . . and that was the night with the Gypsy Woman!" he thought, the next morning. Strange that, after a night like that, his hair was still neatly combed, not disheveled, no one would be able to tell what had taken place . . ."

(The jacket too big): "I made it thinking of a fat man, and that man was you," she said, laughing, "it sounds mysterious—but it's quite simple—perhaps I'll tell you about it sometime . . ."

(in another place): "But now, all joking aside, why did you sew the jacket so big . . ."
He no longer felt so sure . . .

She took the red suit not from the chest, but from the armoire. "The armoire was so empty . . ." He breathed in the stench of naphthalene.

Two rascals in the orphanage get into an argument over who can do the best knee bends. . . life goes on, and one of them was always on one side, and was always falling down . . . the Captain saw the star on his brow, but to the boy the star burned as though it were the mark of Cain . . . and so the mark of Cain became a star and the star a mark of Cain, and so on . . .

For the End

THE CAPTAIN SMOKES his cigars, his wife a cigarette—and from time to time the Chinaman puffs on his opium pipe.

And their smoke mingles, and merges with the smoke from the gas lamp, and forms a little cloud that dissolves slowly in the sky this autumn evening.

the wife is pregnant (or rather *Progenom*, because the child won't be born into this world: not to pass the work on *by proxy*)

While the Captain is at sea, the woman goes on vacation to the woods from time to time. (It can't do him any harm.)

Silent, silent, eternally unreachable, the cat with the silky fur goes by—

Prehistory of the Captain's idyll
(and the doomsayers were almost right).

But what the Captain would prefer is to sit under the arbor, in autumn, when the leaves have turned reddish and the last hornets hum, and read foreign books that he has brought back with him from faraway lands—or else to drink, slowly and meditatively, some strong wine, mellow, velvety, made from grapes that have ripened under different skies. Often his wife sits beside him and smokes a cigarette, the Captain wraps his arm around her shoulder and his gaze follows the fragile clouds of smoke that slowly dissolve in the quiet evening sky.

Is it right to seat three people around a square table? . . . If a
table is square, there should always be four, but there's no fourth
to be seen.

"But there are four of us already, I'm pregnant." If the fourth
could be seen, the meaning would already be complete, and this
story would already be over. And yet it goes on—

The Captain decides to set off on voyages of exploration. (?—
he takes his wife with him, with the green hunting jacket, the
Burgomaster's Daughter looks after the roses. She is jealous, but
after all she's young— eventually the time for voyages of exploration will come for her, too.)

It's just like before, only the taste is different. One starves only
to be better able to taste one's food.

"We care for each other too much, and this is a sign of immaturity. I need to have a few more flings so I can learn not to care
for you so much."

What the Sirens sang comes to pass.

"I have to go in search of what I've searched for all my life . . ."

Who is the wife? It's not even clear if she is fat or skinny, blonde
or brunette. "You have no qualities, if a novelist wanted to describe you, no reader would know what to think. You're a schema,
a formula, perhaps a specter, not *life*—(*if you like*)! Are you young
or old? I know you have gray hair, but it's dyed (black)—are you
gray-haired or black-haired? (it's good you dye it). If for a while
you don't dye it, the roots turn white—that's all I know . . .

If the Captain loved the Burgomaster's Daughter, the Cabin Boy
would stay on with his wife. We all have to recover our youth.
The world has stolen it from us—but probably the Captain gets

over his love for the Burgomaster's Daughter, from now on it's time to be alone—if all goes well, he won't skip a single passage, otherwise what's been skipped will take its revenge . . .

"You have the Sirens, I on the other hand have the song that the Cabin Boy sang with his accordion—I sat down at the sewing machine because I thought perhaps it wouldn't be right to listen—and that was stupid of me because, when I stopped sewing on the machine, the song was over—in the house sometimes there's a dreadful silence."

The red suit has a child.

The bonfire of illustrated magazines.

"Maybe it's because we got a cat instead of a turtle . . ."

"No," said the Captain, and he puffed on his cigar, "maybe there's a border between song and life (he was thinking of the Sirens).

"Yes," said the wife, and she inhaled a mouthful of smoke in her usual unexpectedly decisive way, "there must be a border between song and life" (she was thinking about the sewing of the trousers).

The Chinaman didn't say yes or no, and he went on slowly smoking his opium pipe. In the distance the dog at the tavern barked. Around the house roses were thriving, in the sky the hawked soared in circles. On the attic windowsill, the cat was curled up in a ball. And the smoke that drifted from beneath the arbor mingles with the smoke from the tavern and forms a little cloud that slowly dissolves in the reddish autumn sky.

The triumphs of the gray liberation were so great that even the dogs became free.

Outside: (there are rumors) the movement of gray progress had made new conquests. One could feel it in the air: even a gray dog, according to what was said, had gotten so excited he'd begun to chase his own tail. But he died in the street, and miserably, from hunger, because he hadn't been able to tear off his muzzle. And so he'd become a symbol of the martyrs of liberty and there were plans to erect a monument in his honor.

In the armoire the four items of clothing are hung: the blue uniform, even if it is in tatters.

Serpentine path from woman to woman.

Guide: the Wife drove him out to sea
        the Siren brought him into the world
        the Girl of the Woods led him to the Gray City
        the Burgomaster's Daughter gave him the courage
        to continue his voyage

The hawk was soaring in circles over the rose garden and the sea

Sometimes the Chinaman also came to visit: the three of them sat together under the arbor with the roses and spoke of the tempests and the calms of the sea, of the beings and the specters of the earth, of the stars and the clouds of the sky. But always, when night fell and the gas lamp was lit, they concluded their conversation saying:

"How many things there were," said the Captain, "even the hermit in the woods."

"But he wasn't there for long," said the Chinaman.

The other two gave him a questioning look.

"The Hermit was me," said the Chinaman.

They were thunderstruck.

"How did you manage to transform yourself from a Chinaman into a hermit?" they asked.

"For a long time I mortified my flesh, I fed on roots and wild honey, and I praised God in the heavens. But when the time came, I went away and bought myself a new iron. And then, to my surprise, money began to grow on trees outside my hut."

"Then you really must be very rich, if you know trees where money grows . . ."

"Tree money," said the Chinaman, "blooms in spring, ripens in summer, withers in autumn. In winter, the branches are bare, and then I have to fend for myself until the next spring."

"If you were the hermit, then perhaps you'd know what became of the Girl of the Woods."

"The last thing I heard she had to be whisked swiftly away from a ball at Court (very beautiful and wearing golden shoes): no sooner had a man taken her in his arms to dance with her than she made a dreadful scene and claimed that he'd pinched her (perhaps she was right). But it's a long time now since I've been in the woods and I don't know what's become of her. I know she still had plenty of dealings with the Gray Man, but all she had to do was learn to read and write, and the Gray Men lost all power over her, and in the end she'll marry a real yellow Chinaman"—and he puffed intently on his opium pipe.

"Everything depends on these impossible, unappreciated, uncomfortable trousers that you foisted on me."

"I don't sew anymore."

"But you can buy them premade and tell me you sewed them yourself . . ."

"Yes, and I can also play other tricks on you, I'm full of wicked spirits."

"You're forgiven in advance—that way, I can leave you later with a better conscience."

"And what will you do then?"

"I don't know. I'll decide later on. All the seas are open to me . . . First of all, I want to finish writing my book."

"But what are you writing, really?"

"Really it's my own story . . . the story of a certain sea captain."

"Is there a lot left to do?"

"No, only . . . a few lines."

"Then it won't take you long."

"Who knows, perhaps on the contrary there's a long way to

go."

"I have time."

"But with me lines last . . . longer."

"I have more time than you."

"Who has more time?"

"We shall see. This conversation is included?"

"Certainly, and now all that's left is . . . a few lines. But stop now, otherwise the conversation will come out of the frame. And then there will be a few lines extra. If we don't erase them, the end will arrive right in the middle of a sentence."

The two of them laughed.

"Why are we going to have such silly conversations?"

"For the sake of romantic irony, I think."

. . .

And the Captain wrote the last line.

APPENDIX

FROM NOTEBOOK B, VERSO

The Road to the Castle

EVERYBODY IS RUNNING in different directions, limping, dancing, marching, crawling, climbing—and searching for the Grail. "Perhaps you have it on you?" He turns out his pockets. Nothing.

After the death of Amfortas the Gypsy Woman arrives with the Arabian balm—finally the Captain sleeps with her, his hormones are appeased. He becomes so normal that he wakes up in a furnished room.

the threshold
The gatekeeper was old and myopic—noble, limited, the boss's spy. He observes everything, draws up secret diagrams and statistics. By the time he'd completed his calculations, the Captain had already crossed the boarder a long time before.

The reporters and photographers, hidden everywhere, await the death of Amfortas.

A single drop of blood and the machinery ground to a halt.

The stains on the armor, which doesn't go away with Sidol.

Seen from a distance: the temples destroyed and the village burned

A dead end: anyone who doesn't want to live here has to go back down to the woods and pick up the road just where they left it. And up here everything is, insipidly, an end in itself, beautiful death, but life doesn't move forward, the work outside remains undone.

The king dies because he doesn't want penicillin—he waits for the Arabian ointment, which Kundry must bring him . . .

Kundry is firmly convinced that the circumnavigator will bring him the ointment—he's crazy about me, he's my slave, for me he'll do whatever I want . . .

Dying in a lost post—tradition: not disowning the old style.

Helmsmen heal because they eat sulfonamides, kings die because they don't want penicillin—what subversions in the world . . .

The crossroads of the two masters.
The two roads are the same. They lead into the same landscape.
The two masters are the same. Cold, captivating eyes.

"The wrong road is always taken. And in the end the wrong road is always the right one."

"Yes, and if that's how it is, couldn't one skip the ceremony?"
"No, because then you wouldn't have the choice . . ."

Preparations for blocking his path—but it's only ceremonial (they rattle off a list of prohibitions)

They have to shoot off a cannon—the ball doesn't budge. "This means that another innocent child must have peed in the powder." The blades of the sabers are nicked, the uniform is in tatters, a soiled shirt hangs outside.
The whole ritual is a substitute, the uniforms are welded togeth-

er (autogenous welding), everything is made of *papier mâché*, and everyone is genuinely racked with pain—(necessary to aid the imagination) with a genuinely noble gesture—("my goddess, the imagination")

"But it's a vicious circle, everything's pointless, even climbing up here."
"Yes, but the only path went right through here . . ."
"Why didn't we take another path?"
"There aren't any."

The knights despise the city . . .

The mysterious woman, who the great master went to get (it's the morphine addict)

The last world war had gravely damaged the Castle of the Grail. Insects had gotten in, DDT was everywhere. The chalice had been welded—inflation—a knight had injured one of his legs by falling from a rotted-out staircase, which had collapsed.

CASTLE OF THE GRAIL
lifestyle ←→ life

(Amfortas): "He's only afraid of injections," said the psychologist.

Here's the injection, here is death.
What was this fear, so great that it forced you into efficacious action . . .

Wine

WINE, SEAWATER AND blood
Growing roses and hunting with hawks.
deeper down—where the crystals lay silent

I, a sea captain, I, a grower of roses, I, a falconer.

The sea all around or the virgin forest, the rice paddy, the eternal ice.

The rousing of the gods who'd been sleeping deeply in the glands.

The laws of hell apply to the men of hell—the laws of change apply to the men of change.

Gradually he becomes a drunkard: seeing as everything's gray, he drinks, and the more he drinks the more beautiful life with wine becomes, and the more rigorously destiny goes on plaguing his life.

He recognizes that it's ancient, the eternal battle between Poseidon and Minerva—in the end, Poseidon won.

(poetry: from a tender little wrinkle on your neck)

The cat on the windowsill. If she stays at my house another

twenty-two minutes, I'm going to sleep with the Girl of the Woods. She rubs her head on his arm. He lights a cigar, the cat takes off at a shot. —Stupid like a man . . .

(Maiden of the Woods): the fear that things don't balance out before death.

(The acid gaze of a woman, when he pays the bill.)

The lost evening, feelings of guilt, but an idea was born, much more precious in other categories.

One sip more, one sip less, on which destiny depends—the right perspective—what does the right perspective mean?— That one knows nothing about one's own body.

He drinks with the Burgomaster's Daughter—the "demoniacal" tension—

Everything I do to free myself is too much, or too little. Perhaps it's only a question of one cigarette—but of which one—(if I smoke it, it's avidity—if I don't smoke it, it's renunciation—and both things are equally bad)—

He melts into the song of the Sirens

The last Byzantine (problem of the mosaic)

I can't give up the Siren

He goes into the tavern, he fills up his pen and buys a new notebook to write the story of the sea captain, but he puts the box of matches on top of the cigarettes, then vice versa, then again as before. —Thanks to *you*—

"Why do I always order a quarter liter at a time? It's a never-ending farewell. I am drinking on the brink of death."

A woman with a beautiful fur got up from a group, at a distant table, she moved indecisively, this is the turning point, the
woman took a few steps toward him, she turned to a waiter and
whispered something, the waiter pointed to the room in the
back, the Captain smiled and succumbed to destiny.

drank on the brink of death

One is always searching for a corner

The timid sit down right away at the first table by the door.

and with each quarter liter everyday reality drew further away.

Before him the big Persian rug was rolled out from end to end
(but no, not completely, one end was still rolled up . . .), heav-
en, earth, and sea . . .

The Danish man bowed to the Innkeeper—the Danish woman
curtsied

FROM NOTEBOOK D

For the Prelude

MENSTRUATION—SHE GETS fat, then thin, then swollen, etc. —hair—HUMIDITY—aching back—a day before: very hungry, pastry shop—then: no hunger, and her panties are RED.

(Hourglass): turn over the hourglass BEFORE it's empty— death had been stymied—VANITAS—UNA EX ILLIS ULTI- MA—she has the clocks repaired

The scissors are no longer sharp

After the "ORGY" in the moonless night

In the end the first thin crescent

But one mark doesn't go away, it wasn't on her legs—at a certain point, later, a new mark appears.

COSMOGRAPHER

Milk coffee in the beer—or in the wicker wine bottle empty liquor bottle—empty bottles in the kitchen

cockroaches

withered flowers in the vases—

135

On the teapot the lid of a saucepan

She finds the Captain's walking stick and starts walking around the house with it—same with the black monocle

The wallpaper is peeling off the walls, with bulges here and there—she should order new wallpaper, but she doesn't—

When he finds cigar ashes someplace they shouldn't be, he can't take it anymore—ashes, ashes, ashes . . .

Voyage

(FLORIAN): THE DOWNFALL of us Europeans, of our world—The other was staring straight ahead looking gloomy, because our world was going to ruin. —Long silence.

The Captain hadn't been drowned at all . . . and so the Captain gradually went completely insane . . . and so he leafed through the lyric poems of a suspect poet . . . The most difficult things to throw away are photographs . . .

"The poor gypsy woman . . ."

THE HELMSMAN: tattooed: the Captain is curious, but
              he never manages to find out
              what his tattoos depict.
              "The cannon stuck out of his sweater . . ."
              He heads straight for the virgin

"I was only following orders."

So obsessed by the idea of putting everything in order he forgets to map out the route . . . there's almost a shipwreck.

He dreams of a Homeric village of fishermen . . .

excited—depressed

isolated, he stares straight ahead, he had no desire to see people and complained of being isolated . . .
—he tells the story of his collapse to the waiter

With his powerless hands he pounded on the eternally barred bronze doors

The new methods are good for nothing . . .

Toward the END: headache
                    FIT OF RAGE: breaks the teapot

His native port, once a fishermen's village, life flowed along peacefully between high and low tides, what could have driven him out to the open sea? —Sometimes there was a tempest and on the high cliffs that stood out, as in an artistic photograph, the silhouettes of the women, who observed, paralyzed, how their feeders were swallowed up by the great feeder—they huddled in their shawls . . .

Getting things quickly in order (superficially) before his friend arrives

toward the end: everyone has "betrayed" him

overexcited, he paces back and forth in his cabin: me-two-legs-he-one-leg . . .

he isn't even capable of doing knee bends . . .

for years now he has lugged around something impractical (a broken cigarette holder)

The temptation to love one's enemy

He still had the new thinking
AND the seven paths of liberation.

Ruins: he sets up temples of friendship between collapsed walls and broken columns (or on the island)

He sits like Melancholia

his courtesy is cowardice

The Helmsman's tattoo—the moon (masculine) copulates with the feminine sun—

The red flag
The red light
The Red Cross
(Out of arrogance, he has the red flag raised)

He does woman's work

At night he can't sleep

He jumps out of his bed and moves boxes around (shifts them from right to left). Everything has to be separated.

While he's working he forgets to give orders and the Helmsman saves the situation

To resole or not to resole his shoes. The heels were about to split in two.

Sometimes he eats yogurt, sometimes stuffed turkeys.

The doves in the square, he would have liked to strangle them.

He falls into the water with a sigh of relief.

He lives through death by dismemberment: every day he lost a piece (one piece here, one piece there)

The wind sends his papers flying (or at least puts them in disorder) he starts over again patiently (perhaps the Cabin Boy has left the window open?)

Memories of an old, unresolved business matter begin bothering him.

The tattoo: two half moons sticking out their tongues, but their tongues aren't really tongues.

Destroying his wife's photograph. He destroys his wife.

The die was cast.

He gives orders in a cutting voice. Ready for battle he returns to his cabin and slams the door with definitive severity.

a dark gray streak in the bright gray mist

Plebs, thinks the Captain

Sacred Book

IT WAS AN old edition, published by the Jesuits, of the history of the reckoning of the months, the Sacred Book that the queens used to read, dictated to a eunuch by X. during the summer they were exiled in the cave with the spring of medicinal waters

it began with the invocation to the grandmother of the moon, of the many teats, of the hair made of snakes, surrounded by a flight of doves, by the dance of the bears, over which the cow jumped, while the red rain threatened to flood the earth, it continued with the succession of the dynasties and of the queens and their favorites, with the color of their hair and their true names, inscribed in the month of their birth, erased in the month of their death.

Dictionary of folklore
o my God and my Goddess

he skipped a few pages: too boring

Moon waning: floods, storms, spirits

The bringer of dew
Fertility made possible by the lunar bird

The red cloth before the image of the menstruating goddess

(Moon, moon, always moon . . . thought the Captain.)

The moon goddess does nothing when she sees her son get killed, then frantic grief (even the women wear mourning, etc.)

her favorite animal: the dove—that's why he strangles it

the white goddess the black goddess

Sirens

THE PRINCESS

THE music-hall singer

She blushes in her first ball gown

and the world is before me, and the world is behind me

legs enlaced

"And I speak in no uncertain terms of bed"

"I am my song, like all the others."

"and my smile is wise and sated, and when you are lying there spent beside me I cover you with a warm blanket . . ."

She was the Siren who sang, or they were the Sirens . . .

"and so I barked on in my hoarse voice, and I spoke obscenities, and I laughed, and my cough rang out with a sinister sound from my hollow chest."

"Dissolve into the solitary sound of the organ"—but suddenly, deafening, the yowl of a cat, shrill—and meanwhile the siren continued to roar, she roared between song and life, and

it seemed there was a border, who knows, perhaps the yowl of
the cat was the border, in any case the Captain found himself
suddenly in the water

The Negress—breasts of ice (hard as ice)
The woman—clear voice, perfumed breath

The opposite of an *éducation sentimentale*
(an education in contempt)
Drowning in Eliot.
The Jews who cross the Red Sea with dry feet.
Whereas the Captain . . .

An education in pride
Education in contempt (how much Christian kitsch he still had
in him) . . .

Read: Job
         Odyssey
         Milarepa
         Mysteries of transformation
         The hero with a thousand faces
         Aeppli: Der Traum und seine Deutung
         Hercules
         Ferdowsi
         Strindberg, Legends
         XXX, Au pays des Tarahumaras (N.R.F. 287—August
1937)
         Faust
Polyphilus
Song of Songs

Research: canaries
             corals
             sewing machines
             Trinacria
             gasworks

dolphins

everything is taken by the vortex

A passage where
   the Wife
   the Burgomaster's Daughter
   the Helmsman's wife
   the Sirens
   the Gypsy Woman
   (in advance) the Innkeeper's wife
are a single figure

THE TWO RUGS ARE UNROLLED

Island = belly of the whale
  he was on the island or
    he was in the belly of the whale
or was the island the belly of the whale?

The too-short trousers were a prefiguration of the Peg-leg

"ever since I learned that no one is born and no one dies . . ."
the wheel of things

Yes, even the Chinaman is a sea creature—(perhaps you and the Chinaman are only figures in the song of the Siren.)

But why fable—up to now it was reality, things of this sort happen every day—and yet now the fable begins

There are no lost paradises, there are only paradises overcome— if I'd lost it, then I'd go back there again to overcome it. (A decent person doesn't need lost paradises)

and in the end paradise becomes a hell—and then it goes on— we need this: a fourth part of the *Divine Comedy*, where there's no more hell, there's no more purgatory, and there's no heaven—but this fourth part is not death . . . (following the acceptance of death)

Lay more emphasis on the RHYTHM of life and death . . . seasons—days and nights (menstruation = Captain's shipwreck)

At best we play at being Novalis

Everything that has already been, I can't stand it anymore . . .

X. thrives on the hunger of his ancestors

other shipwrecks in the same place—But no Captain returns—and it's only right that this is how it is . . . one should never be shipwrecked in a place where others have been shipwrecked . . . A real life means: inventing new places where one can be shipwrecked . . . each new work is only the invention of a new death—
This doesn't mean that no captain's life has been saved . . . but (for us) they have become helmsmen . . .

After the next crisis there are hawks again, roses, etc., and the next tavern.
(Hunting each other down in the next tavern . . . The Chinaman: "It's been a long time since I hunted you down in the next tavern.")

"You have opened my eyes!" By the look of things, she had closed her eyes again

Because, in the beginning, there are always two rugs rolled up in the cabin—

NOTES WITHOUT A TEXT

Notebook E

England

CRUSOE COMPLEX[13]

---

13 Here is what John Rosselli, whom Bazlen saw often during his
sojourns in England, had to say on this subject: "According to Bazlen,
this complex was discernible in many English people. 'Walking around
at night,' he said, 'you see so many rooms lit up with people inside
painting the walls of their houses: everyone on his own little island,
like Robinson Crusoe, busy building his private hut with all the modern conveniences.' Bazlen thought that, from the seventh century on,
the English had sacrificed everything they had to the development of
the *homo faber*, not just to industrialization, but to the development
of the critical and analytical side of the human mind. 'Nowadays,' he
said, 'they live their animal life through animals and their vegetative
life through the plants in their gardens.' Essentially, they were now
miles away from any possibility of an integrated life—like Crusoe, he
added, who, finding the negro Friday on the island, had immediately
made him into an insipid slave.

"Bazlen's attitude in this regard rekindled his interest in a whole
'unofficial' English literature—for example, the 'Christian science-fic-
tion' writers Charles Williams and C. S. Lewis; their spiritual ancestor
George MacDonald; the aficionado of the macabre T. L. Beddoes; and
Wilkie Collins, inventor of the psychological thriller, etc.

"One day I quoted him what Virginia Woolf wrote in her diary about Joyce's *Ulysses*, which she, a publisher (together with her
husband) of avant-garde works, had turned down: 'When one can
have the cooked flesh, why have the raw?' 'As a matter of fact,' Bazlen

POWER—Baroque (they're stuck at this point)—Shakespeare is not *the* world (he was a world). Not so much as a mention of the masters of our problems—meticulous, but only as regards what is universally human.

Inventions ("devices")—never creations

"Power": from value to justification (hence also schemes)

Powerless, but with Power's lack of imagination and scruples

Scratch them and you'll find a utilitarian (Huxley for example)

Style becomes etiquette

Unreligious—dissident theorists, but no adventurers—

Merely clever—the pedantry of nonsense

"Don't sit there doing nothing. In a moment you will start thinking."

"You may enjoy it"[14]

The angry young men: they bark.

---

replied, without missing a beat, 'that was just Woolf's trouble, everything was too "cooked"—if she hadn't cooked it so long she would have written better stuff.'"

14 Allusion to an anecdote relayed as follows by Ljuba Blumenthal: "This concerns the wife of a Methodist minister, who explained to me the role of sex in a Christian marriage: 'Naturally, it's one of a wife's duties—but that's okay—so long as they don't enjoy it.' When I replied to her that, in other religions, it's a wife's duty and right, but that never in my life had I heard she should not enjoy it, the woman replied: 'Beh—the Old Testament.' The implication being, of course, that there's nothing the Jews aren't capable of."

"Je fais exception à l'égard des touristes anglais, qui semblent n'avoir jamais rien vu ni rien imaginé," Nerval, "Les amours de Vienne" (1841), in *Voyage en Orient*.[15]

One does not "travel"—one "is dispatched"
(Even in the café: you're made to sit down)

No dishonesty—only crime

Quality without a man (specialists)

"The most ferocious"
The evening of X.[16]

Style is conspicuous on one's person—but privately it's permissible to maintain one's own style.

Coitus compared to urination

Impossible to say of an English girl (as in Tuscany): what an excellent waitress.

---

15 "I make an exception in the case of English tourists, who seem never to have seen or imagined anything." [AA]

16 Bazlen here refers to an episode well recounted by Ljuba Blumenthal: "X. is a woman I know whose mother died at ninety-eight, after living long enough to destroy the lives of all her children, who'd all been brought up to believe they had to make sacrifices for their elderly parents. Once, when Bazlen was at my place in London, X. telephoned and told me: 'Naturally, you know my mother is dead!' I did not know, and she asked us to drop by and pay a visit. Of course we went, thinking this was what must be done when someone has suffered a great loss and would rather not be alone. As soon as we arrived, we heard a fantastic racket coming from behind the door, and discovered half a dozen of X.'s friends—middle-aged women or old maids—all dead drunk, staggering around and bursting into loud fits of laughter, trying to force huge shots of whiskey on us. In a moment of relative calm, I asked X where her mother was buried (I'd known her mother for several years), and X. shouted: 'Don't be silly, how should I know?'"

EROS OFFICE EQUIPMENT Ltd.

MINGLE WITH THE MIGHTY AT MADAME TUS-
SAUD'S

SAVOY THEATRE (Strand!)—Berenice. Antiochus announces the (Titus's) decision (to dismiss Berenice) to the queen. Berenice is both surprised and annoyed.

Prince Andrew: social assistance, free milk, and health insurance.[17]

The inferno of insipidity

ULYSSES

ART (Picasso, De Chirico)

AUTOBOGRAPHY (Mallarmé: at the age of seven I took my
first exam)

INSTRUMENT—WEAPON

CINEMA

THESEUS (ARIADNE) (NAXOS!)

THE UNCONSCIOUS CONFESSIONS OF GROUPS

LESSON: from reading

THE LIFE AND DEATH OF DISEASES

---

17 According to Ljuba Blumenthal: "This note concerns a letter to
the editor submitted to an English women's magazine when Prince
Andrew was born: 'I suppose the Queen gets milk and orange juice
free of charge from the Health Service like every other woman who has
a baby, but, apart from that, she must be an excellent mother: no one
has ever heard of one of her children getting a cold.'"

THE SAINT—THE NEANDERTHAL MAN—THE POET

PROBLEM OF THE NEIGHBOR

ORPHEUS: don't look at woman while you're in the underworld

WIZARD CONSCIOUS OF ALL (THE INS AND OUTS)
OF EUROPEAN ASSUMPTIONS

AGAINST PURITY OF HEART

AGAINST THE TRAGIC

Death

Love and death: in the days of cellular division there was only
death by catastrophe (annihilation)—Death from internal ex-
haustion (conflict) begins only with sexuality—

At the age of 33—Christ—Lorenzo de' Medici—(Buddha at
66).
On the other hand, Titian from cholera: otherwise he would
have continued to paint, always better and better—

Not knowing how to die.

Death in Europe. (The abolition of death.) Pasteur anecdote.
Forty-three years without death.

The new death: on land Messina—on water Titanic ("The
fenced-off ways of death")—world war.
Aestheticism—Rilke—criminality (diverted to the colonies)—
politics of the postwar era

The deathless man: the petit bourgeois—the communist.
Death for the petit bourgeois—resignation or dismissal.
The smuggling of death into communism: the persecution of
the bourgeoisie, the war—(Man is born after the theft of a bicycle)[18]

To invent a new death

Dead or collapsed at my critical age (42 years old), in my situation:

Spinoza	?	Napoleon
Kierkegaard		
Pascal	sister	
Nietzsche	sister	
Van Gogh		
Kafka[19]		

The next redeeemer will be over 84.

Lao-Tse, the only one who doesn't die—he leaves.

---

18 Bazlen is here alluding to the movie *The Bicycle Thief*. In this connection, he wrote to Luciano Foà, in a letter dated March 21, 1951:
"If you're interested, I now add to my hatred of people whose bicycles
are stolen my just as implacable hatred for traveling salesmen who die,
inspired only by the effect that this death had on the whole audience,
though personally I averted my eyes when he died."

19 From a letter Bazlen wrote Giorgio Voghera, December 28, 1951:
"Consider that almost all the culture that has in some way defined
or expressed us during these last few centuries has been produced by
people who didn't make it past the crisis of forty-two: Pascal, Spinoza,
Kierkegaard, Nietzsche, and, if you can believe it, even Kafka, etc.,
etc. —and now the time has come when we forty-two year olds must
finally begin to live."

The Italians

The war veteran: the most subaltern figure, the ignorance in the face of destiny—if he existed (but he doesn't), he would be offended.

"Our trouble is we have bosses who don't care about us."

(The Italians—they live on art, they live on love, and they die in despair.)

(Social assistance—superiority bought so cheaply.)

Crusoe (the real one): on the island for the feeling of freedom— *but* with baggage (*de profundis clamavi ad te*: this he cannot say)—
But instead of a miracle: his old junk.

In the center of Florence: UPIM.

the long thin nostrils of Florentines

X.: gone back to his mother.[20]

The too quickly solidified aspect of the language (from Dante to the *Messaggero*). (Words with accents on the penultimate syllable, no diphthongs, no umlauts, no H, no consonants at the ends of words)

The petit bourgeois pyramid of fascism—everyone afraid of being fired, all the way to the top, M., who lived only in relation to his career

Impossibility of translating into Italian—in other languages translation serves to instill new dimensions of civilization.

---

20 According to Ljuba Blumenthal: "One day a certain someone's lover proudly explained to Bazlen: 'He loves me so much he's left his wife and gone back to his mother.'"

The ceremonies of criminality.

In Latin, there's still v i r and h o m o —In Italian only
uomo—and woman differentiated from man only in sex: f e m a
l e m a l e—The question of how to be human (*Mensch*) doesn't
come up—

Fascism was an attempt to make the Sun State a reality when it
had already become a figure of speech.

Death

Every love story is, without exception, a story of four. (Love is
for two, but love is story-less.) Problem of the triangle (Wagner,
Ibsen, those virility complexes!). Isolde, the bourgeois drama:
T h e f o u r t h i s a l w a y s d e a t h.

Socrates is the first Western plebeian, he abolishes death (the
plebeian is the deathless man). This is why, without any anxiety,
like a satisfied storekeeper, he drinks the hemlock, secure in the
conviction that "up there" everything will be more cheerful.
(From the bowl of hemlock to the mug of beer.) And the sacrifice of the rooster! As if to say: paid in advance and insured.

To die fulfilled and *curious*.

The more anonymous the enemy becomes (because he is), the
more devastating the weapons—it's always a single man who is
hit (though it may be all the inhabitants of Bikini).

N o v a l i s : *l'acte philosophique est le suicide*, etc. Nothingness
reached too quickly—faced with slow-paced nothingness,
distilled nothingness, experienced in every capillary through
the karmic surmounting of the problems of our ancestors (and
not that in the beginning there was fear and hunger).

The art of dying every second—
(to understand that every second stands in opposition to the transformation of the others)

Everything that doesn't want to die has to croak

It's a world of death—once people were born alive and slowly they died. Now we are born dead—and some of us slowly manage to come to life.

The Germans

Instead of distance, the Germans have respect.

Cosmopolitanism—excess of cosmos, lack of polis

The Germans as individuals react collectively
The French en masse react individually
The Italians react individually as individuals, collectively en masse (at home and in Piazza Venezia)

Phallic reaction against progressive cerebration
Hitler *contra* Blum with his lolling head
After Napoleon only the Axis.

No woman is closer to whoredom than Gretchen[21]

Cinema

Complex
Problem $>$ of the

The theater actor "expresses" (can represent his own possibilities

---

21 Allusion to Goethe's *Faust*, Part One. [AA]

in various individuated figures)

The movie actor is (can represent only his own image, which comprises all possibilities)

On stage (false note, natural element), Nature (false note, artificial element)

Theater, a single distance
Cinema, all distances

Cinema is a new art only because it didn't exist fifty years ago

You didn't have to see Duse's white hair
You're required to see X.'s ugly mug

The theater requires you to "look within"
Cinema forces you to look

Russian film: *The End of St. Petersburg* and the documentary cobbled together. (What is chucked out the door alive returns through the window as a ghost.) [. . .]

The artist: how can it be expressed in the most perfect manner . . .
The director: how can I achieve the effect most effectively?

Plato: "It is through the eye that our imagination is most strongly affected, because the sense of sight is the strongest of our senses, even if it cannot perceive the truth."

Problem of distance ("*la mesure de l'homme*")—Dostoevsky < Tolstoy > Gogol   →
(as a psychological problem: uniform size of all phenomena, cut down to the same scale)—

Problem of the Age

Order in place of truth.

The generation of the sexual problem (Freud and Strindberg born in the same year?).

The end of eternal values—the new eternity

The danger of a wisdom without science: psychology becomes moralism

Throw Europe and America and Russia overboard, until we're left alone.

The great complicated ones of the nineteenth century: figures of dissolution, without solutions.

God has been absorbed.

(The Reverend X in America fights like a lion for zippers to be sewn into priests' robes)—

The fear of vampires appears in the eighteenth century (the Enlightenment)

Two separate sets of problems: the man of progress and the man of civilization.

The stratum of insect society (beyond the Western problem of self-preservation)

Neanderthal man: finds out *today* that 1 + 1 = 2 — cultural event?

New possibility for taking stock of the ancient themes:

Benedict of Nursia (nurse)
Saint Francis (father)
Mani (transitional charlatan)

Saints are epigones, martyrs are vampires

Until Goethe: biography absorbed by the work
Beginning with Rilke: life set against the work

The confusion between n e c e s s i t y   a n d   v a l u e .
The confusion between a s s u m p t i o n   a n d   v a l u e .

Smoking in Europe more or less contemporary with the French
Revolution. The first cigarette and the first locomotive.

Europeans feel Western, not central. Only civilization that
speaks of itself as a half of something. All the others are civiliza-
tions of the center.

The decadence of the mystery of the smile:
S p h y n x : the mythical Oedipus
G i o c o n d a : the universal Leonardo
L ‘ i n c o n n u e   d e   l a   S e i n e : the abysmal camouflaged
sentimentalism of the petit bourgeois Rilke.

The great revolutionaries of the turn of the century (Strindberg,
Nietzsche, Wilde, Jarry, etc.)[22]

The saints dwelled in the spirit, the modern mystics, in the
best case, dwell in "sublimation"—that's why their lives speak out
against the word, and blood tends to thain into ink.

22 From a letter Bazlen sent to Alessandro Pellegrini, March 15, 1949:
"I understand better and better the reasons why European artistic
creativity came to an end with the generation of '85; everything done
by the following two generations is the result, it seems to me, of a hu-
manist misunderstanding, and is done without any real necessity (real
necessity can't lead, at the present moment, to artistic expression), and
without any substance."

St. George kills with a sword made from the cross: late in the post-Christian age, a monstrosity from the remote pre-Christian era.

Socrates: Sancho Panza of Plato and Alcibiades. Don Quixote can have Sancho Panza.
The knight has his shadow.
But woe to the knight whose shadow is Sancho Panza.

Putrefactio: as a consequence, up to a certain stratum of consciousness, the necessity of revolution. Evolution, mawkish prejudice of the Nineteenth Century, which knew nothing of the dissolution into chaos and wanted to "abolish" death.

1948 (?): The atom bomb obliges the daily press to disseminate reports on the total harmlessness of the atom bomb.

Tacitus (Rex Warner, *Freedom in Literary And Artistic Creation*, p. 10): "It is easier to destroy a culture than to make it rise again."

Now the opposite: the next culture would already exist if one could just eliminate the remnants of the past.

The problem of "the perfect man" of the Renaissance: the world has moved on, but the concept has not.

Goethe's perfection: not in his statuesque clarity (what does that mean?), but in the rhythmic balance between clarity and madness.

The non-creative: getting lost in an enormous figure.

Now destroying means creating: only what stands between us and our creative possibilities can be destroyed.

How it happens that individual images no longer coincide, that they no longer proceed at the same pace: the image of love, anatomy, meteorology, physiology

The law of the persistence of values: that the value of civilization is added to everything that is of value to progress (and possibly also to civilization).

Uneasiness in the face of everything that already has a name

Of subordinate neuroses

If today a saint did what saints used to do—but the work is gone—
By and large, the specialist does a better job of it

Art

The Japanese painters who renounce their names and sign the name of their master, followed by a number (they adopt the name of the master, and stick a modest numeration after it).

Some guy lives his life and writes beautiful poems. But if a guy *doesn't* live his life in order to write beautiful poems, how ugly are the beautiful poems of the guy who *doesn't* live his life to write beautiful poems.

The *Hitlerjugend* as necessary counterweight to:
    Pavese
    Sunset Boulevard

The indiscreet hybrid in Bosch and Brueghel: Erasmus without the wit . . .

A world takes six days to create . . .

On the sixth day God created man *because* five days earlier He'd separated the light from the darkness—Nowadays, novelists begin on the fifth or sixth day.
Their forebear had, however, divided the light from the darkness already—and it's in the division of light carried out by their ancestor that their maggots therefore writhe

(Joyce: you may decipher my work for the rest of your life—)
The decent person, (who should meditate on one of my thoughts for an hour. (To discover the organization of the artifice—to attempt to experience what's essential.)

Regarding C a r l o   L e v i —only where there's choice is there art—i.e., where resistance or doubt dominate—where, through man's influence, something becomes something else, that where a natural law dominates, by means of being filtered through man there develops another law—the artist who is driven by unconscious reasons to give conscious form to the unconscious— all the rest is bureaucracy, scheming, vanity—

Literature

Thomas Mann: nominalized adjectives
Where culture becomes (almost) wisdom—

Knowledge of *hybris*—Counterpoint of the Tao

Lion:[23] sociological cookbooks
(But in reverse—not: take the so-and-so, but: dissolve the such-and-such)

Shakespeare—world—drama—unlimited power—the pariah.
Balzac—society—novel—unlimited wealth—the poor.
Plan—Organization—Newspaper   (bulletin)—limited

23 This probably refers to an expression employed by Ferdinand Lion, noted German essayist and literary critic.

wealth—old-age care

Western mythology gives us the characters of the drama, not the drama.

The tragic is even lowlier than the comic.

Form is the polar opposite of chaos, not the definitive overcoming of chaos. Misunderstanding of the European aesthetic, and of classicism. The classical artist creates eternal death.

The harmony of Goethe's life: not Apollonian: the lovelier, more rhythmical alternation between form and chaos.

Our "Divine Comedy" has four canticles: in the fourth there's no inferno, no purgatorio, and no paradise. —Sartre's "Divine Comedy" has only one: in itself, this wouldn't be so bad, except it's not the only one, it's only the first one, and he believes it's the only one. —Sartre is not the instrument of the Apocalypse but only one of the *four* beasts of the Apocalypse—which is no big deal!

On the legislative aspect of the great forms (lyric).

Gide, *la recherche des causes profondes* [. . .]. (w i t h a k n a c k f o r n o t k n o w i n g w h e r e t o f i n d t h e m .)

The only solution is inexpressible, indescribable—up to that point, there's nothing but the problematic joy of ever closer description—yet the fact that it's all provisional (consciously experienced) guarantees this joy will be negated.

Oh, a Kierkegaard who was no longer motivated by a Regine Olsen!

Problem of reading: I, at eighteen years old, who found the common ground between Salgari and Kant—it was a matter of reading, not knowledge (the child reads Salgari; people say he'll grow up to be a scholar)

The fact that only bad writers can write b i g novels (the greater the art, the smaller the worlds):
Wilkie Collins
Bulwer Lytton
Rider Haggard
Péladan
(Similar to the problem of Eusapia Palladino)

How we can no longer stand Homer, now that man no longer has a profile

Psyche

The fact that there's no longer such a thing as a psychology, but only psychologies—

Milieu theory applied to Freud, Adler, Jung, etc.

Psyche / Rationality (false antinomy)

Mechanics of the Tao (where man doesn't disappear)—in the middle:
a psychology of the "inanimate"
(the apartments,
the blankets [. . .].)

I Ching statistical

Tea, coffee: a cup of tea is an open lotus flower
a cup of coffee is a spring in an oasis

The next step: a psychological morphology. And somewhere, in the background, no more symbols, but only principles.

The sense of the intuitive is the physiognomy of the sensitive.

The *other* sequence of psychic time (the "unrealized" and the "re-realized," etc.)

Psychic energy: a hundred grams of pralines.

The anxiety of facing the original castrating mother is not the anxiety of facing death, it's the anxiety of facing death before completing the task . . .

The only conceptual tool needed for any psychotherapy:
        S w a m p   a n d   s a c r i f i c e

Narcissist—Problem of the material in which he is reflected
        (Caravaggio—water— [. . .].)

That taking stock is new creation and not a matter of digging or revival: it gives form to what is formless (and not to an unknown form latent within us).

Gandhi

(*except* the Salt March)

Greatness only in relation to the guilty conscience, the lack of clarity, and the lack of level of the enemy.

The other side of Hitler

Fasting without physiological knowledge

suspicious oily simplicity

Christ

Christ could have long flowing locks because Pontius Pilate was bald—(but the Buddha was bald!) and after everybody has washed his feet, in the end Pontius Pilate washes his hands, and the bald are permitted to stay down on earth (having no need to go to heaven).

You drink your own blood or the dragon's blood. The blood of the Crucified is the liquor of those who have no destiny.

Christ was crucified after saying: Father, thou hast forsaken me. Christians get themselves crucified so as not to be forsaken by Christ. It's easy and devoid of imagination.

On the cross one dies either of thirst or blood loss. In any case, from lack of fluid (weaning?)

The cross has Christ's unequal arms equate right and left, and the equation of right and left is love. But top and bottom are not equal, and the lack of equivalence between top and bottom creates morality and ethics: heaven and hell, and thus Christians live in an e t e r n a l p u r g a t o r y .

Christ *was* overcoming and fulfillment.
Christ *is* temptation and a point of departure.

Only Christ can be pure of heart; every attempt to be pure in the sense that Christ is pure is a step back, backwardness, infantilism, reaction—
In the end Christ becomes a paralyzing Superego, purity of heart becomes schoolwork.
Christ the Son becomes Christ the Father.
Every *Imitatio Christi* is an imitation of Christ.

The devil can't be crucified: one of his legs is too short. Five is an evil number (good only when the fifth unit is the center of a circle).

The feet of the crucified Christ don't touch the ground: he renounces the earth. The Buddha renounces his legs.

Van Gogh had to come along to clear Peter's name. He gave his ear for the ear Peter had cut off. (?)

Crusade against Christianity (on my part, or no?)

Christ recognized only the "universally human," that's what he preached, what he suffered for—and ever since then the "universally human" is assumed, foundational, essential—but it's meaningless.

Yahweh wants the family. Christ doesn't want the family. Result: the Christian family.

The cross divides time: BC and AD, the only case of positive and negative computation of time. Before the cross the dragon, after the cross the flower.

A thief was able to ascend to heaven with Christ. The ascension to heaven of the Christian is not the ascension of Christ, but the ascension of the thief.

Only he was able to rise again by ascending to heaven. We have to rise again in order to finally be in the earth. Whoever wants to go to heaven therefore goes to hell.

The Christian ritual: soothing and uncreative.

Christ "creates" a meaning. The saints are puppets of a meaning. The impossibility of a "psychoanalysis" of Christ. The necessity of a "psychoanalysis" of the saints.

The fact that the judgment of Christ, and especially of the saints, does not take everything into account. —Serenity *à côté de* life. —Unawareness in liberation.

The poor in spirit are certainly blessed, but not creative. —As if it were a question of blessedness. In general: the overemphasis on blessedness—
The redemption of the world is a creative process starting from everything that is given, not the renunciation of a (bothersome) part of what is given, so as to eventually gain the favor of one's superiors.
One doesn't go into the kingdom of heaven: one has to create the kingdom of heaven.

Christians are programmatically rigid in their Christianity because they haven't assimilated it—the fact that afterward, on the human plane, I don't have to atone, is the miracle that Christ performed.

That Christ can redeem only Christians.

Reduction of Christianity (which was already a Platonic reduction) to the intellectual element (the Enlightenment).

Will the dead (the unincarnated) be saved by Christianity?

Animals Plants

Some bulbs are kept in a completely dark cellar. Only once, for 1/1000 of a second, a strong beam of light is projected into the darkness. The sprouts grow in this direction, toward the only possibility of light.

The rooster is masculine. Singing, because the day is beginning (masculine). That is why at the third cry of the cock Christ is betrayed.

A physiognomy of the potato: from America (!) to Prussia (!).

The fertility of two extremes: virgin forest and rice paddies

Extremely differentiated aristocratic social orders and myths: South America and China:—South America, order in the virgin forest. China—order among the paddies (in China the rice grows wild). The crudity of the other orders: among the fields and pastures, and the "banality" of European forests.
(Here, the problem of the Greco-Roman profile.)

Problem of yeast and fermentation—grain and egg, bread and wine (unleavened).

Sphere: sun and bomb: and that's the way the elephant and the bulldog approach the sphere.

Snake: beginning and end, with no center. That's why the snake has to be the temptress and the mark on the road. (The queen serpent with the crown on her head.)

The animal can't stand erect. When he wants to stand up, he doesn't quite reach an upright posture, at most (like the giraffe) a long neck. (Problem of the camel!)

Problem of i n s t r u c t i o n :
      creative honesty
      canine honesty

That animals are our own individual qualities
Specialization of qualities [. . .].
Prometheus takes qualities from the souls of the good and bad animals and locks them in the chest of man.

On the feline level . . . I'd be much more flexible (If I were a cat, how flexible I would be)

Jews

There's an animal Savior but no animal Yahweh. (But the elephant is the animal Buddha.)

Yahweh is an asthmatic

Judith, the first suffragette (in the West she'd be hysterical). —
The West: separation at table and in bed
The East: separation at table, not in bed

"You shall not have any God but me." This is a stiff rejection of a higher knowledge. —For the other peoples, it's obvious that, apart from the gods that exist, there can be no other gods. The Jews, by the fact of having been programmatically hardened against other gods, were persecuted by the other gods, whom they didn't want to know about. —So they turned to stone—the one who, *hardened*, refuses the cross, must finally be destroyed in pogroms or in the crematorium ovens of a concentration camp. (The Jews can't "forget" their Jewish God. But how can the gods be forgotten?)

After Christ the Old Testament Jews are an anachronism: at most Christians by religion and Jewish by race.

The Jewish imagination stalls in the face of death (L., that the Jews fear only death.) Christ, the first Jew who voluntarily goes to his death on his own (this is not so!).
Job suffers for the deaths of others, but continues to live and, before he dies, is "rewarded." Only Christ is rewarded after death.
It falls to Abraham to sacrifice his son, so that he, Abraham, might show his beloved God how obedient he is.

The tragedy of the Jews: they cross the dry Red Sea (they immediately throw themselves into the Red Sea, seized by panic). On dry feet at the bottom of the sea. (Eliot—the drowning one—my captain—is saved.)[24]

CROSS

SWORD   CHALICE

FLOWER

Our voyage to the East (opposite the direction of the sun) (pendular motion)

Crusades: you can only go East with a sword and a chalice. Instead the division between sword and chalice. And thus the sword becomes the atom bomb, and the chalice becomes the morning paper.

The West doesn't have flowers (the rose is Persian)—at most *les fleurs du mal*—and the blue flower of the Romantics, which is a *fleur du bien*—flowers have nothing to do with *bien et mal*. (Lotus—India—tulip (alas) from where . . . ?) This is why the West doesn't have great pictures of flowers (all the great painters depict the crucifixion, and the cross)—the Orient, yes. —And why the most inferior figure of European art is the woman who paints flowers.

Take sword and chalice to the Orient, to find the flower. Once it's found, it loses its value—the cross is formed by plucking off its four arms—leaving one point, or the emptiness in the point.

The voyage from East to West.

---

24 Probably a reference to the poetry of T. S. Eliot, "Death By Water" in *The Waste Land,* and to the novel *The Sea Captain*, which Bazlen was writing.

Rosicrucians, skip over the sword and the chalice—hence only magic, demonic anticipation.

Before the cross: chaos: between Job and Christ the destruction of the Temple.
(The Sun States, perfect mandalas—the virgin forest must be all around.)

Bowl of hemlock, not chalice of hemlock.

With the sword, one rushes into the past; with the chalice, one drinks a sip of the past (for the future)—

Tool Weapon Machine

Sword and scissors: the problem of cunning—of a strength that isn't your own—

Tool: at the service of individual creation.
Machine: at the service of the satisfaction of collective needs.
If the machine is used to produce what should be individually created, then you have *le malheur*: and battle (with the sword) becomes mass murder (with the atomic bomb)

South America

Pre-Columbian Civilization: blood where "otherwise" there would be spirit. Not a chaotic *craving*, with form as counterpoint—but form in chaos (this should be expressed more precisely in some other way!)—They had their minds on blood—therefore: the "law of the blood"—not only the rhythm of the blood, but the inexorability of the blood, the justice of the blood, blood like crystal, and then perhaps (but perhaps it's factitious) a transition to salt—
Safe to say that when we think of blood, we forget its salt con-

tent—A mathematics of blood? (An almost intellectual knowledge. Incas, no virgin forest.)

Numbers

13 as good and evil number—Christ and Judah.
10 number of the law and intellectual order.

Hair: an innumerable mass. Otherwise the human body: 1, 2, 5.

Buddha

The third eye of the Buddha. It corresponds to the two circles. The fourth, at the bottom, is missing, hence the problem of alcohol.
The Buddha's nearness to the earth. (Extinction of pain.)
Christ's distance from the earth. (Primacy of pain.)
Buddha, an inverted phallus. —The Buddha is virile—but he gives up virility.
(In the beginning, there was an eye—the two eyes: sword and chalice. —In the end the four eyes, and then a single eye.)

The last Buddha is eternal even in the flesh.

He didn't know the way of alcohol. That's why he forbade it to his disciples. That's why he died from a stomach ache.

Forms

Ellipsis: with overlapping foci: circle.
    With infinitely distant foci: line.

Pendulum: masculine: circle; female: ellipsis.

The man is a special case of the woman.

The Crucifix in the circle: center between navel and sexual organs.
Buddha: two circles (and one ellipsis): navel and solar eye.

Mythology

Orpheus / Eurydice: you can't look at the woman in the underworld—you leave, and she will follow.

Ariadne / Naxos—Naxos is the island with *no* distinguishable character.

Nostalgia for the *golden age*: plebeian, because it doesn't set a duty for itself (our era, an era of conscious duty)
the *silver* breed: the Second generation: heirs and children (and therefore mortal demons).
The Third generation: the *bronze* breed (brutality after being ruined by enervation).
The Fourth: the Heroes [. . .]

Neurosis

Problem of the *threshold for poison*.

[. . .]
the self-satisfaction of the third-class dreams under analysis (by a Freudian)—

Psychotherapy: swamp, overcome only by means of sacrifice (not renouncing, not escaping, not abandoning, not tearing apart)

Notes for a Letter
(May 1944)

It's not about—you understand—denying history—history exists—the thing to do is to overcome it—history (let's indulge ourselves in this abstraction) is realized (it's not a disembodied idea) through the historical part within us, the most transient, the most chthonic, the least crystallized part—the more fully we realize it, the less disposed we are to "history," the less we participate in some immediate activity—it's the voracity, the hunger for life, the misunderstanding, the inadequate aspiration in us that makes history: not the grand gesture that triumphs by abdicating, but the small gesture that triumphs by satiating—those who make history will never have the glory of transmutation, they will have only the satisfaction of satiety, they will have only the self-complacency of being able to assert themselves, the mean exaltation of revenge exacted—they will triumph on the level at which they lived, and they won't breathe the great calm beyond vengeance and forgiveness—
—who makes history?—the people in the streetcar who shoulder toward the exit, the people who start screaming when the ship is about to go down
—See, dear X., pray to the Lord that our dreams don't come true—what we have dreamed we have had already—every fulfillment is repetition and routine—but there is also a hierarchy of desires, and of dreams—every dream that fails creates a higher dream—whoever dreams always on the same level is the bureaucrat of himself—[. . .].)

Perhaps there will be the silence of two bodies exhausted after making love—perhaps there will be the silence of serene solitude, the silence of Stylites—and then there will be the third great silence of death, after death—but the fourth great silence—

The boss is not the incarnation of the idea, since in addition he has the urge of satisfied pride—

my old discovery that a single satisfied proletarian and a single unhappy capitalist overturn all your theories . . .

The refusal to participate in the totemic feast under the aegis of the Amazon.

The fact that I owe everything to having no more money. Too many wild animals have died out, don't take one of the last wild animals from man—every wild animal wiped off the face of the earth is a lost victory.

Italy doesn't know how to lose a war.

history is realized through confusions (not conflicts): the conflicts are an order seen a posteriori, from the perspective of the results of chaos . . .

swap places with a proletarian—I carry sacks, he reads Mallarmé

gift / sacrifice—the foundation of the city

the petit bourgeois pyramid—the end of politics—the error of the thesis of equality / inequality of humanity (the vertical, the horizontal)— common levels and levels of difference, possibility of organizing the common level, impossibility of organizing the levels of difference . . . (because the levels of difference come from contradictions in dialogue—and dialogue isn't organizable)

anthropological hierarchy—the politician as the necessary evil of a biological dynamic

[Untitled]

This book, written only in order to prevent misunderstandings with you, dear X., with you, dear Y., with you, dear Z., with you, dear XX.

How legend coagulates into history, and how (and where) history dissolves again into legend.

(so optimistic that I really don't rule out the possibility that, if things go on this way much longer, which isn't at all out of the question, I may not become, and with good reason, even more optimistic)

I work with historical material, of which I have only a nebulous sense, and that's why it's as imprecise (albeit in a different way) as the historical material the specialist historian tackles in a scientifically precise way—the meaning arises from history, but the rectification of the historical facts doesn't manage to touch the meaning eternally rectified a priori.

Prologue: I say, for example, that Socrates was a plebeian: for us. Don't forget that this is a matter of private mythology. But what real value he had in his own time. But that was another world, and the reference to me (to us) is acceptable.
An iconoclast, but a destroyer of extinct images.

In 1929 my childhood came to an end.
up till now, latency period
next step: the crisis of puberty

. . . people who, because they feel destroyed, consider me a destroyer—and don't have the imagination to see that to destroy them is to open the way to greater values, which negate them—

Not for the enthusiastic iconoclasm of the twenty-year-old, but for the mature, conscious, responsible iconoclasm of someone who has lived fifty years, *living through them*.

I think it's no longer possible to write books.
That's why I don't write books—
Almost all books are footnotes, inflated into volumes (*volumina*).
I write only footnotes.

The book: starting from chance,
        and also emphasizing chance,
        while at the same time narrating
        our uncertain position
        in the face of chance

The worst enemy is the enemy who shares our arguments. (The Antichrist, who looks exactly like Christ.)

Coitus as chaos.
Man: mother→chaos→child.
Woman: child→chaos→mother.
The man is anxious in the face of chaos. Impotence is a masculine trait.
(The "fury" of "evil" in sexuality.)

(Regarding Odysseus): there are some subordinate people (the whole of Europe is inhabited by them) who may believe him to be dealing with flashes of intuition . . . : actually, he's dealing with law

Menstruations: eternal menstruations
      The panic of the woman because she has (not) been impregnated
      (she draws it out)

Sun—long / short   Moon—big / small

Chaos, where every thing becomes every other thing: hence science fiction (?)

The characters of Theophrastos—of Jung—both *right*—it was a simple world with simple mechanisms—

Complication doesn't only come from life, but also from assumptions: the mixture of peoples and ancestors

Hierarchy of themes (instead of aesthetics of forms)

Province, because of roots—but we have roots in the wider world

for an introduction: The modern world divided into two contrasting halves that share all the essential characteristics: stupidity, no sense of the present—therefore, to people from another world that has nothing in common with the two halves into which the world is divided

therefore, the generation that will live through the Third World War

God will not forgive them, because now humanity is grown up and ought to know what it's doing

Innocence after guilt (before guilt: paradise lost)—after all, none of us would want to change places with Adam—The serpent not like a seductress, but like the woman who points the way—she has only shown Adam his task—in Paradise everything was too easy—paradises are always below Adam's level

On the seventh day, God got short of breath—so on the seventh day he had to rest—and so man had to finish up the seventh day's creation, everything God had forgotten or overlooked by using the expedient of a democratic paradise—he has to divide up the world according to values

In other words: God made us creators of his creation—and by creating us and his creation, we create Him.

Noise

The Italians don't distinguish between *Lärm* and *Geräusch*.
In both cases, they say "noise."
The beginning of racket (*Lärm*): the f o r g e .
Hence the connection between racket and tools.

(Progress—racket; civilization, silence. But: silence a f t e r
n o i s e).

For Schopenhauer, the crack of the coachman's whip is unbearable—the world of tools disturbs the world of the work.

Plebeians don't differentiate between work and tool, they think the use of the tool is work (or life)—In the end, they think the racket of the tool is work. (P r o b l e m o f d r i v i n g c a r s .)

(Summer '51:) They hammered for so long that I came to learn that I was hammered flat with contempt for blacksmiths.[25]

R a c k e t and m u s i c (not n o i s e and m u s i c)
Music—racket harmonized by man
                hammering iron is work—
                making music is not work—
I don't like any music because I like silence
Problem of rhythm—
Natural sounds, even if annoying and irregular, never rhythmi-

---

25 From a letter Bazlen sent to Giorgio Voghera, November 20, 1951: "And just when I got better, they started doing construction in front of my house, using machinery from six-thirty in the morning until eight at night—I have no idea why—but I really lived through—no joke—certain phases of the Tibetan initiations—as an experience, it was interesting [. . .] —as a chance to think about my affairs, it was a tipping point."

cal or unrhythmical
Rhythm has to do with the regular functioning of machines not
with the regular functioning of natural processes
Rhythm is always a rhythm of work (or of tools created by
means of work)—it begins with work
There is no rhythm of life

Toward a Theology of Driving

A man in a car goes from Nowhere to Nowhere.
He is everywhere.
And because he is everywhere, everything becomes the same.

(On humanity in little tin cans—elevators, cars)—

The man with the beautiful car—once he was only the man
with the beautiful watch.

[Untitled]

The great (monumental) monolithic stupidity (*Ahnungslo-sigkeit*) of Homericism

Not devotion to God (dissolution of self), not dependent on
the I—but the balancing point between God and me (where
God and the I coincide, the self and the non-self encounter
each other in the best way possible). Neither is betrayed and
both become purposeless, superfluous—
to drive and to be driven
arrogant qua the I (within the I)—humble in the face of God

No rebellion with these stupid ardent eyes, no abdication with
these floppy lips—

dedication is not abdication

God and I, both sovereigns, facing off—only the 0–0 match is
productive
everything else, movement on the same plane

to forget oneself, in the presence of everything,
domination of everything,
there man dissolves, and God, too

estimation of God, estimation of myself
God is no bigger than I am
I am no bigger than God
big and small
blowing raspberries at God
blowing raspberries at myself

face to face (with reverence)

This is the prologue, perhaps we can only write prologues—
there is the age of prologues, the age of the work, and the age
of epilogues.
(But our moribund men were unable to invent epilogues.)

> sweat on the brow doesn't create eternity
> they irrigate only the fields
> that bloom in spring,
> bear fruit in summer
> get harvested in autumn
> dry up in winter
> never to blossom again

The great work is done without ambitions
only culture is made with ambition
The non-destination a priori

All of us, guilty conscience in the face of modern physics (the
only allowable route)

Parapsychology taboo

(Joyce: orchestrated quagmire)

(Kafka: biting off less than he can chew)

devant la guerre la vie personnelle s'efface
        no—*commence*

Autobiography—how, in the moment in which I write, I am convinced of having experienced it

Anti-Odysseus

                                        (the untransformed
                                        the curious)

Odysseus → from the Talmud on down

Hamlet

Faust
↓
The experimental position of modern man

Poseidon versus Pallas Athena
Poseidon (father of the Cyclops Polyphemus)
Athena (only ally)

Penelope, the most barren woman: destroying at night what was made in the daytime (which naturally is always the same thing) is the stupidest thing conceivable; Penelope is the h o u s e w i f e.

Listening to the song of the Sirens, but bound: here is the beginning of the petit bourgeois fear of risk.

Anyone who has a (conscious) goal cannot be transformed—before Odysseus, the absence of purpose, the undulating here and there, that's why Poseidon is his enemy, the god of undulation— and Minerva (that arriviste snob) his protector . . .

The problematic of the modern man: Odysseus no longer enough—instead of moving forward, nostalgia for the lost paradise of Polyphemus.

In the prologue: Alemannic pietism . . .

I speak in concrete terms: my concreteness is the anthroposophy of the subordinate (true anthroposophy can only be subordinate—the necessity—though not for much longer—of maintaining a division between psychic reality and concrete reality)

In the end: And Odysseus, too, is only a fluke.
          this is not a sermon, not a doctrine,
          not an example,
          not a story . . . *it's an order*,
          not an explanation—
          an order.

P a l l a s : not from the mother's womb, no, from the father's head (and from then on the
Athenians have culture)

in conclusion: the new man, valid for a moment
          —Odysseus is eternal—therefore he had to wither
          —the new man is not eternal (we don't care for flowerings)
Eternities wither—but the moment creates the moment—the new Penelope is eternal, and creates an eternally new Penelope.

Odysseus—he had to retain his unique soul (to recover his unique soul, otherwise chaos)

In conclusion . . . and there's still a vague discomfort in the face of modern physics.

Not the stupid phrase: Odysseus is the petit bourgeois . . . but: with Odysseus begins that form of life which the petit bourgeois represents, in a form of degeneration . . .

Maybe a lot of things were forcibly included—but they were forcibly included in a way that made a lot of sense.

The destination is formed by living.

He who, out of fidelity to a woman, is constantly getting caught up in adventures, in order to escape from adventures, and doesn't take notice of what he encounters on his adventures, eventually, untransformed, finds the woman again, untransformed as well—the creative life comes to an end and the Christian family begins.
Rigid *fidelity is not trust* (both of them must accept chaos) . . .
Organic fidelity . . .
Rigid fidelity . . . The doubt of Philemon and Baucis . . .

The insipid soul corresponds to the intellectual . . .

The nostalgia for paradise lost: Odysses's sense of guilt for having murdered Polyphemus (to have one eye was more comfortable) . . .

Why so many books are now based on the *Odyssey*. . .

the metamorphoses of capillaries—myths *en bloc* . . .

Starting with Odysseus: fear in the face of adventure (justified, because previously every hybrid and indiscriminate thing spelled adventure . . . which establishes our value . . . but it's our only value . . .)

(the fact that works have to be arranged on a single plane, a unilateral perspective—there are tangential planes—perhaps they're the *right ones*—the work is understood only in terms of its performance—hence with a view to the petit bourgeois, and the creator is a petit bourgeois *malentendu* (the genius's order is the petit bourgeois' chaos)

To attend to thoughts (because Odysseus had thoughts, otherwise you're glossing over them, like the anthroposophists).

The song of the Sirens, to the exclusion of death
Birth of aesthetics
For the first time division between song and death

rigid order isn't a solution—order in motion, yes!

Space (Polyphemus)—direction (Odysseus)

the mutual, rigid cleaving together of Odysseus and Penelope—
which remains barren
Athena: i.e., fidelity according to the rules

The fool looks with tears in his eyes across the sea—

S u s p i c i o u s Odysseus is afraid Calypso is a trap—He lacks the imagination to see her self-surrender, and he isn't even a physiognomist—

Near the climax—the fact that every form, at its highest possibility of fulfillment, lasts only for a second—the uninterruptedly creative—but this is impossible, because form arises from chaos—and so disintegration, which is part of the birth of a new form—
Only those who accept disintegration are creative, there's also the creativity of the negative—it's human to be able to do nothing, to live, the art of not delaying death—

Pan is dead—of boredom

culture oblige

In the name of that class, an unjustifiably arrogant minority, who live off a minor discovery, whose interests (not to speak of capital) have already been eaten up—

Not to have goals is bad, uncreative,
To have goals is bad, bureaucratic . . .

We are not iconoclasts, but we want the development of images— images that have not been developed must be destroyed.

the development of images is the development of the world

Penelope: work for work's sake . . . why? In order to resist temptation.
Even Odysseus doesn't want to be tempted . . .
Because Christ has to resist temptation, but not modern-day man . . .

Odysseus doesn't create order, he creates direction—i.e., for a long time intellectuals live following a clearly marked line—but the clearly marked line is in chaos . . . (Croce and his peasants.)

Everything that crosses our paths and that we reject by following some other thing, is not experienced, and turns against the other thing . . . but there is fidelity (remaining faithful) and we know that *the woman who has been transformed makes her way to the man who has been transformed*—(and then that's not infidelity) fidelity without the sense of guilt . . .

He escapes from his adventures, for the sake of fidelity, and thus forces Penelope into rigidity (*communication mystique* between them)—and with a reciprocal sense of guilt the world does not move forward . . .

In every form of desperation there's a component of *coquetterie.*
"Pure" desperation would be death.

The just one becomes such only through (subsequent) confirmation from the outside (M a n i)

The self-assurance of the demonic gambler, who wins only to
plummet straight down into hell . . .
The only way is (always) the wrong way.
No Way is the right way.

but since there are only false ways (but since every way is a false
way) every way leads to the destination and every way is right.
(Woe to anyone who thinks that the place where he finds himself on his way is the end)
(because every road is right and every road is blessed—)

Up to the end, every way is a wrong way—wrongness means
not accepting the way you've taken

Odysseus—once he has eliminated the risk—studies the law of
beauty

the way beyond death—not to get bogged down in death . . .

Odysseus: he discovers the future. "But we want to forget about
the future . . ."

In a world of the unknown, to discover the continuity of the
known—but, in a world of the known, to read about adventure
into the unknown . . .

The adventurer, but not hand to mouth—the great adventurer
of God—

Odysseus and the Sirens: and so the critic is born, and soon it's trotted out that the sirens of X sing worse than the sirens of Y, and the sirens get wind of this, they want to sing even better, and so it comes to pass (that all the sirens sing out of tune)

the critical reader creates the poet inhibited by criticism

The Odysseans' apex. Erasmus, and together with his portrait, the portrait of a hybrid emptiness.
     Eagerness for the quest becomes indiscretion
     Being centered in oneself becomes impious
     The human measure becomes excessive
     In other words: a spirit in the mirror

The Greek gods, atomized like so many gnocchi

Regarding the petit bourgeois: he gives his tithes (the Orthodox Jews—the orthodox communists, and America)—nowhere near the threshold of sacrifice—with no risk—there's no risk of being ruined

[. . .] that classical noses have no sense of smell

It's not that in the beginning was the image; in the beginning everything is a wonder—turning from wonder to wonder—longing for a world without wonders, longing to dominate a world—and so i m a g i n a t i o n b e c o m e s the c a p a c i t y t o i n v e n t (ingenuity)

The need for the birth of reason had necessarily to arise on an archipelago: a life dragged around by the currents, threatened by maelstroms, abandoned to the winds

Where there is no problem of existence: no one is thirsty, no one is hungry—and where when you arrive the people have a feast

Horrible frictionless couple: he runs away from love and seeks out his image in the mirror: husband and wife have the same qualities—the other three women have qualities he wants to overcome

Puns: the emergence of self-irony (intellectual jokes, no magical knowledge of common roots)

Poseidon *refuses* him passage. (*In the end*, the dominion of Poseidon, but Messina, Titanic, etc.)

Calypso / Athena Conflict: she (or her father) knows all the depths of the sea—but Odysseus longs for the shore of his homeland—we are all black with the soot of our homeland, and we are always longing to return to the depths of the sea— The forces are driving him (every life, with its meetings, chances, strokes of luck, and other twists of fate, is just the play of the forces within us)

and he must not pay any mind ("they cannot conquer his heart') to:
1) the seductions of the wise soul (of magic)
2) the attraction of destiny in Circe's directionless sensuality
3) the playful childishness of Nausicaa's innocence (she would like to marry him)
in order to find again the clever soul of Penelope
(W h y has Odysseus gone away?—How one doesn't go away, one is thrown into a common grave via a world war)—

Odysseus spends his days with Calypso weeping with nostalgia

On the banality of Odysseus's admirers and of poems about Odysseus—going straight from Odysseus to B l o o m — (and the hero becomes Hemingway)

(I am writing in Rome, while a movie version of the Odyssey is

being shot: A d d e n d u m : how the filmmakers, as the last
Ulysseans, see Odysseus)

Odysseus "not a psychologist"—with the intellectual's typical
tactlessness: and persecution mania he becomes distrustful and
makes Calypso swear she won't pull any tricks (because he is
projecting and he himself pulls tricks)

He can't eat of the lotus—there'll be trouble if he forgets

Cyclopes: they rely on providence

He falls into a deep sleep when (borne by the Aeolian winds)
in the distance he sees the fires of the homeland (Kafka—who
falls asleep in the castle)—the fires, not the smoke—the unconscious wants to push him into the distance again

as prologue:
    that in place of the truth, order is established
    Truth, that last unconditional element, that silence
    into which *all* words flow—Since the truth has become
    conditional

From Notebook N

([. . .]. SIMPLICITY, A CONQUEST of complicated people, complication, a conquest of simple people . . .)

Analysis kills the heart: when it dissects from below. But analysis that examines the heart from above . . . !

Romanticism: as transition from convention, which is truth, to *realisms*, which have only one thing in common: the abstract element

Not taking a stand against the brain, but against its hypertrophy at the expense of still salvageable qualities, which are no longer dangerous, and, if integrated, are precious—Its greatest work, knowing its own limits: an intelligence that makes you frustrated and stiff is stupid.

The first commandment:
respect your father and mother, if they are respectable.
Know how not to respect them, if they are not
(in a solid culture, they are always respectable)

Third, always be courteous, with friends and enemies. Know how to defend yourself and how to kill, with courtesy.

Fourth, love work—don't slave away like a serf—love even the work that is performed within you—while you're just lying around—renewing yourself

Second: *Garder ta pureté sexuelle*—this is the most difficult—to know how to be impotent with the impure woman—

The exaggerated reverence for intelligence comes from the days when it was still difficult to be intelligent—

a writer who isn't an employee

the mere fact that he had [a need] to create the work speaks against this individual's vitality—

We know from experience that
experience doesn't count

The socialist who dies near the end of 1899 knowing that on January 1, 1900, the sun of the future will rise—and who's told about the Europe of '39 '40 '41 '42 '43 '44 and after

that up to the end point, there are always hierarchies

just now the *Observer* (the *Observer*, I say) reports that Koestler (Koestler, I say) has acknowledged that on the basis of the experiments of a Medical Society (a Medical Society, I say) in California (in California, I say) what has passed for *objective reality* is created by the expectations, not of the observer, but of whoever confers the task on the experimenter—

Spaniards who do the work
rolling their eyes.

For Eichmann: [. . .] The non-individual man is beneath guilt.

The anchor of humanism is lodged in shit.

From Notebook C

THE STUDENT TOLD the master: "Yesterday I did a good deed—all my money to a poor man—it was so simple."
The master said: "It was wrong, it wasn't a good deed. Yesterday you could have made a start with your money, you might have found yourself—and he has done only harm with the money."
"I'll do it tomorrow with the money I'll have then—I want to toil and sweat."
"But you could have done it yesterday, who knows if you'll still be able to do it tomorrow—and you might have liberated the world from labor and hardship—now you have to start all over again."

"If you were wise, the beggar would not have approached you—the fact that he approached you is your limitation, your mistake, your condemnation."

"The very fact that you're approaching the master is problematic."

The master smiled: "It was all pointless, now I can reveal it to you, I myself was the beggar, and also the second beggar."

"Then it's wrong that I didn't find my way to you immediately."
"No, because both beggars were hungry, and nothing bad would have happened in the world . . . "
"But you said that I let a crime occur, and that a beggar was

195

hungry . . . "
"Look out the window: the beggar is sated, the crime punished
. . . "
"Then the deed was good . . . "
The master, mockingly: "If you like sated beggars and crimes
punished . . . "
The student was confused . . .
The master: "Then you love the hunger of the poor and the
victory of evil."
The student was confused . . .

"And that's why creation isn't possible?"
"Yet, if I'm a good master and you're a good student, I will have
learned from you and you from me . . . "
"Then I want to make an effort to learn . . . "
"Then you wouldn't be a good student, but a fool."
"And if you learn from me?"
"I'd be an idiot . . . As long as there are masters and students—
don't be a student; that way, you can help me not to be a master
anymore . . . "

Prejudice: that there has to be
an end: you speak of the end:
"You will succeed . . . "   now is the beginning and
"At neither of them . . . "   the end: that's why it's so
"The work can never succeed?"   b e a u t i f u l .
"Don't you know it can never succeed? Don't you also know
that today it succeeded?"
The student went away, it was evening. At the crossroads, a
beggar . . . Was this the good one or the bad one? . . . The student
gave him alms—And that's w h y the history of creation hasn't
stopped . . . The work was done: everything was as it was in the
beginning, when alms were given, right or wrong.

"Then you're a guide?"
"No more than you are because you approached me . . . And the
fact that you approached me is my limitation."

"And if I hadn't approached you . . . "
"That would be my sterility."

"Are you starting to figure it all out?"
"The master: I can only figure it out if you become my master . . . "
"Then the encounter was no accident . . . "
"But you're a real putz if your student doesn't approach you by accident."
"And if I show you the way . . . "
"Then we'll both be up a blind alley . . . and the only one who will be able to get us out of it will be the student who approaches you . . . " said the master. "But you don't have any students."
"So all three of us will be up a blind alley . . . "

"It's all wrong, because I'm not the last master and you're not the last student . . . there are still plenty to come before we come to the end . . . "
"The end? In the end, there will no longer be students or masters . . . "

"And how can we get beyond masters and students?"
"If you become my master and the student of your student."
"But what about my student?"
"Your student is a charlatan, otherwise he wouldn't have become a student of yours, a student of my student."
"Then he has to tell you directly, that you are the master?"
"No, because there would only be a master if you became my master."

[. . .]

"But what would happen if I didn't give alms?"
"You would have been another person, and the beggar, too, would have been another person. You alone can meet your beggar. —You cannot give and not give alms to the same beggar."
"And if I had been another person, and the beggar, too, had been another person? And if I did not give alms?"

"Something bad would happen in the world, because he would have been a good beggar—and the pain would have been pointless . . . "

"And so it's inevitable: if I give, it's wrong; if I don't give, something bad will happen. There's no salvation."

"You continue to misunderstand," said the master. "You, as you are, have done wrong, because you gave alms to the beggar. — And you, as you are, would have done wrong by refusing him alms."

"What should I do?" the student asked.

"Be another person, and give the right beggar the right alms."

"And then?"

"Then you're no longer you, and the beggar is no longer a beggar, and the master is no longer the master."

"Should we say, then, that this discussion is pointless?"

"That can't be said, no, because if we stop now, we're leaving behind the plane where we've been, and that can only be done when we're at the limit—convenience and impatience are now things of the past—not h o l y   i m p a t i e n c e —only sinful impatience; not the impatience of the person who foresees the end, and has already come to the end, only the impatience of the mind that knows it can't go forward this way, because he doesn't go forward." (Arguments.)

"But am I one or the other?"

"We'll see once we've arrived at the limit"

"But is there a limit?"

"Yes, because we speak words and think thoughts."

In the end it's a question of taste—do we want to give alms?

These are the latest reports on the history of creation.

You sound like the Salvation Army.

Salvation is singular. Armies are condemned to defeat . . .

Why . . . ?

Because it's the same between the two of us.

Naturally a solution cannot be arrived at—but the very fact that the dialogue has taken place so near the end of time . . . however distant it may be, as ever—which is to say, at the end of all time.

"Who knows what I'll encounter now, the time is ripe for something new."
But when he came to the crossroads there was a beggar who was asking for alms.
The student felt confused—he was the beggar, he was the criminal, he was the master—but without thinking about it he gave alms, and he knew it was not a good deed.
Then the beggar bowed down and asked modestly: "Can I become your student?"
The student was confused. "Gladly," he said, "but why have you chosen me?"
"Because before I was your teacher, and everything you know you learned from me."
"But if I didn't give you alms, what would you have done?"
"You never know"—said the beggar—"maybe I would have starved, maybe I would have become a master. But now I'm forced to come and learn from you . . . "

"I wanted to do good."
"That was the hope, but is the good the good, or only simple-mindedness, enthusiasm, haste?"

[Untitled]

He decided to change his shirt to receive the angel. There was a knock at the door: he opened up, but it was just a student.

The "perfect" welcome of the master.
Order:
The drawer: invitation to the opening night of an exhibition, envelopes with postmarks from distant countries, an eraser—and, strangely, a rind of cheese.

A nice person, thinks the master: too bad for him—but he sees my order in my disorder and doesn't see my disorder in my order.

The master reflected and looked straight ahead—the history of creation was motionless—the angels were superfluous—But you could throw away the cheese rind—make order a little at a time in the drawer—the history of creation was proceeding apace . . .

They knocked—quickly, with his feet, he shoved his shirt under the couch.
He opened up: it was the angel.
"How tidy it is," said the angel, "I came too early . . . I'm on time, but I can see my messenger (because I sent you a messenger) has done a good job announcing me.
"You sent me a messenger?" asked the master in surprise.
Surprised, the angel replied: "Didn't you know the student was my messenger? Students are always the angel's messengers."
To think that something like this should happen to me, thought the master . . .
To think that something like this should happen to me, thought the angel.

And so they talked it over, because the master and the angel are honest people.
"It all comes down to the fact that you threw away the cheese rind," said the angel.
"Do I have to keep the cheese rind in my drawer forever?" asked the master (stammering, confused).
"What better place would there be for it?" said the angel.
The master didn't know what else to say.

"Plus, you weren't thinking: why put on a clean shirt to receive the angel?"
"Yes, that was my mistake—but these things go hand in hand, if I had forgotten about my shirt, I wouldn't have needed the

angel, I would have kept the dirty shirt on."
"Forgotten shirts are neither clean nor dirty (they are over-
come)."
This was the angel's message (annunciation)

Alms given at the right moment.
The money in the hand,
the open hand
(but who knows if the man to whom the hand belongs is the
right man)

In the end, no poor men, no donors
To the open hand the hand that receives

A fraction of a second of silence on the earth.

From Notebook P

THE BEST DON'T have any bad neighbors.

We have no models, we have only precursors.

There's no such thing as paradise lost, only paradise overcome.

The second cousin of the unknown soldier. (All Italians know (believe) they are the second cousins of the unknown soldier.)

The master discovers the problem, the students invent the answer.

There were slaves who lived only to help drag a few stones to help build the Pharaoh's pyramid—Certainly very sad—Had they been free men, they wouldn't have been able to do so much.

Something that should be applied in the deepest sense (without any paradoxicality): *De mortuis nil nisi male.* (To spit on the corpses of martyrs while they're still warm.)

The divine only believe those who are divine themselves.

The most difficult thing: to make blood of the spirit.

Megalomania is the first step toward greatness.

With us, the flood.

(Totemism ended with Darwin.) After Darwin totemism changed its name.

(Sad that you don't understand that every revolution is a revolution of slaves.)

Already said so many years ago: the flesh doesn't bind, only stories do. Contents of the *Thousand and One Nights:* the caliph kills all the women he goes to bed with and only marries the one he doesn't go to bed with, but who tells him stories.

The course of social progress is unstoppable and the sun of liberty is already shedding its first rays: we emancipated the slaves and in their place we ended up getting waiters.

Books of astrology supply the material: the level should be in ourselves.

X. speaks of his nostalgia. I feel sick. Only those who know what nostalgia is know what I suffer.

Understanding everything means forgiving something

No: dance around the fire—dance around the void.

The only thing that counts is first-time-ness

Those close to us ought to be kept at a distance.

People think we're dealing with eternal truths: what we're dealing with are adjectives.

Don't teach people anything: they are capable of learning

In a civilized country the use of the plural (by one spouse or the other) should be grounds for divorce.

On the problem of education: children declared themselves willing to sit still in the room for hours on end without making a sound, provided that the adults skipped around and shouted for hours outdoors.

Even the dead are "being developed"—and, eventually, we'll live in a world of the developed dead.

We can rightly envy the naivety with which (Strindberg suffered and) Weininger committed suicide . . .

(From an old notebook—1935?) He saw for himself the inexorability of God, he felt he was made in the image of God and therefore was inexorable. So he became an instrument of the inexorability of God—but he was really just vicious.

He was so smart he didn't understand his housemaid.

So the West is in pieces . . . The pieces bring luck . . .

Wars are the public private affairs of a mass with whom I share a few merely anatomical characteristics. In the worst case, I may die in a war, i.e.: I have been unable to escape from some camouflaged plebeian inside myself and so must suffer the consequences . . . Whereas others may, in the best case, die in a war, and then at least become "the fallen" (otherwise, at some point, they would die of cancer) . . .

Claustrophobia in the cosmos

The "neurotic" in 1951: showing symptoms discarded by lords

He was too strong for this weak, tender little woman: so he had to die.

Finally, a woman with whom you can avoid talking.

There are no wrong answers from the oracle: there are only wrong questions, based in wrong attitudes.

The diabolical temptation to love our enemy.

How does he always manage to be so lively?—He is never alive—

. . . and in the best case, depth psychology!

Intelligence is a tool—and this tool has ended up in the hands of morons

Against modesty . . . and whoever is satisfied with it, the best thing that can happen to him is to enjoy it

Between us and the truth is God. You have to go *through* God— you can't skip over him.

Political program:
space without people   Dictatorial rule by
freedom from the State   a free man—
a place in the shade   but he doesn't become
the right to silence   a dictator

One dies only out of stupidity.

Kafka etc.: making things so difficult is too easy.

They think what I say is for the most part paradoxical—as a result, I can say, with pleasure and perfect knowledge of the facts, that what others say is for the most part not paradoxical—

I have no ear for music—I can only differentiate silences.

The more assumptions, the more devoid of assumptions

Who shouts *Viva!,* shouts from fear.

In the smallest hut, there's no room for us.

The veil of Maya has become particularly frayed.

Forgetting is nobler than forgiving: this man is very noble and enumerates to her, with painful precision, all the things he's forgotten.

From a notebook, end of 1921: [. . .] The Jews lose their heads so wildly over every little thing that, chased by the Egyptians, they run straight into the Red Sea.

Progress—from peasant idiocy to urban banality

Do not take Proust's name in vain

Introduction to Svevo
First Draft (November 11, 1934—9:45 p.m.)
Milan–Astigiana

TOO MANY BANALITIES have been written about Trieste, the city of "dissent" and of "the melting pot"—undeniable banalities, true and indisputable like all banalities, and put forth, like any self-respecting banality, to serve as the context for a truth that is far more individual in nature [. . .]

It's telling that psychology arises only where the need for examination arises, both in cultures that aren't completely "solidified" and at the point of contention between two different cultures; see: the "psychological" Jew.

Now Svevo, a "Jewish" psychologist, in an un-"formed" environment. —Trieste, city of silent renunciations and un-expressed tragedies: man, overexposed to diverse influences, a diversity that . . . poles that couldn't be more opposite, from which, through maximum tension, the liveliest spark may arise, a spark that flickers and dies out in the futile efforts of the "impotent" genius, for whom the already-formed language is not enough, and who cannot find his own: *Däubler*.[26]

—The culture of Trieste: the libraries to be found on the "stalls" of the "ghetto," everything else is for now, in spite of my great respect, *belanglos* [irrelevant]—for example Stendhal.

—The tombs of many Spanish kings, dead in exile, and others, reminiscent of the cemeteries of the birds, on down to the

---

26 Theodor Däubler (b. Trieste, 1876–d. St. Blasien, 1934), author of the "lyrical epos" *Das Nordlicht* (1910).

twentieth century.

And with that, the possibility of the birth of that rift from which "psychology" is born: uncertain, almost, . . . not so much the knowledge of was der Mensch ist [what man is] as the fact zu wissen was der Mensch nicht ist [of knowing what man is not]: not noble, not consequential, not causal.

but our continual parasitism, not one cause but many causes, and love, and why we are the way we are, and the need to rationalize, and everything becomes a symbol, and man without limits—where one ends, where the other begins, and why we act—and everything, even reduced to the most basic level, fails to satisfy—and life lived "by proxy," etc., etc.

Every gesture has its own meaning, agreed-upon and inescapable; every word has its own precise outline, every sentence its premeditated cadence. And even the episode itself, more the humanistic taste for repetition than the immediacy of first sight.

—And the romantic masterpiece becomes an example of classical prose.

—understandable then that the aesthetes have never been drawn to the shirtsleeves of the Triestine bourgeois: their towers of imitation ivory.

—solidified culture, triumph of specialists. The novelist, being non-specialized, does not exist.

—Zeno: a more complicated and less mechanical game of references and interdependencies.

—there's no place for the unexpressed.

—the different premises of Italian literature and of, shall we call it, Triestine literature.

—and from this arises the inescapable link between the possibility of creating these figures and the absolute lack of style.

—overheated genius and dead-end exaltation.

—and we must not forget the debt of gratitude that the honesty of tomorrow's hero owes to the honesty of yesterday's coward.

Preface to Svevo

EVEN IF I have no desire, in this brief introduction, to play the game of seeking out the cause of causes, it will be necessary to say something about Italo Svevo's historical moment and environment in order to come to terms with how, on the fringes of Italian culture, such an unusual figure could arise—and a figure who has so little in common with the "cliché" of the Italian "man of letters."

Nothing will better reveal to us the gap between Svevo's work and the work of his Italian contemporaries than the different premises from which the formal informality of Svevo arises on one hand, and on the other the excessive, and anti-natural, formal perfection of Italy, which will also make clear to us why this figure could not become "enmeshed" in the prewar literary world and could not receive his full (?) recognition until a few years ago.

Prewar Italy: the country with the most solidified culture in Europe. The noteworthy fact that, from Dante on, to confine ourselves only to language, the language did not change, and therefore it was the culture of maximum form. Form born from an admirably blended unity of background and from an a priori synthesis, in which, as a logical consequence, every need for expression therefore becomes a game, a search for a new, ever more refined equilibrium, set apart from each other by a nuance (let's leave this word, spontaneous product of the pen, in all its caricatural Bovaryism)—and under which—with immense respect to all exceptions to the rule—the overheated effort of the genius, in his attempt to bring together what can't be brought together, to smooth out what can't be smoothed, to reconcile the irreconcilable, will hardly be noticed.

A world, therefore, already polished to a shine, with no adventurers or pioneers of culture; "the problem" resolved a priori, no call for a revolutionary of the form to arise, everything already being the logical consequence of logical consequences, every gesture indisputable and accepted in full, no sense of lacking for "cover" between gesture, word, and environment, hence the Italian man of letters is left with no more than a game consisting in making different combinations, expressing old feelings in old forms, and continuing to polish, shine, and refine words and cadences that have already been overrefined, passed through the filter of dozens of generations.

Every gesture has its own meaning, agreed-upon and inescapable, every word has its own precise outline, every sentence its premeditated cadence. And even the episode, in a narrative, is presented more as a pretext for the learned game of style and the humanistic taste for repetitions, almost hieratic in its repetitiveness, than with the immediacy of first sight. So much so that the greatest romantic masterpiece comes to be and to count not for the humanity that shapes it, but as an example of "beautiful writing." Culture solidified, triumph of the specialists: specialists of the head, the eye, the ear, critics, painters, musicians, and there's no place for that immense dilettante, the novelist . . . lack of that breach, that rift, which gives rise to uncertainty and doubt, the fathers of observation, introspection, the first step, the only premise necessary for "psychological" interest.

On Trieste

WELL . . . BUT I'M afraid I haven't lived in Trieste since 1934, and that I haven't set foot in Trieste since 1937, and all I can tell you are very old stories: I was born in 1902, sixteen years of Austria, then emancipation, and then, until 1934, sixteen years of Italy—later I was liberated once more, but by then Trieste was no longer in the picture—we'll see how many times it befalls me again—

The Austro-Hungarian Empire in the last years of the first prewar period . . . a world with very different standards than ours, today—there were, it's true, some national struggles, but with standards that now no longer seem real— in Trieste, they brawled from time to time, they were serious, as serious as you could be in those days, and there were always some skulls cracked, some legs broken, and various abrasions, it was written up in *Il Piccolo*, they could allbe declared completely healed in seven or eight days, but the Bora, the wind in Trieste, made for disasters far more serious than those committed out of civic fury—it was one of the rare cases in history where the elements were more pernicious than man.

They used to call Franz Joseph the Emperor of the Gallows, and they lived under the "yoke," and they passed hours of "grim servitude" . . . but, if I'm not mistaken, he only had thirty-six people hanged (maybe I'm mistaken, but I don't think so), about half of them in 1848, when he became emperor, and then only to settle accounts opened by others—so that leaves about twenty people in seventy years, including Oberdan,

211

whom Franz Joseph did have killed, it's true, but only because
Oberdan had wanted to kill *him*—

Austria, a rich country, equipped with an inflated,
meticulous, bureaucratic machinery that, of course, could seem
ridiculous and pedantic . . . but it functioned perfectly, with
slow, precise, conscientious, generally incorruptible employees,
with a religious respect for the laws of the state—also because
they were well paid and had no need for tips, handouts, or
blackmail to make it to the end of the month—with a state
salary, you could live well enough for the needs of the time,
and more than well enough for the needs of today—consider,
for example, that one of my old friends in Trieste, the first
person of real culture I ever met in my life, was employed by
the post office—he wanted to live in peace, he had no career
ambitions, and by spending all his years of service behind a
counter until he could take his retirement, he was able, with his
single salary, to get a decent apartment with four rooms, a fine
library of a few thousand volumes, art books, for the most part
bound, to purchase a violin and a grand piano, to get married,
to send his son to school, to go to the café or drink a glass of
wine every night, to go to the theater, and to take an annual
month-long trip, during the vacation season—today it may
seem strange that a person of real culture should adapt himself
to an employee's life, especially at a time when everybody had
"every door open" to him, but to be an office worker in Austria
was conceivable for people who weren't keen on rushing in to
the "battle of life," who preferred to think about other things,
it was an ideal solution—a slow-paced and quiet working life,
with little responsibility, which guaranteed all the necessities of
existence, and not just material ones—and it wasn't a barren
life either: besides having as a colleague the painter Fittke, who
was a fine and not insignificant painter, even by non-provincial
standards, the whole world paraded past his counter, in Trieste,
and just observing the way English, Danish, and Japanese
sailors signed their receipts, he learned much more about the
world than most people who've conscientiously traveled it from
end to end—and then there was his free time, when Fittke, a

shy and quiet impressionist from the days when Impressionism was still a living thing, painted, and quite a lot, in the hours when he wasn't at the office—

The world, or at least that part of the world typically considered to be the world, was rich: Austria was a rich state, Trieste one of the richest cities in that rich state in that rich world—it was only after the First World War that I heard talk of unemployment for the first time, before that, those who didn't take the initiative (and it didn't take much) of getting to work on their own account, if they looked for a job found it the same day and were faced with an embarrassment of choices—they easily earned what they needed to get by and even brought whatever they had left over at the end of the month to the Trieste Savings Bank, a savings bank that was open even on Sunday: except on Sunday you could only deposit, not withdraw, probably to ensure that, in the enthusiasm of the benders that lasted from Saturday night until Monday morning, people didn't drain their accounts (although it wasn't easy to drain them): benders that I can't describe until you consider that a longshoreman who did two shifts certainly earned a great deal, but a great deal more than the director of a bank branch earns today, and I, whose childhood house was at the border of a patrician neighborhood and a working-class neighborhood, remember that on Saturdays I couldn't get to sleep because of all the drunks passing by (this is not to mention that they'd also give drinks to their donkey, their *muss*, and would wander around Trieste with their drunken donkey), singing *no go le ciave del porton no torno a casa*,[27] which is why the *fraia* lasted until Monday morning, when the door was opened —an almost Pantagruelian world, where everyone worked a lot and ate even more, where everyone drank and made love, and despite all the nationalist rhetoric the problem was all hail Spain where everyone drinks and eats—and no one even complained about taxes, and I tell you about this because, later, the fiscal problem became a

---

27 In Triestine dialect. "I don't have the door keys, I can't go home." [AA]

really serious problem (but here I should tell you what I saw in
emancipated Istria, and this isn't the place)—but at the time I'm
telling you about there was, if I'm not mistaken, a commission
composed of citizens who monitored the taxes, and in the rare
cases where the declarations may have seemed not too plausible,
the interested party would be called in and everything would be
sorted out to everyone's satisfaction (i.e.: to the satisfaction of
the party and everyone else)—in general, Austria was fair and
tolerant because it was old, because it retained the sediment of
ancient experience, because it had all the dignity of a ceremoni-
ous man on his deathbed; the constitution recognized the same
rights for all Austrian subjects, and the bureaucracy, loyal to the
constitution, really committed no injustice. You mustn't forget,
too, that they had the sagacity to stock the nerve centers, the
cities where the national problem was most delicate, with their
best functionaries, chosen for their tact, who knew, within the
limits of the possible, how to patch things up while causing the
least possible irritation (at the time it didn't always seem so, but
considering what we saw after . . .), but Austrian subjects were
easily irritated, and they had every interest in being irritated;
in fact, until 1918, I attended German schools (naturally I was
irredentist, but I'll tell you about that later) and I can assure
you that in classes composed of a mixture of Italians, Germans,
and Slavs, in more or less equal measure, I don't remember (in
spite of the undeniable patriotism of certain professors come
down from some German-national Bohemia, and in spite of
four years of war) having noticed any offensive reactions, or
ironic phrases, or charged words of hate against Italians or Slavs.

And as you've asked me for anecdotes: to give you an idea
of what lawfulness consisted of during this period, let me tell
you something that happened to Svevo: a little girl in his family
(I seem to remember it was his daughter Letizia, but I'm not
sure) calls up a friend her own age and in a fit of patriotic furor
began, on the telephone, to sing a song outlawed in Austria,
no doubt an "anthem" (woe to anthems), the one by Mameli
or the one by Garibaldi. A telephone operator (the automatic
telephone wasn't installed in Trieste until a few years after the

first war) heard them singing and broke in: "Watch what you do, girls."—The little girl tells Svevo about this, and Svevo tells Felice Venezian (one of the Triestine irredentist leaders), who, overjoyed to have acquired such a serious argument against the oppressors (violation of the telephonic secret), in no time flat is at the house of the Director of Austrian Mail and Telegraphs to protest violently, because a telephone operator intervened while two kids were singing an anthem outlawed in Austria—the Director of Mail is appalled and fires the employee on the spot (violation of the telephonic secret!), and Svevo, to appease his Zeno-like conscience, goes looking for another job for the telephone operator fired for having violated the telephonic secret of two little girls singing an anthem outlawed in Austria.

And the situation was delicate: a city that speaks a Venetian dialect, surrounded by a countryside where everyone speaks a Slavic language, the most intellectual part of the bourgeoisie, who feel cut off from the country to which they think they belong through language and culture (even if they don't understand "Tuscan," and even if the culture . . . but let's not speak of culture), and who are therefore obliged, well into the twentieth century, to have recourse to the rhetorical phraseology of the Risorgimento, who carry the flame, who believe that Italian is a genteel idiom, musical and pure, and that Florence is the city of flowers, who believe that in Rome they milk the she-wolf to nourish their offspring, who offer votive lamps, who stick Lions of Venice everywhere, who tremble, invoke, throb, hope, suffer, wait, yearn, pine, burn, sacrifice, protest, pant, lust, and long, and when they put on *Nabucco* at the City Theater, the thought of all the shopkeepers, brokers, directors of banks and insurance companies, doctors, lawyers, importers, and exporters sitting in the orchestra seats, the professors and teachers sitting in the balconies, the students and shopgirls "piled up" in the peanut gallery, *va sull'ali dorate*,[28] and the excitement is such that it could, as they said in Trieste, "bring down" the house. One of my teachers, who took his first trip to Italy after having

---

28 Allusion to the "Chorus of the Hebrew Slaves" in Verdi's Nabucco (1842). Literally: "goes on golden wings." (AA)

been emancipated, brings me back a book as a gift with the dedication, "the which a small token of a great affection," and one of my cousins, who later became a civilized person, around the age of eighteen draws a very De Carolis-esque postcard for the National League, with fine black and red lines, with an altar, a broadsword, an open book, a pomegranate, and this motto, "Well to us does it behoove to win the battle," and I, in the children's encyclopedia, find a poem not a word of which I understand, but which I like so much I end up committing it to memory and walk around the house shouting: "When Jason from the Pelion / pushed the firs into the sea / and ran first to cleave / with oars the breast of Thetis / so sang the Odrysian bard,"[29] until one of our servants asked me what language I was speaking. A Triestine poetess, on the Grignano vaporetto, said to her son, who'd just thrown his wooden sword on the floor: "Dario, gather up that broadsword."

The other part of the bourgeoisie, the less cultured, continues to conduct their business, invest their profits in reliable ventures (so that everything's lost at the end of the war), go to Tergesteo, talk about business more than politics, but are nevertheless dragged along in the wake of homosexuals, tremble and rave at the close of whatever act of the *Puritani* ("let the intrepid trumpet sound"), buy National League stamps, pay their dues to the "Patria" society, the National League, and the Philharmonic, while the ladies swoon at Ibsen's *Ghosts*, and when Oswald starts stammering, Mama, give me the sun, they have to be picked up and carried out of the hall. I'm not exaggerating: one of my aunts was among these swooning women.

So, in the city you have this bourgeoisie—and just a stone's throw from the city, on the Carso, you have Slovenian peasants, on a poor, rocky, barren soil, where, except in the sinkholes, they have to tear a few square meters of arable land out of solid rock. Primitive, insulated by outmoded myths, with no cultural traditions, proud with all the susceptibilities of an easily (and justifiably) wounded pride. The Italians couldn't feel more

29 From Vincenzo Monti's poem "Al signor di Montgolfier" (1784), lines 1–4 and 17. [AA]

superior than they do to these people, and this superiority based on a high school diploma (the *maturità*), based on their life being insured by the Assicurazioni Generali (this was a world where everything was insured), based on their commercial connections with foreign countries: the Italians make sure it's felt. I don't know if at that time in Trieste there was any possibility of understanding between Italians and Slavs, but I know that every Italian family that could have Slovenian servants (and the contact between Italians and Slovenes was reduced, aside from a few shopkeepers, vegetable merchants, etc., to a rapport between the bourgeois Italian family and the ex-peasant Slovene servant) and that treated them with humanity, without hauteur or a sense of cultural superiority, were always more than satisfied with these servants: hardworking, loyal, attentive, more intelligent than their masters, quick to assimilate and learn, but on the other hand too quick to take offense, barricading themselves in a stubborn and vindictive opposition. But in general, with their inflated sense of superiority, the bourgeoisie despised them (*sciavo* was an insult) already for not understanding Italian (but they would have been horribly astonished if the Slovenes had despised them for not knowing Slovene), provoking in them a mute resentment, which smoldered. On the other hand, thanks to the quickness with which Eastern European people assimilate European culture, these servants, if they found themselves in favorable circumstances, easily took on an elegant polish and, just as Budapest was more Parisian than Paris, Ljubljana was more Viennese than Vienna. (Marriages in Sicily.)

I told you I attended German schools and that I was an irredentist. My family belonged to the less intellectual bourgeoisie that I mentioned. So it was German schools for me, as for most of the bourgeoisie; this was the period when it was widely accepted that "those who know languages have the world in hand," as though there were a limitless need for hotel concierges! So, until I was seven, I didn't have any political feelings at all. But at seven, my first vacation in Italy, in the "kingdom," or in other words in Friuli, above Udine. And at the hotel, a big "pro"-National League party, tricolor flags speeches usurpers invaders hangmen domination foreign anthem by Garibaldi anthem by Mameli royal march. And a lady, this fat and this tall (I'm not exaggerating), with a mustache, I'll never forget it, and may God never forgive her, when she heard I was attending a German school, she explains to me, with all the rancor she was capable of, to me, a boy of just a little more than a meter tall, that she is one of the oppressed and that I am an oppressor, which I found so upsetting that I immediately resolved to become one of the oppressed at any cost, and this I think I managed rather well. So, down with Austria, the invader, the clod, and the bootlicker—and this with all the enthusiasm of a boy who still plays at Indians, suffering half to death at having to attend the German school, and underneath it all a sense of inferiority I can't begin to tell you about.

So, the city fought for Italianity, but Austria, undaunted, concedes everything. Trieste receives everything it needs, to the point that, I was told, one of the biggest ruses of irredentist politics consisted precisely in demanding and simultaneously being seen to refuse an Italian university in Trieste. If they had gotten one, they wouldn't have had any more arguments.

So, this city that speaks a Venetian dialect, and this countryside that speaks a Slavic dialect, are entrusted to an Austrian bureaucracy that's irreproachable, but that speaks German. A world of high bureaucracy, composed in large part of aristocrats with little blond daughters with governesses, with Bösendorfer pianos, with old Vienna porcelain, with Biedermeier furniture, who permit everything, who (and with more style) are more liberal than the irredentists, who every once in a while are forced to prohibit something when one of the many Sem Benellis wants to come to Trieste to stage a demonstration of the Italian lack of tact; who only make arrests when nothing else can be done, deeply displeased to have to do it, and then great scandals, obscurantism, medievalism, interrogations at Parliament, and long live liberty. And this peaceful, well-fed, equitable life goes on until 1914, near the end with a subject

30 Allusion to a popular song of 1911 written to promote the Libyan war: "Tripoli, bel suol d'amore." [AA]

for even greater enthusiasm: Tripoli, beautiful soil of love,[30] is about to become Italian to the boom of gunfire.

The Italians had their *Società Ginnastica*, the Germans their *Turnverein Eintracht*, the Slovenes their *Sokol* affiliated with the *Narodni Don*, and all of them did their cartwheels and knee bends for their respective political ideals; the city continued to make money, the oppressors did their best to oppress, and the oppressed did their best to feel oppressed.

And suddenly 1914: Sarajevo, the funeral procession of the mortal remains of Franz Ferdinand and his wife, which traverses the city, a few days of vacation from school as a sign of grief (earlier I pray to the Lord that they may kill two archdukes every month); followed by eight or ten months of Italian neutrality; the royal subjects return to their kingdom, most of the Italian families go to Italy, young men of military age cross the border with Austria, which pretends not to notice; then, in May 1915, the intervention, I go to Barcola with one of my tutors who tells me about D'Annunzio's speech, about the war that won't last more than three months, and about the liberty that we'll enjoy when the war is over, in three months' time.

Now, though, before we continue, shall we try very quickly to get a sense of what these Triestinos are, this Triestine culture, this city about which it was said, and the Triestinos took no offense (quite the contrary) that it was a melting pot? At first sight, I'd say that Trieste was anything but a melting pot: a melting pot is a receptacle into which the most disparate elements are put, melted down, and out of which comes a homogeneous fusion, with all the components distributed equally and with consistent characteristics—now, in Trieste, to my knowledge, no such fusion ever took place, at least not one resulting in consistent characteristics (in the sense that a "Roman," a "Milanese," a "Sicilian," if they're typical, if you go into a café you'll recognize them, but just you try to pick out a "Triestino," if he's not talking)—there was the possibility of what the Italians call "dialogues" (when they're chic), the possibility of numerous encounters and rapprochements between elements that normally never meet, but all that came out of it were attempts, approximations, never totally definitive figures, God's experiments went only so far. People with different premises, who have to try to reconcile the irreconcilable, who obviously don't succeed, produce some strange types, adventurers in culture and life, with all the strangest and most tormented failures that result from such a concoction: Trieste had (I don't know if it's still the case) one of the highest percentages of tuberculosis (the second generation of urbanized Slovenes), insanity, and suicide in Europe. The mixing takes place at the physical level, and when there's a blending of Slavic blood—the primordial Slavic health—with a certain Latin refinement, what comes of it are wonderfully healthy and harmonious bodies: what you see on the beach in Trieste is difficult, I am told by people who know much more about sea bathing than I, to find in other cities. Indeed in this regard, I'm reminded that on the occasion of a referendum held by American journalists concerning the seven wonders of Europe (an affair of some twenty years ago), they cited (after the differences in the price of gasoline in the various European states) the bodies of the young people of Trieste.

And just as there is no single Triestine type, there is also no one Triestine creative culture; to create a homogeneous work with such premises would have been impossible. Trieste, for these reasons, made an excellent sounding board (moreover, it shouldn't be forgotten that despite its cosmopolitan characteristics—which are only cosmopolitan when compared to the non-European level of the Italian petit bourgeois—it's a quite small provincial city of 250,000 inhabitants) and it really didn't produce anything that in any way whatsoever introduced a new element into European culture (I don't say that it didn't produce a few respectable works, but cross it off the map of Europe, and even the world, and Europe would remain as it is). Culturally, the first important event that made Trieste famous was the murder of Winckelmann, a rather obscure business with homosexual undertones. Then, more than a hundred years ago, the first propeller experiments were done in Trieste, by Ressel. Then, in the nineteenth century, as in all provincial cities, Trieste had its indispensible provincial intellectuals, humanists, and rhetoricians, who composed perfect sonnets and perfect regional histories, but who now serve only to provide names for streets, or places to rendezvous with girls, under their monuments— and it also produced a painter of historical pictures, Gatteri, and a man named Domenico Rossetti, who must have had some influence in his time, since one of the longest streets in Trieste bears his name, and he has one of those monuments to him I mentioned (where people arrange to meet each other, in the morning to go on excursions, and in the evening to stroll with girls), but may I be struck dead if I, who am Triestino and who am what they call a cultured person, know what he did with his life, or why he's famous. But let's leave the Academies alone now, and speak of those madmen who did research under their own steam: now that alchemy has become one of the deepest psychological problems and modern physics has picked up some of its themes, it would seem that the last European intervention in favor of alchemy may be a book by one Adolfo Helfferich, published in Trieste just under a hundred years ago.

And consider that the foreign artists who ended up in Trieste are among the least categorizable, that strange line of Burton Lever Joyce (Burton of Arabia, known as the translator of the *Thousand and One Nights*), and Stendhal, and Hamerling, and the strange childhood of Ferruccio Busoni. And what gives a particular flavor to Triestine culture is the proximity of Duino Castle, where Rilke lived as the guest of the Princess Thurn-und-Taxis, where the *Duino Elegies* were conceived, and where, at the turn of the century, the most *highbrow* European culture passed through (having therefore popped over to Trieste).

I see the particular tension between two different cultural configurations particularly in a Triestine poet called Teodoro Däubler, whose name you must know. A cosmic cultural out-pouring of visions from a shoreless river, and, on the other hand, a need for narrow, angular forms, which produced a quite peculiar screeching, which condemns to failure the work of this man who was one the greatest visionaries, almost (almost) on a level with Blake and Lautréamont.

And then Trieste furnished another interesting specimen:

Italo Svevo, a Triestine Jew educated in Swabia (whence his pseudonym)—whose body of work was one of the very rare living contributions, in my opinion, that the literature of the Italian language made to fin-de-siècle Europe. Now, it seems to me that the fin de siècle was, contrary to what's usually said of the decadent spirit, the last European moment when literature (and perhaps also art) made a real contribution to European culture. It was the moment of Van Gogh, Nietzsche, Wilde, Strindberg, Jarry. Now, in that moment, Italy's only contribution was the work of Svevo, which couldn't have the wide appeal it deserved, and which has the particular misfortune of having been too differentiated, too subtle, and too nuanced to be understood at the time it was published, and, on the other hand, superficially and structurally, to be written in a style so conventional, with such stiff nineteenth-century *gaucherie* (superficial elements, yes, but still bothersome) to be immediately digestible today.

So, even if Trieste wasn't a source of any great creative value, it was an excellent sounding board, a city of uncommon seismographicity: to get a sense of it, you'd need to have seen the libraries that ended up on bookstalls in the ghetto at the start of the last world war, when Austria was in ruins and the Germans were leaving or selling off the books of people killed during the war. A whole great unofficial culture, books that were truly important and completely unknown, lovingly sought out and collected by people who read that book because they needed to have that very book. All the stuff that passed through my hands, where I discovered stuff I'd never expected to come across, but most of it, whose importance I hadn't yet understood, slipped by me. Even now, when I hear of books that are totally unobtainable and have been reevaluated over these last twenty or thirty years, and which I'll never find again, I remember how they passed through my hands, on the bookstalls of the ghetto, thirty or so years ago, covered in dust and ready to be sold off at a lira or two each. I'm talking about the libraries of Germans, Austrian naval officers, and so forth. If the situation had been reversed and it was the Italians who were leaving, the stalls would have collapsed under the weight of Carducci, Pascoli, D'Annunzio, and Sem Benelli, with a side of Zambini and other men of ill omen.

And it was a musical city, too, where everyone sang, and sang well, little songs with a characteristic cadence, recognizable to the naked eye, where popular songs were almost born, with a Teatro Comunale where the success of an opera or a singer was valued only a little less than a success at La Scala. After all, if you consider what I said about research, experiments, and so on, didn't Busoni, who wrote some foundational texts about modern music, who performed musical experiments in other countries that may have failed but were still significant, spend the first formative years of his life in Trieste . . .

But now let's go back to 1915.

EDITORIAL LETTERS

MUSIL, *Der Mann ohne Eigenschaften*

I'M SORRY THERE's such a hurry. It's a complicated thing, and to give you some idea of what it's about, I'd like to write you at length and translate a few excerpts for you. But seeing that there is a hurry, I'll send you back the three volumes today, and I'll jot down for you, as best I can, a few words that may—I hope— help you make a decision:

Regarding the level of the work, there's no question, and (despite the reservations I'll mention and the innumerable other reservations I could mention) it ought to be published without hesitation. Regarding its symptomatic value on every page, and regarding its absolute value in many parts, it remains one of the biggest of all the great non-conformist narrative experiments undertaken since the First World War, works that are almost all based on the predominance of a single element, employed beyond the limits allowed by pedantry (Joyce, for example, the association of sounds; Musil, the precision of thought).

There's much to be discussed, however, from an editorial-commercial point of view. Here, I have to play the devil's advocate. And, as the devil's advocate, I have four arguments. The novel is:

1) too long
2) too fragmentary
3) too slow (or tedious, or difficult, or whatever you want

227

to call it)

4) too Austrian.

1) *too long: 1674 definitive pages*; minus *307 pages* initially considered definitive by Musil, so much so that they'd already been printed. Later he had second thoughts, took back the proofs, and was still rewriting them the day he died (thus, in this part, you'll find chapters not redone, chapters redone, one chapter broken off in the middle); minus *150 pages* of chapters finished and unfinished, with no continuity between them, and in which there's almost no hint of how the novel was supposed to have concluded (though, in the most general way possible, one does get a sense of it, and I'll tell you how).

2) *too fragmentary*: the first part is completely finished; disorderly chapters follow; no hint at a conclusion. It's not one of those great torsos, like Kafka's three novels, where—despite the gaps, the half-written chapters, the imprecisions and contradictions—you can see the book through to the end. Here, you intuit the historical arc (the novel begins in August 1913, and you know that everything will go south in August 1914; but long before Sarajevo, I'd say in the spring of 1914, it stops), but what happens to the individual characters?

I myself, even though the book is worthwhile for countless other reasons that have nothing to do with the actual plot, after having spent virtually two months reading it every day, feel a bit disappointed, because, all things considered, I, too, would like to know who lives, who gets married, and who dies.

(By the way: I've been set on the trail of all the other posthumous fragments of the novel, as yet unpublished, to see if it's possible to reconstruct the ending. They're in Rome, where Musil's widow died a few years back. But just a few days ago I learned that Rowohlt is reprinting the book in Germany, and that he's commissioned a German by the name of Frisé to come to Rome to sort out the manuscripts. This Frisé will arrive in Rome in a few weeks, and then, maybe, this reservation of mine about the novel's fragmentariness will fall away. I'll see when he gets here, but it's possible that months and months will go by before any of it begins to come clear.)

3) *too slow (or tedious, or difficult)*: in spite of all the action I'll tell you about, everything progresses on the basis of essays of dozens, scores, or hundreds of pages, very often in the form of authorial comments, or in the form of the characters' reflections, or in dialogical essays. I translate for you, literally, a posthumous note by Musil on the subject of his book:

"Readers are accustomed to demanding that they be told about life, and not about the reflection of life in the minds of literature [sic] and men. This is surely justified only insofar as this reflection is a poor, conventionalized copy of life. I try to give them the original, and thus they will have to suspend their prejudices."

4) *too Austrian:* everything takes place against the implicit backdrop of pre-1914 Austria, and is packed with allusions to forms of life, habits, institutions, bureaucratic machinery, etc., from that world, which are unfamiliar to Italian readers. This wouldn't be a bad thing, books are published and understood with far more exotic premises, but there's too much to be lost in translation: the physiognomy of names and surnames, which are so symptomatic and clinically precise it's astonishing, and which themselves are often enough to characterize someone almost completely; a particular *négligé* of diction (I don't mean dialect, but almost the cadences of specific coteries) that creates "the atmosphere" and gives body to the characters, and that in Italian would necessarily be lost.

I implore you to take these four reservations on the part of the devil's advocate very seriously. And as for the *subject*, I'd like to tell you about it in the minutest details, but then I'd have to write you pages and pages. All things considered, there are subjects upon subjects, the story of at least a dozen leading characters, who are more or less interconnected (I say more or less because in the two thousand pages published so far everything isn't yet connected in full). All these subjects, all these stories, are constructed around the following skeleton:

In the month of August 1913, a group of Austrian aristocrats decides to prepare a big fête to celebrate the seventieth anniversary of Franz Joseph's "reign of peace," which will take place in 1918. The committee's meeting place is the house of the committee's muse, an ultra-cultured ex-petit bourgeois endowed with soul, front and back, who's now quite arrived, having become the wife of a very highly placed foreign affairs official. A great German Jewish financier falls for her (a monumental portrait of Rathenau) and gravitates toward the committee partly because of her, partly—it seems—out of interest in certain oil wells in Galicia. The protagonist is employed as secretary of the committee: the "man without qualities," the spokesman and perhaps self-portrait of Musil, who, being a mathematician (like Musil), obsessed with precision, thinks with an unassailable inflexibility, and with a more than exemplary ease, richness of ideas, associations, and culture, and therefore thinks about everything that's happening or that could happen, always a bit beyond the conventional limits within which things are commonly accepted by the characters and by others, and within which they have a—however conventional—form and consistency and justification, to the extent that everything might be something else, and everything is taken to the point of absurdity and disintegrates, and you can imagine the disaster that results.

For more than a thousand pages (on top of everything else), the committee is very busy searching for the central idea of the fête, and can only decide to make the decision to form subcommittees to decide to make the decision, etc., until it's decided, in view of the fact that Austria in 1918 will have had nearly seventy years of almost uninterrupted peace, to stage a great *Friedensaktion*, an "action of peace." This is in the spring of 1914.

Mind you, this is only a very rough skeleton, around which are built:

—the quite numerous love stories and adventures of the protagonist, which on one hand lead to a *coucherie* with the wife of the high official, on the other to a (wonderfully delicate and warm) incestuous idyll with his sister, crammed with a few hundred pages of intelligent dialogue, and accompanied by a work composed by the protagonist "on the psychology of feelings";

—his sister's estrangement from her husband, and the encounter with another man, naïve, stupidly systematic, and a bit
puppet-like;

—the great financier's pompous and cautious love for the
official's wife;

—the story of the financier's black servant and the official's
wife's maid;

—the financial-familial affairs of a minor Jewish bank
attorney who has a quasi Junker wife, and a daughter grappling
with those blond young people who ten years later will be Nazis;

—the idiotic considerations, but with a truly luminous intuition and an almost impalpable delicacy, of a general who is
trying to lift his own spirits;

—the sexual murder of a delusional vagrant, which (the
murder) besides all the problems concerning the limits of
consciousness and responsibility, sets into motion ninety-some
pages on the inconsistency of every legal formulation;

—the voiced disagreements and unvoiced divergences of a
young couple's *ménage*, which isn't working anymore,

etc.

etc.

etc.

Now, all of this, which may seem very lively to you, proceeds
only by means of reflections, essays, dialogues, digressions, descriptions, historical diagnoses, etc., and after a while is read
with a great deal of effort, often with boredom, even though all
of these essays are (with the exception of a few irritating pedantries, a few isolated oversimplifications, a few witticisms that
I would not say are too easy, but that I would have preferred to
be more difficult) characterized by an impeccable precision of
thought and style, and by a sensitivity of associations that often
surpasses the most beautiful pages of Rilke's prose.

After which it occurs to you that through these intermina-
ble dialogues, essays, treatises, feuilletons—and after having
been abundantly irritated and bored—a living world slowly is
coming into being for you, the people (whom you thought you

knew chiefly by way of abstract thoughts, etc.) slowly take on the density and form of the greatest novelistic characters, that the plot, which you hadn't noticed, is a pleasure, and that you haven't been bored, but have been enjoying yourself, getting involved, that for two months you have lived as part of this world, and that you have fallen in love with Agathe, the sister of the man without qualities.

And I haven't told you about the miracle of the web slowly formed by threads stretched between one idea on page x of one volume and another on page y of another volume—or about the vast sense of the political game, and the landscape, and the truly respectable knowledge of mental illnesses, and here, too, etc. etc., etc.

However, even though Italian readers are at an infinitely higher level than they're commonly deemed to be, publishing a book of this kind is a rather huge risk; to read it takes time, patience, a cultural background in common with the author, and so on. Now, I would not rule out that it could be of interest, or that some other factor that makes it fashionable might enter in (for example via the new German edition, its publication in other countries, an essay by someone who's taken seriously, etc.). But I don't want to have the responsibility, even in small part, for having thrown a publisher into this venture.

There's no time to give you a more comprehensive picture of the book. If need be, ask me specific questions and I'll answer right away. And I repeat to you what I wrote you about *Freundin bedeutender Männer* [The woman who was a friend to important men]: it's a youthful play, much simpler and easier, so much so that, if I'm not mistaken, Musil repudiated it. But it's very accessible to the public, and if it's still as enjoyable today as it was when I read it twenty-five years ago at least, it should be a very successful comedy. Which (perhaps—though there are almost no common determinants between listening to that comedy and reading this book) could somewhat pave the way for this fragment of two-thousand pages.

(to Luciano Foà, Casa editrice Einaudi)

Science Fiction

TWO MONTHS AGO I was quite fascinated by a few stories (I didn't have the patience to read a whole novel) found in American anthologies, but my interest waned almost immediately. They're interesting because they forebode a new atmosphere and a new geography (certainly not arbitrary) in which the world will live in a few decades, after the Third World War, and which I won't be around to see with my own eyes. But such painfully bad literature I couldn't bring myself to persist with it, though I know that this infiltration of a new visionary dimension is crucially linked with a third-order level of culture, and intimate forms which are, so to speak, very porous. And this intimate polenta is spreading. Today, along with your letter, I received the new issue of *Aut aut*: you can read for yourself Camus's article on Wilde, which has a truly repugnant plebeian banality. And a few days ago Einaudi sent me complimentary copies of Neruda and the Lorca plays. I didn't expect very much of the Neruda, but it still offended me more than I thought it would. But the Lorca (unless I'm wrong about the poems, but I don't think I am) was a huge disappointment: you saw what lack of a great and *inflexible* intimate form, what mawkishness and Bovaryism lay beneath the poetry, and the Homeric solidifications (*c'est tellement facile* [it's so easy], and in an age of new chemistries they're just comic strips, comic strips, comic strips!), and the *justes* chiaroscuri of the Mediterranean sun? and bugger the

233

wretched eternal themes! (Don't you think it's high time to introduce a rating system based on a hierarchy of themes?)

(to Sergio Solmi)

SOLOGUB, *The Petty Demon*

REREADING IT TWO years ago, which is to say twenty years after first reading it, I had the feeling of finding myself in the presence of one of the most perfect, or at least one of the most lively, books I know from that immense period which goes from the end of the century to the First World War and which, now past the latency period that follows a few years after the death of the writers and the first death of the books, is about to resurface, and in which the less-than-thirty-year-olds of today will make exciting discoveries and find the nearest, and hitherto unknown, roots of all their motives and problematics.

The only reservation, raised by Quarantotti Gambini, is that everything Sologub understood or was conscious of he explained too much. This is true, but with the two exceptions, it seems to me, of Hamsun (particularly in *Mysteries*) and Thomas Hardy, all the books of that period, to our taste, explain too much. It was the moment when the new psychological formulations were born, and the best and most modern narrative literature was right on the line between creating spontaneous images and formulating common determinants. Think how unreadable probably the greatest fiction writer of that era has become: Pontoppidan,[31] who was the first consciously to create a character in which man and destiny are one and the same, and he was

---

31 Henrik Pontoppidan (1857–1943): famous Danish novelist, who was awarded the Nobel Prize, ex aequo with Karl Gjellerup.

forced to explain it so exhaustively that his most beautiful novel is nothing for us now but the programmatic development of a so to speak psychological discovery.

Now, regardless of how much is explained in Sologub, you see how much is not explained, how much is not "understood" by the author, or understood later, and which has been imposed on him with such a violent autonomy that, behind the aestheticisms, the tricks, the emergence of the *ballet russe*, the calculated effects, everything unfolds in the great and genuine world of the soul; it reads as if we were separated from our dreams by a transparent gauze. I confess, for example, to stick to a very obvious element, banal if you like, and that in a contemporary author would be "easy," that reading about the woman in the doorway, smoking, and particularly those last puffs of black smoke at the end of the book, gave me goose bumps; and everything, you will see when you read it, under that perfectly measured liberty of the time, is more authentic, more mythic (excuse the word), more dreamlike than in any other book from the first quarter of the century. The stories of Heinrich Mann,[32] in comparison, are constructions of wire, not just on the outside, as indeed he wanted them to be, but, *hélas*, even on the inside.

And then there is a wish to dose (and the dosage is successful) good and evil, white and black, which, however mechanical clever people may find it, brings about a balance of lights such as I have not often encountered, a strange montage of naturalistic turpitude and greco-apollonian-stylized-decadent-*ballet russe* "beauty," so balanced as, in all of modern literature, you see perhaps only once in a while in some of Forster's intentions.

(to Luciano Foà, Casa editrice Einaudi)

---

32 Around this same time, Einaudi had asked Bazlen's opinion about the possibility of translating a selection of Heinrich Mann's stories into Italian.

ROBBE-GRILLET, *Le Voyeur*

TODAY YOUR TEN days of vacation ought to be coming to an end, and I am sending you back *Le Voyeur.* [. . .]

After about two weeks, it's almost completely vanished from my mind. From the little that's stayed with me, I can tell you that

—I read it very carelessly, it didn't grip me, and I don't think you'll disagree with me;

—as far as true substance, it seemed to me an insignificant, shamefully belated fragment by Dostoevsky or one of the decadent Danes;

—the "problem" of the simultaneity of times and places (which will probably become the slogan with which Robbe-Grillet will make a areer) is resolved only on a plane of impure cinematographic ability;

—the only valid talent he has, it seems to me, is the meticulousness of his descriptions. The trouble is that the meticulousness is not consistent throughout the book (which, if it were, would really deserve one of those fashionable adjectives such as "hallucinatory," or "magical," or whatever) but at some points it's denser, at others less, with the result that the densest bits leap out of the book as bits of pure skill.

But these are all secondary affairs. What's remarkable is the fact that a man, probably young enough, genuinely intelligent, sensitive and intuitive, with genuinely open eyes, can spend one or two years of his life with the sole purpose of creating a "machine" that puts a reader in the position to relive a few days of a small-time peddler small-time criminal ruminating an alibi. Robbe-Grillet is one of the many (almost everyone) who are paving the way for the Third World War; and from a culture reduced to this state, there's nothing left to do but emigrate.

The trouble is that all that remains to us is innere Emigration,[33] which is very noble, but uncomfortable. (Am willing to consider any counterargument.)

(to Sergio Solmi)

---

33 "Inner emigration": an expression used in Germany to indicate those writers who did not emigrate after Hitler's accession, despite their opposition to the regime.

DODERER, *Die Dämonen*

I SHOULD START by saying I don't like it. Of course, the *Leistung* [the performance] is considerable. To manage it in a few words (I know it's imprecise), we admit that *Substanz* [substance] and *Leistung* are divisible; it might be said that, in some good writers of little substance (Thomas Mann; partly also Joyce) the *Leistung* becomes substance, but in Doderer it only serves to conceal, to mask, an absolute lack of substance, a pure void. There's only trickery, a great superficial elegance that doesn't make up for the fundamental hubris, a quite parasitic, and, if you scratch it, quite banal intelligence, and a demonic ambition. Strange that Cases[34] likes it: it's the quintessence of everything that exasperated Karl Kraus. After the *Strudlhofstiege*,[35] of which I'd only read a part, for me the thing was settled. After your letter, I started reading the *Dämonen*. At the moment, and with great effort, I am on page 200. Probably perfect as a "machine," but *unspeakably boring*. They tell me there are some very lively chapters about the underworld (in fact, even in the pages that I've read, the lower it goes—socially speaking—the more readable it becomes); surely it's hard to find chapters (or pages) more dead than the ones I've read so far. If I go on with it, I'll

---

34 Cesare Cases, a German literature consultant to Einaudi, was a connoisseur and admirer of the work of Karl Kraus.

35 *Die Strudlhofstiege; oder Melzer und die Tiefe der Jahre*, Doderer's previous novel, published in 1951.

write to you again, but I'm not sure I will.

(to Luciano Foà, Casa editrice Einaudi)

GOMBROWICZ, *Ferdydurke*

A FEW QUICK words on *Ferdydurke*. You know what it's about, I'm not telling you the story, you just wanted my impression.

I would say absolutely YES!!!

It gave me a world and a half of pleasure; and it's one of the most honest allies you can have in the true revolt against "love," "art," the immortal principles, and all the other horseshit you know.

In the first pages, I had to overcome a certain suspicion: of a sophomoric, provincial, prefabricated humor. But there's something hyper-complex even in the naivety, something subtle in the obvious, something refined in the mechanical, that really got me. I was swept along by the verve (and with some small reservations) by the inner logic of the tale.

Gombrowicz is (albeit operating on very different premises) of Jarry's tribe.

The first two-thirds things run along so smoothly, it's a treat. Then, it seems to lose steam—or rather it really does lose it (and it smacks a bit of, maybe not guilty conscience, but let's say of Gombrowicz the Grand Liquidator, easeful and erstwhile Polish gentleman, facing off with Gombrowicz the "Just" and Enlightened One), but he bounces back pretty quickly, abandoning the servants and masters while they're busy trading blows, everyone as moronic as everyone else, and launches into the great final love story that is the definitive declaration of failure of all the

Portuguese monks and nuns of this world. (I've said that, in the literature of this century, I know of only two love stories: that of Ulrich and his sister, in Musil—and that of Marie du Port and the boss, in Simenon. It seems to me—but let's wait for this first, spellbound phase to pass—that I'll also add this securely anti-abelardichéloïsic story of Ferdydurke and Isabel.) It's a genuinely respectable, genuinely healthy book.

(to Luciano Foà, Casa editrice Einaudi)

JARRY, ETC.

In the particular case of Jarry-Elskamp-Boschère, etc.,[36] there may have been some direct influence. Not only because Jarry was an extremely boisterous and unwieldy individual, which must have made him difficult not to notice (even if it was also difficult, at the turn of the century, to understand the authenticity of his charge—in both senses of the word) but also because, in Elskamp's case, they had the *Mercure de France* and, better yet, Rachilde in common.

But the direct influence doesn't seem to me a problem. The problem is that all three, and all the etc., belong to the other French literature (in fact, Elskamp and Boschère are Flemish), which for us is the most alive—and that has been completely overshadowed by the Latin *clarté*, by the *ville lumière* (what horror) with all its courtly-empirical literature, and by the most superficial, most vacuously overheated, most ornamental, and least disturbing part of romanticism with all its aftereffects. The Gothic was born in France, France is Gothic, I told you about the enormous impression that Paris made on me, two and a half months ago, when I found myself in a *contemporary* Gothic

---

36 Max Elskamp (1862–1931): Belgian poet, who settled in Antwerp and whose work, of a great formal refinement, is inspired by Flemish art and folk traditions. Jean de Boschère (1878–1953): Belgian poet, writer, and designer, who settled in Paris and whose first collection of poems (1917) exercised some influence on Eliot, Pound, and the Imagists.

culture (that is, no cathedrals or chiaroscuro, but plenty of modern physics, modern biology, and almost too much cabala).

There was an uninterrupted gothic-initiatory-alchemical-religious tradition, but ever since the Empire, only the provincial and the "poorly adapted" kept on with it, and they didn't have a seat at the table (Paris in its freedom has been dreadfully lacking in intellectual audacity). —When I say religious, I mean seriously religious—not Bossuet or Lamennais—and it strikes me as symptomatic that perhaps the deepest Catholic personality of France, the Abbé de Caussade, is practically ignored by French "culture," and that his *Traité de l'abandon à la Providence Divine,* one of the few truly *pure* Taoist texts to come out of the West, only circulates in a poor little sacristy edition. That no one could see a piece was missing became staggeringly obvious in Huysmans, who fell under the influence of De Guaita[37] just as much as he did, later, of that very dull abbot who "converted" him. There are hundreds of publications about the relationship between Huysmans and the Abbot, their correspondence has been published, and so on. There is not a single volume, to my knowledge, about the relationship between Huysmans and De Guaita. And De Guaita was anything but dull: in his youth, he was a close friend of Barrès's—and he gave many great parties, and made such a racket he couldn't go unnoticed.

Think of what we talked about years ago: about Nerval and Rimbaud becoming "intelligible" along the lines of third-order initiatory and alchemical treatises. The influence might also be demonstrable philologically, but it doesn't matter. What matters is that their function is—spontaneously or not, who cares—that same process of *consecutio*[38] of states (not to call them by the too faded name of images) which also *functioned* in the direct or indirect authors of the treatises.

(About Nerval's death, moreover, there were strange legends, quite fantastical, but certainly no less plausible than the un-fantastical version of his suicide, which to me—based on the few

---

37 Stanislas De Guaita (1861–1897): French occultist, author of the *Essais de sciences maudites* and *Le Temple de Satan.*

38 Meaning both "the sequence" and "the attainment" in Latin. [AA]

facts known with certainty—seems very improbable.)

Think that it took a hundred years, not to notice (nice, amusing, narrow, superficial, banal) Stendhal, but to notice that Balzac, in addition to novels, also wrote novellas. —And think that, in the other France, Eliphas Levi[39] had, and has, more readers than all the Vignys and Lamartines put together (real readers—the schoolchildren who, with great reluctance, are administered small doses of Lamartine etc. in anthologies don't count).

And so on, and so on, and so on. —Sometime we'll talk about it more in depth. But I think that you'll find all the connections you're looking for, and very organic ones, in the French "culture of the soul," banished from the culture of the "mind" (which as far as we're concerned, with few exceptions, is getting to be a very faded and passé social culture). Yes, dear Sergio.

(to Sergio Solmi)

---

39 Pseudonym of the occultist Abbé Alphonse-Louis Constant (1810–1875). His most important work is *Dogme et Rituel de la Haute Magie.*

TOMASI DI LAMPEDUSA

Suspicion of *The Leopard*: extremely justified. However, it doesn't fall into the category of work with polenta two centimeters beneath the surface, the enthusiasm for which allows us to glimpse the abysses of inconsistency in our best friends (*The Bicycle Thief, Christ Stopped at Eboli, Dr. Zhivago*—and I'm already writhing when I think of the publication of Saba's letters)—it's the book of a well-read provincial; with real culture (quite old-fashioned) in his blood; responsible; deeply *soigné*; rather congenial; and, what is taken quite seriously in Italy, rich (materially speaking). —As a construction it's sloppy, almost a polyptych with uneven spaces and all sorts of discordances between one tableau and the next. You sense the need to get it all out, urgently, clumsily, as much as possible before dying. It's not all that great; but still, the worst page is worth all the "tokens"[40] [. . .]. In sum, a good Technicolor production by and for decent people.

Between "art" and Technicolor, if I'm going to the movies, I prefer Technicolor and certainly not *A Man Escaped*. —Have you seen it? It's worth it to get a sense of where we are. Along with all the paltry, spare, anti-rhetorical misunderstanding, uncompromising with the public's taste (but I poor devil am the public!), renunciation of effects, absolute honesty, and other

---

40 "Tokens" [*I gettoni*] was the name of the famous series published by Einaudi and directed by Elio Vittorini.

such Bovaryisms, the director had the shamelessness to rob me of three-quarters of an hour of my life to show me a nobody who (of course under threat of death) is secretly readying the rope for his escape, in a cell, alone. Seeing is believing. (I think it won first prize in Venice.)

(to Sergio Solmi)

ORABUENA—*Gross ist deine Treue*

September 1, 1959

I TOOK A look at Orabuena's *Gross ist deine Treue* [Great is your fidelity]. I should begin by saying that it was enough to see the name of Walter Nigg, who wrote the *Einführung* [introduction], for me to start foaming at the mouth: he is the *religiöser Deuter* [religious exegete], not of Switzerland, which might be tolerable enough, but of Switzerland for the use of the Swiss. Everything seems true = *echt*, even what Kierkegaard says of course, and if you're not careful you don't notice that it's made of Emmenthaler. —I conquered my revulsion and read the first chapter of the book. Which is so human, good, just, polished, clean, well intentioned, and sincerely lived through and suffered that I feel really guilty spitting all the poison it deserves upon it. Everything has the exemplary simplicity of "long long ago," and it's written with a similarly exemplary modesty; a *menschlich* [humanly] respectable Homericism boiled down to the most basic terms. The trouble is that every Homericism, in a time when man no longer has a profile, seems to me, in the biggest sense, and thinking in terms of what's happening now, which is, at present, like it or not, the only creative task, criminal and "reactionary," certainly more dangerous than the capitalism that exploits the poor proletarians. —Besides, it will be a very beautiful book, certainly *achtungseinflössend* [respect-inspiring], and I'll bring it with me to Ronchi, where I'll leaf through it a little less inattentively.

(to Luciano Foà, Casa editrice Einaudi)

SADÉGH HEDAYÁT—*The Blind Owl*

IT'S A WOEFULLY sordid book, and certainly not one with an atmosphere I love, but here, the horror isn't gratuitous, there's no wallowing like in all the books you know. It reaches a plane that opens up only when everything else has crumbled, gone to pieces, dissolved. I don't much like to talk about subjects, and in this case more than ever, the "subject" might be counterproductive. I, for one, would dismiss the book out of hand if I knew the protagonist, reduced from the first to rather unsavory circumstances, sees, through a crack in a wall, a very beautiful girl who offers a blue flower to an old man sitting under a cypress, a girl the protagonist can't forget, and whom he then goes looking for without success—in fact he can't even find the crack in the wall anymore—until one foggy night he finds her sitting on a stone outside the door of his own house, lets her in, discovers she's dead, cuts her into pieces, and neatly arranges the pieces in a suitcase that he'll get rid of with the help of a little old man who bursts into sinister laughter, and who shows up at just the right moment with a funeral carriage pulled by two rawboned horses. After burying the suitcase and returning home, the protagonist lights up an opium pipe and drops into a past life, which is less spectacularly dismal than the present one, but suffused with viscous sufferings—etc., etc. You told me, luckily for me, that you want to read the book yourself, and so I can allow myself to stop here (if I'd had to tell it to you from start to finish, I wouldn't have written in this tone).

This is the "subject"—what is not the "subject" is that I do not know of another story like this one (perhaps some poems, a few phrases by mystics, a few fragments by Novalis), where all realities are superposed—material reality, "psychic" reality, opium visions, karmic life—are blended, form part of the individual, *are* the individual—but where the individual also disappears, is only his shadow on the wall—the shadow of an owl—a blind owl.

I don't know if it's the most beautiful story to appear in I don't know how many years, let's say since Kafka's stories—probably not. I do know, however, that I can't think of any other story (after Kafka) born of the same necessity, with the same violence, and with the same suggestiveness. I say *born*—not *written*—I don't know what he had in mind when he started writing it. Surely, many parts, especially toward the end, were born as they were being written—the themes are treated so organically they can't be the result of cold preconstruction. You will see.

I told you it was the first book I read in London during my bout of pneumonia, and that it became enmeshed with the half-delirium of the fever I had during the trip. What I wrote you might seem too determined by the moment in which I read it. So let me assure you I reread it "coldly," slowly, and with careful attention about three weeks later—and in fact found the weave of the text even tighter and some of the excesses even more justified.

On the cover flap, there's talk of a "Persian disciple of Sartre"—probably because existentialism is "dirty" and because this book is "dirty"—already from what I've told you, you can tell it's the least Sartrian book imaginable—everything is determined in the most inexorable way—"choice" exists—but only after becoming the blind owl—a shadow on a wall. Quite parenthetically, this is almost beside the point, since the *Blind Owl* is not miserablist literature—but I found in *The Times Literary Supplement* this passage I wanted to copy for you (it's from a serious article, and I don't think it's made up): "Just so did the present reviewer hear a well-dressed lady in a Piccadilly bookshop asking for 'something squalid.'"

WILLIAM MARCH, *The Looking-Glass*

HERE WE'RE ALREADY on a more obvious plane. In any case
it's an exceedingly beautiful book (don't be suspicious if I'm
writing only in superlatives, but I'm talking about four books
of about forty I've read for you, plus many other morganatic
readings—and perhaps there will be months—very likely so—
during which, if I use any superlatives, they'll unfortunately
be negative ones)—which is to say, perhaps it's a bad book,
but it's the bad book of a REAL writer. I realized this partly
while reading it—the episodes and figures "leapt up" before my
eyes—but partly, and perhaps more so, when after finishing
it I picked up other books of narrative prose—in comparison
everything was flat, anemic, sterile, made of a synthetic plastic
material (an image that applies, even after the William March
hangover has passed, to almost all Anglo-American narrative
literature). Read the pages I'll point out to you later on, and
read the introduction to the *March Omnibus*[41] that you have in
Turin (and on the basis of which I asked you for the book):
you will understand what I mean. He's a madman with a raw
soul, and the characters impose themselves on him with such
vehemence that, for better or worse, he is able to establish them,
render them, chew them over, and develop them—but never
to abolish them, with the result that, in the book, he is forced
to put *everything* in; coordinating when he can, making things
plausible when he can (which is made easier by the fact that
it's not a linear book, but an interweaving of destinies that is
supposed to be a portrait of the South) and, if he doesn't find
any other way to go about it, encapsulating short stories in
the living flesh of the narrative. I can't say anything about the

41 A selection of works by William March collected in a single
volume.

"subject" here—there are (so it seems to me, thinking it over) dozens of subjects, which is to say: dozens of destinies linked either by encounters with each other, or just by the landscape they share; the subject is supposed to be the South going to ruin—with a finale (the last chapter, in New York, rather bad, and very much stuck on out of no real necessity to provide a conclusion and give a semblance of organic unity to the book) in which the escapees from the South (*not* all are ruined—it's a book of shadows and light) listen to the radio (this is at the beginning of the war), which urges the women to do *your* share to preserve our democratic way of life by using Elsa Fletcher's remarkable, vitamin-fortified beauty preparations.

The great defect (which prevents *Looking Glass* from being the greatest of American novels) is, I'll say again, that March succeeds in dominating his characters (and with what effort) but not in achieving a balance among their individual destinies, and so there's an imbalance (of narrative form—but never of density, never of distances—except in the last chapter), which, particularly reading the book in one sitting, irritates you, or at least makes you uneasy. Even so, it's one of the rare American novels of this century (next to which all the others look like—if this makes sense—Caldwell)—and it's just a hair away from being a masterpiece. Do it and *launch it*.

(to Luciano Foà, Casa editrice Einaudi)

GOODMAN, *Empire City*

I'VE LIKED GOODMAN *very much* for many years—ever since I read, in a New Directions anthology and in a few magazines, some of the short pastiches that would become (but perhaps they were a bit less dense with subject matter) chapters of *Empire City.* He is a member of the most desperate generation, but he's the only one, perhaps, who tries to overcome despair, not by a cretinous American optimism, or by believing in some formula that doesn't cover the whole problem, but because, truly, you really get this feeling, he wagers on good and not evil, and wagering on the good means creating the good. In his company I got a breath of fresh, clean, "youthful" air, whose youthfulness does not mean innocence or lack of experience. Of course he's a bit distant from us, he remains an American, and worse yet, an American Jew (and I believe, worse yet— I'm not sure, *aber es schmeckt danach* [but he seems to be]—a homosexual American Jew), he has the right to be much less *désabusé* than us, to wager on tools that, for us, are barrenly mechanical (psychoanalysis, architecture, economic solutions, education, etc.); but anyway he isn't stupid, he not only knows their limits, he also knows the horror of these things when they fall into the wrong hands—and his one naivety is, perhaps, believing that they can fall into the right hands. But even here it's a bit ambiguous, he doesn't know but he knows— and everything becomes a bit programmatic, utopian, preachy, a bit of a game, entertainment—there are some pages (just a few) that read like the Bible written by Cocteau. Certainly, in those accounts, even occupational therapy becomes *irgendwie* [in some sense] lyrical—and there was joy, and there was the future, and there was spring.

[. . .]

Its intention is to be the great *Entwicklungsroman*.[42] On the jacket there's mention of Wilhelm Meister—I would think rather of Parsifal; the story of the boy Horatio Alger who grows up. But in what I've read (and as far as I can tell also in the other 300 pages, which I've only skimmed) the boy Horatio serves only as a thread to tie together a dozen different characters (all sympathetic) in the struggle against sociolatry. Everyone's sympathetic—the enemy is not personified, it's a suffocating anonymity rationally nourished by synthetic vitamins, which is given vent in world wars. There is no subject, though the characters meet, get married, part ways, and die—the book is crammed full of random gimmicks brought on by no narrative necessity, but necessary as a starting point for observations or games. In the course of these, many things are really well said, honestly thought, or at least very nicely convoluted—a good part is superfluous, almost obsessively repetitive, and just plain circuitous.

[. . .]

I'm unable to find a common denominator for this tangle of characters and considerations; these characters that aren't flesh and blood but have only an allegorical flatness (I have to write quickly and don't have time to find the exact formulation—what pops into my head is something along the lines of "heraldic charm"—or emblematic lyricism); and these considerations that have, in certain sentences, a charge of true prophecy—that are almost monomaniacal, often *outré* feuilletonism; often a truly agonized diary, and just as often full of Jewish petulance, Cocteauian Talmudism with no ground beneath its feet.

And I can neither tell you to read a few chapters at random,

---

42 A novel of growing up (literally, of "development"), distinct from but related to a Bildungsroman ("a novel of education"). [AA]

or point out the finest or the ugliest passages. All my reservations (at least most of them) concern the whole, the excessiveness, the ambition to write *the* great polemical-utopian summa. And certain pages that, read in bits and pieces, I liked very much, read in the context of the whole, I found suffocated and suffocating.

Despite all that, I lean more toward *yes* than *no* [. . .]. It's probably an unsuccessful book—but more respectable than almost all the securely successful books currently being published. It's a healthy book whose healthiness isn't stupid (a very rare thing). And it's a book of that third America that's little known here—i.e., with none of the democratic-puritan-gymnastic character of the books that Washington insinuates through the USIS, or even of the criminalsexualdecadent pre- and post-Korean war books that are all the rage.

I have a sneaking suspicion it's a bad book, and perhaps Goodman is more insubstantial than I think. But he's a good friend of ours, and slamming the door in his face would embarrass me.

(to Luciana Foà, Casa editrice Einaudi)

MINET—*La Défaite*

THIS IS THE only book (except for the few that I wrote you about right after my illness) that has truly made an impression on me since I've been in London. It's the "confession" of a guy who knew Daumal and Gilberte-Lecomte as a boy and who lived as a vagrant in Paris. I've never read a book where the restiveness is so instinctive, and so *echt* [authentic], and so far from any possibility of compromise—and there are pages, particularly in the central chapters, on the exaltation and euphoria of freedom that cut to the bone, that made me feel genuinely ashamed of the life we're all leading. It has nothing to do with the vacuous barkings of the angry young men—Maurice Sachs, compared to him, is just a spoiled kinky *fils à papa* [daddy's boy], a small-time speculator and a big-time narcissist, but very cautious.

The break with his family in the provinces, the flight to Paris, the attempts at work, the break with his employers, homeless in Paris with one shirt and (I think) a single pair of socks in a bag, hunger that instead of being a source of anxiety is pure joy and confirmation, adventures, a bit of homosexuality that's never out-and-out prostitution, the friendship with Daumal and Gilbert-Lecomte, with other literary men, with the rich, and with strange figures from the slums, a liaison with a rich woman, the "career" that begins to insinuate itself. And twenty or so pages at the beginning, before he starts to tell his story, of regret, and of real nausea concerning his settled life.

The beginning is no good, rings false, justifies all the misgivings of those who read it after me, and only reread after
reading the book does it become clear he is seriously desperate
(but the false notes remain). There then follows a much more
convincing part, albeit somewhat naive—then (somewhere past
the first third of the book, if I'm remembering correctly) there
are some absolutely *hinreissend* [ravishing] pages. If, as I hope,
my series[43] comes to pass, the book has to be done without
discussion—but even if it doesn't come to pass, I'd tell you to
do it anyway: yesterday I was in Oxford, where I spent one
of the most nauseating days of my life. —If we don't help the
Minets of this world to win (and I know their limits, and their
stature, and their inconsistency), there's really nothing left but
atom bombs.

RAY BRADBURY—*Dandelion Wine,* a novel

Which then turned out to be so many short stories; the (surely in large part autobiographical) tale of a boy, from the first
summer morning of 1928 to the last summer evening of 1928.
It has only one fault (I don't know how major it would be for
others, but for me it's extremely unsettling): that there's summer, there's childhood, there's a certain genuine poetry, there's
a great variety of inspired inventions (but never, happily, the
exceptional for the sake of the exceptional), there's a great variety of characters, even weirdos (but never invented out of that
nasty frigid taste for the grotesque for the sake of the grotesque),
there's sympathy, a world observed from a quite personal perspective—there's spontaneity, a great deal of technical ability,
and an exemplary economy. Which is to say there's everything
it takes to write a tiny very beautiful little book (naturally also

---

43 A series of mostly autobiographical texts that Roberto Bazlen had
proposed, in these same months, to the publisher Einaudi.

a big very beautiful book—I said tiny little book because this is an unpretentious book—indeed, this unpretentiousness is another of its positive qualities).

But: it's written by a writer of science fiction, probably more original and distinctive than almost any other—but who in any case has accepted certain literary conventions, certain American standards, certain commercial limits—they've become part of his own flesh and blood—and they make their presence felt. And in this book (which is not science-fictional—these are stories, often unusual, but which might happen to any American boy) they clash with everything else, they create a kind of screeching that makes you physically ill, and lead you to forget all about the summer, conjuring before your eyes instead the pages of *Harper's Bazaar*. Perhaps in this regard I'm pathologically sensitive, and to be on the safe side you'd better have someone else read it. As far as I'm concerned, I'm obliged to tell you no (mind you, if there were only two or three stories with a science-fictional element, the whole book would be all right). Pity. *Le malheur de n'être pas high-brow.*[44]

(to Luciano Foà, Casa editrice Einaudi)

---

44 "The misfortune of not being highbrow." [AA]

P. J. JOUVE—*Le Monde Désert*

Here a personal statement must be taken into account. Also I read this on a train, crossing Switzerland, in a hellish sleeper car of a hyper-rational type I didn't know existed, where in the daytime there's no banquette but just a metal chair in a metal room, so it feels like you're in the electric chair on an interplanetary trip. In Amsterdam, I read to page 34, then left off. On the train it was cold, I passed a nerve-racking night on wheels, I had a nasty feverish feeling and a sneaking sense that my pneumonia was coming back again. To chase it away, I picked up the book where I'd left off and found myself confronted with the monologue of someone in a pneumonia-induced delirium. Read coldly, maybe it would have struck me as calculated, artificial, a bit of a stretch—but read under those conditions I realized that it had a photographic precision, and everything that might have seemed to be mere "style" was in fact ingeniously concise. And on the strength of this I read the whole book at a gulp, and I have to say it had me *"gepackt"* [enthralled]. (I had read all of Jouve's other novels as they appeared, and had a ;fond memory of them, but of very passé things.)

Jouve is from Geneva, born and brought up in a world of high, deodorized ideals, and only rather late, after a lyrical work washed in Omo detergent and soaked through with pacifism and European responsibility, discovers (the war, *der Mensch ist*

schliesslich nicht so gut,[45] Freud, his marriage to Blanche Rever-
chon the psychiatrist—and throw in a dash of Elizabethan theater, too) the flipside of the mystic flight, with particular attention paid to blood and viscerality, or rather to the visceral soul.
And he starts writing the novels you know about ambiguity,
or rather the *entrechangeabilité* of the crystalline mind and the
blood-soaked soul.

This is the story of the son of a Genevese pastor (*entr'autres*,
Paolina's great-grandnephew,[46] but except for a few hints at his
great aunt it's a completely self-sufficient book) who believes
that he has triumphed over Geneva and achieved a great Apollonian serenity, with slight deviations toward a hygienic-athletic
Dionysism and plenty of practical homosexuality. And through
a homosexual scandal, a marriage with a Russian woman, "artistic" aspirations that he confuses with accomplishments, he
thinks from time to time that's he being "liberated," but in reality he's going through a series of crises (there's one with really stupendous dramatic force near the beginning of a book),
doubts, depressions, euphorias, he goes more and more to pieces, and two-thirds of the way through the book he ends up
killing himself in the Rhône. The third part: the widow's love
for a poet, his friend: it isn't stated, but you sense her chances
at happiness (not of quiet adaptation) are ruined forever by her
experience with the ruined boy from Geneva, and immediately
after the wedding she flees with her son, and, as far as this book
is concerned, disappears. The husband looks for her in Paris,
also goes to pieces, and ends up in a permanent state of nonex-
istence. [. . .]

There's just enough of the *oeuvre d'art* to be annoying, I
know—but there's something very tense, very dramatic, and beneath the lean angularity (which is deliberate) there's a real richness—done with short chapters that are real gems; and all the
gems put together make a book reminiscent, in certain aspects,
of the moral novels that represent the worst of Gide, but it has,

---

45 "Man is not, after all, so good." [AA]

46 In reality Paulina, the protagonist of one of Pierre-Jean Jouve's
earlier novels, *Paulina 1880*.

for me, a transparency and an unreserved anxiety that—again, for me—Gide's little novels never had, even when I read them at the right moment, as a boy.

(to Luciano Foà, Casa editrice Einaudi)

BROWN—*Life Against Death*

IT'S AN INTELLIGENT, clear, fully thought out book. [. . .] He teaches the reader how to read and think through Freud, as is only right, from back to front, organizing what Freud wasn't able to organize, doing the sums that Freud didn't get the chance to do—or at least to write down.

Let's be clear: it's not as though I want to propagandize for the *Weltbild* [image of the world] that comes out of it (man continues to have the profile and the qualities of Renaissance Europe—which is to say he's working with a man who no longer exists—and you know I rule out the possibility of there being a plausible psychology until psychology has absorbed parapsychology as well—and here we're still very far from that), I take the book for what it is and what it wants to be (not as I wish it were), and I must say it couldn't be done any better, and no one else could have found room for so much new freedom within such old and narrow bounds. He has really managed to scrape away everything (a great deal) petit bourgeois that Freudians and neo-Freudians have crystallized around Freud (I'm not forgetting the degree to which Freud, by dint of his birth year and environment and cultural premises, lent himself to this end) and without ever overstepping; *he has written the work of Freud* twenty years after his death. The reevaluation of childhood sexuality, the reevaluation of death, the reevaluation of imagination (which, though Brown doesn't realize it, becomes identical with the archetypes of Jung)—does it seem like small potatoes to you? There's one thing that really struck me: the episodes determined by individual history are moved even further toward birth—which is to say we're getting further and further away from superficial functionalism, and closer to a global show with a much more coherent and much deeper link between man and his destiny.

All this, I repeat to you, always remaining within Freudian limits, applying Freudian laws, using Freudian terminology—only clarifying certain of Freud's contradictions (which were inevitable, if you consider that Freud's work was constructed slowly, over fifty years, through a series of new discoveries that seemed to overturn the discoveries that preceded them) and thinking through to their final consequences all the thoughts that Freud had no choice but to think halfway. This is the first part of the book, and it seemed to me exceptionally well done. *Perfect.*

The second is, more or less, a diagnosis or interpretation of the present situation of humanity employing the means derived from the first. If you accept the first (I have accepted it—again, for what it is and what it wants to be), you cannot dispute the second. You can't be happy that someone invents a plausible new language and then immediately get upset because he speaks it. Just as you can't, on one hand, recognize (and you've told me that everyone has recognized it—and I recognize it, too) that it's an important and stimulating book, and on the other hand have doubts about whether to publish it. Few important and stimulating books are born in the world. And why, if we found it stimulating, shouldn't others be stimulated? Others (and especially in Italy) need it more than we do.

(to Luciano Foà, Casa editrice Einaudi)

DORNER—*Überwindung der "Kunst"*

IT'S AN EXCEPTIONALLY intelligent book, one of the few books about art that has impressed me in I don't know how many years. No *Kunstgeschichte* [art history] (convincingly demolished along with all the *Geisteswissenschaften* [moral sciences]), but a large-format theory of changes in perceptions of reality, hence of changes of reality during the course of, shall we say, the evolution of humanity—a theory that takes its cue from, and understands, art, or rather the organization of perceptions that lead to art. And it provides an excellent hypothesis-key for understanding the phenomena of modern and abstract art, etc.

Moving from the primitive a-dimensional world to the static three-dimensional western world, and from there to a future "hyperspatial" reality (of which we already see many signs— very plausible parallels with modern physics—Einstein and Planck used to attend his lectures) of pure energies. —Which is to say from magic to the ascendancy of a formal spiritual idea; the dissolution of this in the Enlightenment and Romanticism, which brings about the first signs of reality experienced as becoming, not as being. (Very amusing, but also very profound, the part about the smuggling of magic into spiritual, three-dimensional experience; and the part about rationality being closely linked with the *Erlebnis* [experience] of the three dimensions, etc., etc., etc.).

The examples are perfectly apt; they provide a new vantage

point from which to look at a work of art, and also provide an organic background for each and every interpretation of what is happening in the world of art. In any case, whether right or wrong in its applications, we have to come to terms with what Dorner says.

But I should warn you to take what I've said with a grain of salt. It's still, I think, a good book; fertile; and he knocks almost all Italian art historians out of the ring. But "a grain of salt," because in Venice I read it in a hurry, almost just to orient myself, and was convinced. Now, however, I've spent several days with Dorner, up until yesterday, and am writing you perhaps still too much under the influence of a book that hasn't only made me truly *think*, but also made me truly ashamed of all the prejudices I drag around with me, and all the many ideas that I'd only let myself think halfway through. In any case, I have too much of an ax to grind with Art and Love and Eternal Values and all the rest to be able to judge impartially. Not that I've lost my mind: these ideas are in the air (even if the *Kunstgeschichtler* [art historians] know nothing about them: to know something about the air you'd need to know how to breathe); they've already been expressed in certain specialized fields ("philosophy," biology, particularly in modern physics, to which Dorner continually makes reference, etc., etc.), even perhaps better expressed, because they have (had) a field whose boundaries were less blurry and thus the possibility of a more coherent terminology and stricter formulations; Dorner himself doesn't reach the final consequences: he's still working with man as he exists today, that is, with a man whose qualities, in the course of evolution, have changed a good deal, or a great deal— not with a man (the most plausible hypothesis at the present time, and to my mind the only convincing one) who loses existing qualities or acquires new ones "as if it were nothing" (with regard to man, Dorner still has some leftover magical notions, some leftover Enlightenment and Romantic thinking, which are at odds with his great clarity in matters of art and culture generally); and whatever other objections you like. But:

Of the attempts so far made to see art from the outside, I'm only familiar with those made by people who have nothing to do with art. If they understand it, they understand it with their heads stuck in *Kunst* [art], etc. —and down with aesthetics, elevations of the soul, eternal divine proportions, *Ausdruck* [expression], and all the other horseshit we know. Dorner has a cool head (but warm eyes): he has understood that, given the absolute auto-transformability of the absolute, art ceases to be a symbol of eternal values and so ceases to be "art," that the eternal ideas are reduced to eternal determining spiritual forces. And so no eternal styles, and nothing to do with all the etcetera. Rationality = eternity = three-dimensionality = beauty (!) = "art."

I'm writing you in a hurry, pell-mell, making haphazard use of some of the notes I made while reading, and probably you have the impression that it's a rather abstract theoretical book full of frigid, philosophical terminological *jongleries*, but in fact the book is quite alive, lived, even with its slightly portentous popularizing democratic background (at least in the theory of the museum), which is certainly not the part that most fascinated me. Do it without question: an excellent antidote to Worringer and to the many books of *Kunstgeschichte* that have been and will be done.

(Luciano Foà, Casa editrice Einaudi)

BLANCHOT, *L'Espace littéraire*

SIX MONTHS AGO, I wrote you from Venice about the general impression I had of Blanchot after reading his novel and trying (trying) to take a look at two or three others, and I also mentioned my desire not to think about Blanchot again for a few years.

I don't remember exactly everything I wrote, but I clearly remember, among the negative things I listed for you (there were also some positive ones) was the sense of inconsistency that laid bare for me some of his *jongleries*, some of his wild goose chases, involving such solidifications as *le désir* and *la nuit* and *l'angoisse* and that of *la mort*, which I especially recommended to you, solidifications that have decayed in French symbolism and in post-symbolist classicism, and that in any case no longer contain the whole chemistry that brought them into existence—and that therefore, if you think about it, are pure folklore. In the final analysis, crass and disagreeable folklore, like "popular" folklore, even if it's on an seemingly less uncivilized plane, and to which, for the sake of convenience, we lend our complicity with a quieter conscience. Not that there aren't already some solidifications that have been born of the new chemistry—but "experimental" literature (which probably hasn't produced a single book worth a book of Blanchot's) at least has the merit of conducting its search on this side of the watershed, whereas I felt that, despite his many chichi flourishes, Blanchot was dragging me back to the other side.

With these assumptions, I started leafing through *L'Espace littéraire*, at first only with reluctance, then also with irritation at finding him less of an irritatingly spiritual acrobat than I'd believed him to be, until I found myself confronted with the chapter "Le Regard d'Orphée," and here I gritted my teeth, because as so many previous experiences have taught me, as soon as Orpheus comes into the picture (and then Eurydice!), I find the key to all my intolerance.

And I found myself confronted with six *stupendous* pages, not written on this side or the other but *on* the watershed, where the elusive paradoxicality of the artist / work relationship is expressed as I've never found it expressed before. Then I continued leafing through, and then I began from the beginning and saw a preliminary note that I'd missed, where it's said that the center on which all of the book's considerations converge is precisely "Le Regard d'Orphée."

I'm sick today and don't have much ability to concentrate [. . .] but I think even if I were well I wouldn't be able to draw up a systematized exposition of the book: you're in a hurry, and I've only flipped through it (though twice). It can't be much of a success: the Rilkean derivativeness can, for good reason, be infuriating; superficially, it may remind you of one of our hermetic critics, but intelligent and consistent; etc., etc. —Anyway, a book centered on these six pages is to be done without question: I assume full responsibility.

To give you an idea of it, just read pages 179–184. (And in that case, compare them with the idiocies about Orpheus at the end of Marcuse's book,[47] a book that you've signed on.)

(to Luciano Foà, Casa editrice Einaudi)

---

47 Herbert Marcuse, *Eros and Civilization*, published by Einaudi in 1964.

DHÔTEL, *Le Plateau de Mazagran*

I DON'T FEEL like insisting here, because I love it and love is blind; and although I see its faults (my love is only myopic), I don't mind them. I know I read it the way I read *Le Grand Meaulnes* when I was seventeen, and I know that, today, *Le Grand Meaulnes* still gives other people goose bumps; but since I first read it I haven't had the courage to pick it up again. What's certain about the story of this small-time Parsifal in love with a rather elusive woman he's figured out how to get a grip on—and who goes to the Plateau de Mazagran to look for the bad man, and finally ends up in the grip of a much simpler but equally elusive girl who was so obvious to him that he never gave any thought to whether she was elusive or not—is that I devoured it, from cover to cover, in a single sitting, completely forgetting I was also reading it for the purpose of telling you something about it. Thinking back on it, it doesn't hold up, it's an attic full of hand-me-down romantic decorations, and passé passé passé, and whatever else you might say—but if on the other hand you consider that almost everything that's published stands on really foul and filthy feet, it's a basement full of equally hand-me-down realistic decorations, and not passé because it has never existed, I don't think we should dismiss poor Dhôtel without giving him a second thought.

(to Luciano Foà, Casa editrice Einaudi)

SANSOM, *The Body*

HE (IN THE first person): a not unsympathetic and not implausible lady's hairdresser (or rather an owner of salons) who—having arrived at the age when the body begins to show the first symptoms of breakdown and, along with the body, everything else starts breaking down too—on the basis of rather vague clues, begins to suspect his wife of being unfaithful. —She: more complicated when she seems less, less complicated when she seems more. A not ostentatiously enigmatic but rather quite impalpable mix of Anglo Saxon wifey-dolly and real woman. (To me she seems the only not superficial and not oversimplified creation in the whole book.) The other man: in the business of cars and garages; good-natured and with the well-intentioned and oblivious joviality of everything unwieldy and vulgar.

Novel of jealousy: "gnawing" uncertainty—indirect espionage—clandestine investigations—double-edged evidence—increasingly painful anxiety and increasingly humiliating situations—whiskey—down and adrift until the last big bender. At which point he'll open his eyes and realize everything was his own fabrication—just when the other man, who's taken a car trip with another woman, has had an accident and lies dying in the hospital.

Sansom is a discovery of Lehmann's (at least I think so—in any case, he may as well be) and like all the fiction writers that Lehmann discovers (the poets he discovered came with different

270

troubles), he has that anonymous *sensiblerie* that's based on the sophisticated knowledge of what English highbrows consider the unfathomableness of the human condition (poor Malraux!), taking the leavings of Maupassant and Chekhov and sweeping them in the direction of Proust and Woolf, raising a good deal of Dostoyevsky's dust.

In other words: an extremely publishable book that nothing can stand in the way of: it's up to "standards"; it's well done; it has an excellent brand name, the Hogarth Press; it's sanctioned by *New Horizon*.

Middle-class decor well rendered; secondary characters ranging from the pathetically sordid to the insignificant (but scarcely less pathetic), well drawn, and particularly effective when they approach the grotesque. Psychology, development, atmosphere, telling details: all in perfect order (less in order is the fact that I noted everything without boredom, but never managed to feel myself implicated in it—but chalk this up to my insensitive heart and my megalomaniacal need for the great themes, etc.)—what more could you want?

Wanting more (i.e., wanting what it would always be right to want) would be obstructive: first of all, the fact that in a world that, fortunately, isn't Moravia's world, jealousy has ceased to be a central theme. Indeed, if you think about it, it never was. Okay, Robbe-Grillet, and Proust. But (1) even then, those poor men! and (2) for Robbe-Grillet it was just a pretext to set up a problem of perspective or for a descriptive geometry, and with barren results as you know—and Swann's jealousy is encapsulated, almost a foreign body: a boil or a tumor on the body (which isn't too athletic, anyway) of the *Recherche*.

But what wallowing!

Butor, a person I like, has stopped going to the theater because he can't stand the idea of those people going up on the stage evening after evening at the same time, repeating the same words and gestures, living through the same feelings over and over. Actually, it's a rather bloodcurdling idea—but it's much more bloodcurdling to think that in Europe there's a man (among countless others more or less like him) who's not stupid, who has some not despicable qualities, probably not too poor as far as humanity goes, who for who knows what reason, it must be the demon (but now the time has come at last to establish a hierarchy of literary demons!), goes to his desk for a whole year, for however many hours a day, breaking his head to "create" a hairdresser grappling with his sense of inferiority when he compares himself with a garage owner. What kind of world are we living in? *À quoi bon?*[48] As for *à quoi bon* and the reasons (which are neither "cynical" or inhuman) that now (now! —seventy years ago the opposite was true) it's time to quit it with "small" characters, with purely descriptive dramas on a single plane, with the microscope turned solely on the center of the infection, I'll write to you some other time. I have several other things I'd like to do today, a particularly quiet day. But these are things that need to be made clear.

(to Luciano Foà, Casa editrice Einaudi)

---

48 "To what end?" [AA]

HAMSUN, *Mysterien*

WE'VE TALKED ABOUT it often. Now I've finally reread it (after forty years). There's a certain datedness to it (the book is seventy years old), which is easily overcome and shouldn't affect our opinion. Dostoyevsky is much more dated. Besides, Cases told me, if I'm not mistaken, that you're doing Pontoppidan. Now, when I talked to you (perhaps with René), as well as explaining why, for me, Pontoppidan is important, I made it clear that all the parts that take place in the literary circles surrounding that character whose name in the book I can't remember, but who in reality was Brandes, not only have a lower and more antiquated tone than the rest of the novel, but I think that, for us, they're unreadable. In *Mysteries* on the other hand the antique part doesn't weight us down, any more than it does in Hardy or Stevenson. I mention these names because Hamsun, too, seems to me one of the last great European novelists (one of the writers of novel-novels—coming before the dissolvers). From these few lines, you understand that I'm saying yes. And not only because of the historical importance (which *Mysteries* has: the protagonist, Nagel, is one of the great paradigmatic characters, one of the very greatest, in the line that with Werther on one side and Adolphe on the other leads to Leopold Bloom. And here's the Great Unhinged, prey to the unconscious, conjured into being ten years before Freud's first psychoanalytic publications).

Nagel: who with a yellow suit, a white velvet cap, a wad of

money in his pocket, a couple of suitcases, a violin case (empty, with clothes and papers inside, because he cannot play; in fact he'll play extraordinarily well, but he'll end on a false note that gives you the shivers), perhaps an agronomist (who knows), checks in to a small hotel in a Norwegian coastal village, talks talks talks, pals up with a half-wit who's perhaps not a half-wit, talks talks talks, drinks, falls hopelessly in love (but maybe not) with a young beauty, talks talks talks, drinks some more, poisons a dog, gets more and more and more excited, makes really screwy but basically quite fair Nietzschean speeches, wants to marry (but maybe not) a woman of a certain age, talks gets excited drinks, gets into the most unlikely scrapes, tries to poison himself but fails, until eventually he falls ill and throws himself into the sea.

Psychologically, too, it's an extraordinary portrait. The antidemocratic tirades when he talks talks talks may seem, if you take them to be Hamsun's arguments, a bit faded. But as Nagel's speeches—the most apt insights in the most inapt form or environment—they are very convincing.

Read it to someone who knows how to jump for joy when (on several occasions, for example Miss Kielland's engagement) the flags are hoisted. Otherwise, *everything* I've said to you is a waste of breath.

(to Luciano Foà, Casa editrice Einaudi)

EDSCHMIED, *Der Marschall und die Gnade*

IT ENDS (IN my literal translation):

"Your last wishes?" His voice trembled.
"To be embalmed well," he answered calmly. "I have prepared everything. He can be in Santa Maria in half an hour."
"How can you say it so calmly?" the admiral asked. He stood up, weeping, looked out the window, and greedily inhaled the scent of heliotrope that, carried by the evening breeze, permeated the room.

THE END

As for the rest: it's a book by an old gentleman who comes from a world of great culture; who's had a lively life; who was, let's say fifty years ago, considered to be at the cutting edge of the most conventional literature for having invented an expressionist style all his own, extremely rapid, and unreadable even then, and for having introduced "new" subjects—a man who's traveled all over, who's lived for long periods in very colorful countries, who's certainly observed a great deal. And who has, if nothing else, all the cosmopolitan *aisance* of a man who's "seen the world." So even in this book, despite the ending (you'll note that I picked out the finale for you, and this was, however necessary, a dirty trick on my part—the banality of the many pages that precede it is much less glaring), there's a sense of life. There's a lot of bad writing (even worse than bad: conventional and anonymous) but there's no narrow-mindedness. On the contrary: there's an innate feeling for the great game of politics, which happily or not has been one of the prerogatives of the German grand seigneurs (to be clear: with all due respect to the others, the only great artist who preserves an aristocratic position, who knew how to play the great political themes, remains I think Schiller—without whom—as no one ever bears in mind—even Maurois's biography of Disraeli would not have been possible. But here, in my rush, I'm letting myself get carried far too far away. So stop).

There's not much I can tell you about the subject matter: I read the first chapter three or four times—it's a novel about Bolivar, partly in the third person, partly in the first (fictitious diaries). Then yesterday and today maybe a hundred pages, jumping around here and there. Storyline: very skillful. Dialogue: conventional and never indecorous. Direction: excellent work. Actors: well schooled though showing no special talent. Costumes: plausible. Makeup: the fake beards are not immediately noticeable. Photography (cinerama): perfect (at the edges of the frame, the objects are just as in focus as they are at the center). Color technician: good (Agfacolor). Sound technician: not bad. Smell technician: excessive. Period consultant: first-rate. Distinguishing characteristics: none.

To be clear, I would give:

4 Oscars to *Gone With the Wind*
2 Oscars to *The Leopard*
1 Oscar to this.

(to Luciana Foà, Casa editrice Einaudi)

SHATTUCK, *The Banquet Years*

QUITE DECENT—I would certainly say yes—an excellent volume for the "Saggi."[49]

A few years ago I told you (in person) that the time had finally come to write a book about our ancestors, about what has really and directly determined us (I'm convinced, for example, that it's true Marx has pestered us more than others and that certain basely *practical* consequences of his work have forced us to take *practical* positions that without him would never have come about—but that something of our confidence and our way of thinking, or we might even say, if we're brave, something of our freedom, we owe much more to Wilde than to Marx). Now, of the four figures that are the subject of this book, at least two and a half (Henri Rousseau, Jarry, and ½ Satie) are, in my opinion, among the most important of our grandfathers, with whom, for better or worse, it would be worth coming to terms directly (and not, as in the case of Jarry, through the intermediary of a nephew—Ionesco—: continuing to treat your grandfather smugly without getting to know him seems to me too easy).

The book is a mixture of *Kulturgeschichte* and *Kulturkritik*, anecdotal history, literary history, and literary criticism about the "origins of the avant-garde in France," very intelligently centered on four Parisian figures from the turn of the century

49 Collection of nonfiction then in preparation at Adelphi Edizioni.

(the three I mentioned to you and Apollinaire).

As for period and ambiance, it anticipates and overlaps with that American's book on Gertrude Stein we were talking about in Turin.[50] And despite some reservations on my part, you were very much in favor of it, saying that for the topic alone [. . .] it was a book that must be done. Now, about this one I have fewer reservations; it's livelier, deeper, more (genuinely) clever. And the non-narrative part is not impersonal, it's the fruit of experience, and it's full of good ideas for understanding modern art (for those who know how to experience it).

And it's also very entertaining. It becomes a bit more boring in the fourth part—but that's also down to the fact that, next to the other three, Apollinaire is a nobody (just to be clear, and to avoid having it seem I'm speaking in paradoxes, I realize that this nobody wrote some beautiful poems and that he was one of the aptest propagandists with incredibly far-reaching (practical) consequences; but set him next to the other three, and it shows!).

(to Luciano Foà, Casa editrice Einaudi)

---

50 John Malcolm Brinnin, *The Third Rose*: Gertrude Stein and Her World (Boston: Little Brown, 1959).

GRODDECK—*Das Buch vom Es*

GRODDECK: FIRST GENERATION after Freud, doctor who really knows how to heal, inventor of the term *Es*[51] and practically all psychosomatic medicine (in his time, with many reservations and a great deal of opposition, only hysteria was seen to be psychosomatic), infernally intuitive, non-systematic, theatrical, amoral, unprejudiced (even by today's standards, forty years later), quite individual, and with all the fascination (and single-mindedness, and mania) of someone who intuits a law for the first time.

He also wrote a picaresque-psychoanalytic-pornographic novel, and a book about language; but this is the book that is truly his: letters to a friend in which, with many digressions, he speaks of her symptoms and his own, of the cases he's encountered, in a fireworks display of symbols, analogies, and associations, attempting to show the influence of the unconscious on all physical phenomena.

At the time—I read it immediately after it came out—it was a shocking, very entertaining, not always acceptable book, and sublimely pornographic. I reread it (in part) and have no idea what impression it would make on someone who picked it up today for the first time—probably it would be less upsetting and more acceptable, just as entertaining, and only slightly obscene.

---

51 Typically translated into English as "the It." [AA]

Groddeck was forgotten (I'd forgotten him, or almost forgotten him, myself). Now he's being rediscovered, and Durrell, in addition to the insignificant preface to the German reprint, has written a little book about him. In my opinion, it ought to be translated: apart from any other considerations, it's one of the four or five classics of modern psychotherapy. But see what impression it makes on someone who reads it now, so late.

(to Daniele Ponchiroli, Casa editrice Einaudi)

H. D., *Bid Me to Live*

H. D. (HILDA DOOLITTLE) comes from the world of the revolution in Anglo-Saxon letters around the time of the First World War (imagists, vorticists, D. H. Lawrence, inventors of experimental poetry, etc.), a generation which seems to me to be the last to "live literature" while also living a lively life.

And that's the sense you get in this book—but it's justified. To my surprise, it seemed less passé and out of tune than I imagined (it's true that at a certain point one reads: "That time in Corfu Castle when she reminded him that love is stronger than death"—but that was the only part that made my skin crawl). Which is to say: passé all you like, but on the other hand we have to recognize that for the past forty years poetic experimentation hasn't taken a single step forward. A month or two ago I sent you a guaranteed up-to-date novel by Gisèle Prassinos.[52] I was not completely convinced, though as I wrote to you it's taken seriously by people I take very seriously (e.g., Breton). But all her tricks (cuts; flashbacks; narration that blurs into evocation; impressionistic touches apparently unconnected to each other): I've found them all—and found them more necessary—in this last book by a nice old lady who published it at

---

52 *La Voyageuse*. Paris: Plon, 1959.

seventy-five (after having I think published almost nothing but poetry and theoretical writings all her life) and who died a year later, six months ago.

A roman à clef, quite short, in eleven little chapters composed of highly crystallized paragraphs, all done with exemplary economy. An autobiography more stylized than made up (but then they lived in a stylized way): one character, for example, Rico, is a convincing portrait of D. H. Lawrence; idem Frieda; and almost all the others, too, are easily identifiable.

London, the First World War, air raids. Souls even more disoriented and tormented than usual, holed up behind blackout curtains in makeshift apartments. The protagonist (in the first person) ruminates her poems, is in crisis, has an intellectual husband in the service who now and then comes home on leave, and with whom things sometimes go well and sometimes don't. In steps D. H. Lawrence, who upsets teases embarrasses fascinates disturbs rejects and almost overwhelms. But she saves herself and ends up staying with (and/or *with*) a less demanding intellectual in the countryside, where she can ruminate her poems with greater efficiency. As you see . . .

Even so, I am (almost) saying yes. It's a very intense little lyric novel; it's an interesting document about the last "poets"; it's a world that's beginning to have some interest shown in it (in essence, even if more in England than America—though Doolittle was American—it's the world of William Carlos Williams).

(to Daniele Ponchiroli, Casa editrice Einaudi)

TUMLER, *Der Mantel*

THIS SEEMS TO be a contradiction: it's a very recent German novel and yet it's readable.

And even more than readable: it's the only decent *nouveau roman*, and not just the only one from German; it has a substance, a decency, and a harmony that even the most conspicuous French *nouveaux romans* don't have.

Don't expect too much, it's not earthshaking: it's a modest book (in the best sense of the word "modest"), but it has a theme, it has intensity, it has polish, it's necessary. It's not gamelike or frigid like the (extremely intelligent) books of Butor, etc., and (though it is Gothic) has none of the pompous self-importance of certain Germans you know, nor the puffed up and overheated verve of other Germans you know.

Nouveau roman because it progresses by way of contradictory perspectives, suppositions, attempts at interpretation, stories about real things and invented things that are rectified or not, commentaries, plausible but doubtful intuitions, etc., etc., etc. And the "I" that narrates, naturally, is not the protagonist, but he inquires, he reflects, he ruminates, in an effort to understand why the protagonist has done something. And he has indeed done something, but what it is remains ungraspable; his reasons are many and graspable, but who knows?—because (if I remember correctly, I'm quoting from memory, from the book I mailed you from Florence) "actions are—always—unrecognizable, for reasons are thought, while actions on the other hand are dreamed."

The protagonist is led to buy a nice new coat; he goes on a trip—to go visit his wife, or rather another woman, or rather to visit both of them, or rather who knows—during which he doesn't use the coat once; he hitchhikes back home and, on his journey, a little woman (an extraordinary, kick-in-the-ass character who made me furious) steals his coat, or rather she doesn't steal it because it gets stolen from him, which sets him looking for the coat, and when he finds it he gives it to the little woman, for whatever reason. But something has happened, the protagonist has taken a step forward and he's less closed off. And I, too, as I read and followed and didn't follow, in the end, for whatever reason, became a slightly better person.

I repeat to you: it's not a great book, and it makes use of all the fashionable tricks. But it's authentic, the plot (which actually doesn't exist) is perfect, everything's well balanced, with no pedantry, the city and the countryside have roots, the people are (often very, often sufficiently) alive, and there's one chapter (the fourteenth, I believe) that is *stupendous*. Definitely do it, even with the risk it won't catch on.

(to Daniele Ponchiroli, Casa editrice Einaudi)

June 16, 1962

C. BURNEY, *Solitary Confinement*

OF ALL THE books that have passed through my hands these last few months, the only one in which there's not a single word that made me feel ashamed for the author. It's a book that recounts an experience and I know generally you don't want to do those. But since you've made various exceptions for war, resistance, and bad Germans, I would advise you not to rule it out before giving it a very careful glance.

This is an account of eighteen months of solitary confinement in German-occupied Paris, and that's all it is. There's no before, and there's no after, which anyone else would have made his main course (deportation to a concentration camp in Germany). There's no melodrama, there's no Anne Frank, there's no terror from the threat of execution. There's only solitude and lots of hunger with a few interrogations thrown in, and not much else. But this reckoning with solitude is made (and told) with a purity, a profundity, and a modesty that makes it—for me—*the only* defining book of the Second World War I've come across, and the only one I respond to with my whole being.

W. GADDIS, *The Recognitions*

EVENTUALLY I'LL HAVE to declare bankruptcy as a reader of novels. Just under 1,000 dense pages: on page 30 or 35 I couldn't stand it anymore: I tried to skim and ran aground 200 pages later. All I know is that it's an immense minestrone, like, let's say, Durrell's *Alexandria Quartet*, and I wouldn't rule out the possibility that it swells into success as with Durrell; that it's a kind of *Faux-Monnayeurs*, and has the pretensions of the Great *Kulturkritik*, creating characters who are all forgers (from the concrete forgery of paintings to the more subtle forgery of morals); that it's written and composed with an ambition and tenacity that can pass for intensity and style; that it's a compendium of highbrow American culture with the whole kit and kaboodle (local color—even local colors; symbols; alchemy; patristic literature; pederasty; etc.); that (on the back cover) Stuart Gilbert, who ought to have a pretty good ear, approves of it—and that there's even a blurb, however evasive and tight-lipped, from [Robert] Graves (and that means a lot, because it's out of the question that Graves should write something he doesn't feel); that I've tried to foist the thing on two different readers of novels and neither has finished it.

In sum, it strikes me as a very good fake made by an exceptionally vicious forger, and I recommend searching out a more accommodating reader than my two. I don't rule out the possibility that it's a book to do, and one with a fairly good financial prognosis.

(to Daniele Ponchiroli, Casa editrice Einaudi)

O'CONNOR, *The Edge of Sadness*

EXCELLENT PROSE WRITER. Read about a hundred pages. Forgot
them. Knew that he won the Pulitzer Prize. Picked up the book
again. Read about twenty pages. Fell asleep. Gave to a woman
who reads novels. She wasn't able to finish it.

Irish author. Milieu: the Irish in America. The Irish know
that the Irish are boastful, bombastic, bumbling, extremely colorful, and deep down very good people, very human. And every
Irish author creates boastful, bombastic, bumbling, extremely
colorful characters who are deep down very good people, very
human. Plus of course the Catholic problem: thus the protagonist is a very human priest, a bit of a sinner, but not too much.
—Bernanos tepidly translated. Have whomever you want read
it. As for me, the last Irish novel of my life.

(to Daniele Ponchiroli, Casa editrice Einaudi)

BETTELHEIM, *The Informed Heart*

AFTER YOUR PHONE call, I calmed down a little. We're dealing with two books here: the first, by Bettelheims (plural), goes to page 107—the other, by Bettelheim (singular), is the two hundred pages that follow. This second book is a beautiful one about the concentration camps—which allows for many deductions, even if they're not as general or definitively resolutive as Bettelheim thinks.

As an example of fair-mindedness and understanding capable of overcoming all resentment and all presence of past suffering, I found it very moving, and I had a great deal of respect for it. (By the way, very much in parenthesis, were someone to publish, for example, an update on Anne Frank's family situation—not cynical, or petty, or inhuman—but decently reasonable rather than indecorously sentimental—I would like that.)

So, if in general you find it right to publish books that comment on the concentration camps, *yes* absolutely.

[. . .]

All my rancor and my reaction is directed against the Bettelheims (plural) of the first hundred or so pages—what I consider the first book, which in my opinion is unpublishable. To explain myself, I have to write an "essay"—and here we finally have a subject for a solid essay. But in the few hours I have left, I don't have time not just to write but also to organize the few ideas that have occurred to me since you phoned me.

That's why I'm going to write you about them in haste, and perhaps they'll be more toxic than necessary, disorderly, incoherent, expressed in extreme formulations made necessary by haste, which may make them seem paradoxical: *aphoristischer Beitrag* [aphoristic contribution] in an effort to create a perspective from which to judge the Bettelheims. To try to understand, and to translate them calmly.

Let no one come and tell me that you or I or [. . .] live in the era of technology and are under the thumb of mass culture. What's really going on is that we're living in a world of our own and in an era of our own, and that every once in a while we find ourselves confronted with annoyances caused by people who live in the era of technology and under the thumb of mass culture, annoyances against which we defend ourselves with more or less brilliant results. We can also fall flat on our faces, naturally: we don't come out the victors every time. After all, the fact that these people bother us and can represent a problem for us is a mark *against us*. Our duty is to try to understand, and when we understand they won't bother us anymore. It's not a question of fighting against the idiots, it's a question of us creating a world in which the idiots don't count. More or less (never completely—*Heilsgeschichte wäre erfüllt*),[53] this can come to pass.

All anyone can do is react against the banality that he has inside himself. Myself, I don't have anything of the mass in me; therefore I don't get angry with the masses. I have another banality in me, and that's the banal reaction against the mass. And I get angry with the Bettelheims who react against the masses with words that have become the words of the mass.

Why do I say that the reaction against the mass is a banality? Because it has become one. It's obvious that the first people who understood the danger of the mass and who, in order to denounce it, found the first words, which were *theirs*, and said them with a tone of their own and an accent of their own, they weren't banal. But these words have been worn down, and now they're in the mouths of an anti-herd herd who react against the

---

53 "The history of salvation would be fulfilled."

prefabricated world with prefabricated reactions; in our case, with a prefabricated terminology that seems more dangerous to me than the terminology of the masses. The danger for us isn't the masses anymore, with whom we have nothing in common, the danger is the anti-masses masses with whom we still have something in common, whether we like it or not.

Parenthesis: Like during fascism in the era of N.E.I.[54] The fascists could not be the real enemies. Dominant though they were, in the era of N.E.I. they didn't exist anymore, or perhaps they'd never existed; everyone knew a priori that they'd be deflated in turn. The danger came from the antifascists who, instead of trying to understand, were fighting on the fascists' level and reduced themselves to a negative of whatever positive, but with arguments that could have been ours, too. The only real danger, as far as I'm concerned, is the right argument or the right word in the wrong mouth. The problem isn't with words, the problem is with mouths. I, with my reputation for speaking in paradoxes, invented anti-anti-fascism. Less than twenty years have gone by since then. Have you seen what's happened? Close parenthesis.

Who are the Bettelheims? The Bettelheims are a mass that has come to grips with the dangers represented by the other mass. They used words that were correct in the mouths of an individual but that in the many mouths of the many Bettelheims have become words of the masses. The Bettelheims are superficially more alive than those who aren't even Bettelheims, and not just superficially more intelligent than those who aren't even Bettelheims, but their words propagate the same death as everybody else's words. *Making it clear that in some cases the salvation of a world is not a problem of ultimate truths, but only a problem of terminology.*

54 A reference to Nuove Edizioni Ivrea, a publishing house founded in 1941 by Adriano Olivetti, with a vast program of works of psychology, politics, religion, and literature, whose creation took for granted the fall of fascism. Roberto Bazlen was one of the most active collaborators in this initiative, until August 1943. After the war, the Nuove Edizioni Ivrea was transformed into Edizioni di Communità, with a more limited program.

Thus, if I don't want the first book—the one by the Bettelheims—among the "saggi," it's not because of what he says, which if nothing else is reasonable, it's because of certain words that I hope Adelphi will never publish (unless it's to take a stand against them), words like *integrated* or *adjusted*.

To publish it now, with the first books (in five years it would be one of many, and would be neutralized by the many), would seem to me too much like a program, a statement of position: propaganda for the USIS, for the closed-off welfare world [. . .] Bettelheim is an intelligent man, even if the background he writes from is mechanistic and stupid. I repeat to you that I can only subscribe to what he says—on the condition that you consider it a purely practical manual. But unfortunately it's a manual that implies and even postulates that all psychology (who knows what he means) derives from the old misery, i.e. the mishmash of little petit-bourgeois, petit-intellectual mechanisms found in the small city of Vienna fifty years ago and transported to the Lebensraum of American sociology with one single aim: welfare, and if possible financed by some foundation.

In other words: None of us wants a tile to fall on anyone's head. To this end, we're even willing to publish a book warning people to be careful when they go out walking in the streets. (A Pedestrian's Manual.) But to publish it in a way that gives readers the sense, even confirming and leaving no doubt, that all physics (both ancient and modern) is resolved by the law of gravitation, and now that we've come to grips with it we can all go to sleep, that's another kettle of fish altogether. That would be a dangerous book. In that case, what to do? Two things: (1) a practical campaign (which can also be carried out with flyers) to educate people about not walking too close to walls; (2) printing difficult books that deal with modern physics and what goes further than modern physics. Hoping that readers will go further still.

The first book, the one by the plural Bettelheim, is based on a psychology that corresponds to the physics that definitively resolves all problems with the force of gravitation. And furthermore, with pretensions of revelation: he reveals that, beyond psychology, there is also environment, and he gives environment a determining function (while the second book, by Bettelheim singular, seems almost to deny an environment as unwieldy as the concentration camps in order to focus entirely on the individual reactions of the individual). And this at a time when "environmental psychology" is a proven fact, or even when (admitting that in general we can still tell the difference between psyche and matter) matter is becoming a *Spezialfall* [special case] of the psyche (which is why I'm putting my money on these books of parapsychology that still don't seem to have been written, whereas there are almost too many on "energy-matter").

I understand very well that there are people who are still on the way and who need to be educated. But we need to come to some agreement about where an education ought to begin. Otherwise, it would be better to give up on the publishing house and donate the money to a society for the eradication of illiteracy, or else to start out by publishing primers. As for these people who believe in environment and don't see the psyche, or vice versa, I don't think they're worth us wasting our time.

(to Luciano Foà, Casa editrice Adelphi)

NEUMANN, *Krise und Erneuerung*

FOR REASONS THAT I'll tell you in person, I can't manage to concentrate and am forced to confine myself to a few general considerations. In every case, the reason I'm favorably inclined toward Neumann is the same reason I was unfavorably inclined toward Bettelheim: the implicit background of knowledge and experience. Neither of them say anything very new. But Bettelheim invites people you'd like to make think to give themselves over instead to the security of four little banal, predigested formulas whose application soothes the conscience and even puts the world to rights. —Neumann confronts them with big, very fertile questions, and with a feasible and creative task (although it's a fairly difficult and not fully achievable one).

I repeat: he doesn't say anything "big"—but it strikes me we should renounce these big statements and new ideas a priori, at least when it comes to semi-popularizing essays—it's very likely that, for a long time, formulas (not yet outlined in full) will be found in, or will be coming out of, specialized works.

So I'm not putting the emphasis on what he's saying—and I can't even put it on who's saying it: he's only a model student of the Jungian school. How he says it, then, is even worse: with a gauche-and-Boche ponderousness that occasionally makes you want to tear your hair out.

But the *background*: it's vaster, more open, more comprehensive than our world has provided. It's the only one that leaves room to breathe and may even be digestible for Italians (it remains within the biologic-Kulturgeschichtlich-psychological limits—and doesn't involve structural jumps—psyche→matter—which, although it annoys me, is politically an advantage).

The ideas, in very broad outline:

Western-patriarchal division of heaven and earth (following the experience of matriarchal unity).

With a subsequent restriction (withering) of heaven and the removal of the "terrible" part of the divine—which leads to the secularization of the individual.

Which at first, despite every primacy of reason, continues to occupy its central position in a harmonious cosmos.

But which has deflated

as the cosmos grows ever more vast and unknown;

as the past becomes longer, origins vaguer, and history less and less normative;

as, with the discovery of other cultures, a unique culture becomes one among many.

Deflation, relativity, insecurity, anxiety—with attempts at overcompensation by means of intellectual inflation.

In spite of which (or rather as a result of which) a profound sense of loss and isolation (hence the *Krise*) with possibility of *Erneuerung* [renewal] only through the experience of our shared (bio-psychological) bases, which are beyond all relativity.

(to Luciano Foà, Casa editrice Adelphi)

Spectaculum[55]

I TRIED TO read Nelly Sachs, but after a few scenes, without noticing it, I was already in the middle of reading those two (very beautiful) acts by Beckett, which gave me new faith in humanity (probably the furthest thing from poor Beckett's intention).

It's embarrassing (and may seem like low-level cynicism) to take a stand against Sachs, with her quite real pain, and her quite real (it's a word I never use but in this case it's the right one, in every sense) "inspiration," and her fascinating purity. But at a certain point I experienced a real compassion for those poor Nazis, *forced* by Sachs to be so inhuman. It's not one of Mr. Bazlen's paradoxes; the *abgrundlose Menschlichkeit* [boundless humanity] of the one *belongs* to the *abgrundlose Unmenschlichkeit* [boundless inhumanity] of the others. And such purity will continue to create such dreck. From what you've written me, in Germany the dictatorship of Sachs should be in the ascendant. Here, luckily, we have no need of it. So it's absolutely NO! to this play. But if you get something else from her, send it all the same. Perhaps it will be less repugnant.

(to Luciano Foà, Casa editrice Adelphi)

---

55 *Spectaculum V.* (1962), collection of theatrical works by contemporary authors published by Suhrkamp Verlag, Frankfurt-am-Main. The collection includes among others the plays *Eli* by Nelly Sachs and *Happy Days* by Samuel Beckett.

SADEGH HEDAYAT

SADEGH HEDAYAT WAS born in 1903, *The Blind Owl* was written around (or before) 1930, his suicide occurred (if I'm not mistaken) after 1950. So obviously suicidal that two people I'd told about the book, but not about his death, asked me if he killed himself immediately after. If you consider that twenty to twenty-five years went by between the drafting of *The Blind Owl* and the suicide, it's enough to give you goose bumps.

Outwardly, there's something of the *école du regard* (the whole thing is absorbed by the plastic), but really no more so than in the Grimm tales, or most folklorist literature, or Sologub. In fact I, *irgendwie* [in a certain sense], got much more the sense of Novalis in his *Abschälung* [exfoliating] of one reality after another—a reality of the actual, of alcohol, of dreams, of hashish, even of karma—in an effort to achieve (and this owes nothing to Novalis) the ur-, ur-, ur-, pre-every-kind-of-wisdom obtuseness which is the defining characteristic of the blind owl.

There's no question that, for many years, this is the only book that really shook me up. (I don't know if I told you about it—remind me when we see each other to tell you about it at length) that the book "came to meet me" (literally) two years ago, the day I arrived in London with a bad case of pneumonia, a fever of over 104 degrees, and the delirious hallucinations I had that night in the sleeper car became impossible to tell apart from Sadegh Hedayat's.

As for the French (beyond *l'école du regard*, which didn't exist in his lifetime), there are many elements that bear the mark of Maeterlinck. Reading only *The Blind Owl* you won't notice it—to see it, you have to read his stories too (certainly very important from a Persian perspective—he's the first, I think, to have invented an equivalent of the naturalistic-decadent-stylized turn-of-the-century European language in Persian—but as far as we're concerned, his stories are really awful).

(to Sergio Solmi)

MCLUHAN, *The Gutenberg Galaxy*

THIS IS A book by a small-scale maniac, obsessed by causality, trying to establish a causal connection between linearity and fragmentation in terms of typography, and the intellectualization of a large part of the social and cultural phenomena of the last four and a half centuries. It rather irritated me, and, personally, I wish I could be done with causal *Geistesgeschichte* [history of ideas]; however confused and mediocre it may be, a book of astrology gives us more to think about than a hundred monomaniacal little studies like this one do. However, the way in which the question is approached may represent a step forward for a great many Italians: even if it is a bunch of virtuosities strung together, there were sometimes intuitions that I found really "illuminating." So: *hélas*, yes.

(to Luciano Foà, Casa editrice Einaudi)

CAGE, *Silence*

FOLLOWING AN UNUSUAL path, I've ended up coming to the conclusion that, all things considered, publishing it may be the right thing to do. But only as essays *by a musician*; so on the condition (and here I'm in no position to judge: I don't know, understand, or have an ear for much modern music) that Cage's work has real importance, not only symptomatic importance, but importance as an invention, or at least as a way of posing problems, in this strange thing that will or won't turn out to be music but that's surely a confoundedly significant sonic adventure, the richness of whose consequences it's already possible to glimpse. A great many of Adelphi's readers will find themselves in my position, perhaps even aggravated by the fact that they have greater biases for or against (it's not a given that a Cage enthusiast is by definition more respectable than an admirer of Tosti) than I do, and for this reason I think a very concrete introduction would be indispensable, an introduction that's historical and analytical and extremely clear, without shibbolethic words presupposing knowledge, and one that situates Cage in a complex of problems explained in such a way that I can understand them; and that doesn't come at me with the usual business about the "leap," and "if you don't get it right away," and how I'm still a product of that other world, etc., etc., which are the usual evasions practiced by nebulous enthusiasts. I know (about this there's no arguing) these are problems that can be formulated with simplicity, and that, if clearly formulated, anyone who isn't an idiot will understand them.

So, a preface, and writings *by* a musician. In that case, a lot can be forgiven him, whereas, published simply as essays falling somewhere between a general proclamation and a manifesto or revolutionary self-portrait they would be unforgivable (even if the unforgivableness is mitigated by a fairly authentic freshness, by a nonchalance, and even by a style and rhythm that are authentically personal. And in their turn, freshness, nonchalance, and style become aggravating again if one considers that they're only made possible by simplistic shorthand, *Ahnungslosigkeit* [naivety], and American slapdashery—and here we are again confronted with my misgivings about Homer and the insoluble problem of what measures of value apply to a publishing house that brings out books for the European readers of 1963).

In the preface, Cage says that the critics consider his music to be Zen or Dadaist. As far as the music goes, there's nothing I can say (but then there's Alan Watts who spoke out and declared that it has nothing, *bei Gott*, nothing to do with Zen). I, however, have plenty to say about his writing. Zen, *bei Gott*, NO! And it's fifth-hand Dadaism, therefore not Dadaism at all. Zen: it's possible (it's even certain—it's even happened to me) that starting from some combination brought about by chance or deliberate irrationality (both of which can be found in Cage's bag of tricks) an intuition is born, a (small) flash, and you believe you can glimpse something beyond the break; but I'd say that, between Cage's own sophomoric-anarchoid haphazardness and the deep and *gerichtete* [directed] irrationality of the Zen masters, there's a certain difference. Maybe I'm mistaken; maybe I'm making small-minded judgments. And I'm prepared to revise my opinion the moment someone, reading Cage, comes face to face with the UNIQUE revelation, and stumbles into satori.

DADAISM: Dadaism, dear Luciano, was an important and *unique* event that by definition can have no history. By definition, it's undiscoverable, inimitable. By definition, it can't have a school, a second generation, different manifestations. The more time goes by, the more you become aware (if you didn't notice it straight off) of the intensity, the friendly impatience, the sincere and natural irritation of those young people who lived in a *Raum* [space] where Aeschylus and Goethe and the Kaiser and Dante and Racine and Jean Paul and Mallarmé and Cervantes and Hegel and Keats and Manzoni and Kant (and you can continue on for pages and pages) were still alive and were *lived through*, and all of them together formed the *living* Kultur. If you don't have a sense of what this Kultur was, you'll never understand the sacrilegious charge and High Blasphemic value of every *boutade*, every groan, every raspberry blown by Huelsenbeck and Ball and Tzara and Schwitters. And now, forty years later, these American kids show up with their anti-puritan conformism and their intolerance prefabricated by the *flächenhafte* [flat] (and I'd just mentioned Raum to you) teachings of colleges and American "culchur" in general, and they believe they're doing the same thing, but they're only anti-ghosts of ghosts, not life that wants to live taking a stand against life that doesn't want to die. Yes, dear Luciano.

To bring home to you the grotesque inconsistency of these people, their lack of any *Ahnung* [hint] of seriousness (in the least pedantic and passé sense of the word), look at page 45, I think (it's on the right, so odd, and it definitely begins with a 4) the episode where Cage consults the I-Ching, which dryly delivers him a knockout, and Cage *does not agree*. It's a buffoonery worthy of Molière. It seems almost unreal. And, even if they're less blatantly ridiculous, you can find dozens and dozens of such things. Which, according to our criteria, liquidates Cage with no possibility of appeal. The trouble is that the "new" doesn't necessarily have to be born from values measurable by our measures, and that it may only blaze its trail over a terrain less solidified, less arteriosclerotic than ours (or rather mine). And that the problem, in these cases, is no longer *was ist* [what is] but *was daraus warden kann* [what can come out of it]. With the result that in Amsterdam, the wavering between *was ist* and *was daraus warden kann* in Cage's case completely paralyzed me, and I haven't been able to write you. Until I did what Cage did, i.e. consult the I-Ching (question: what position to take toward him?). And the answer, very clear, dry, and ambiguous, was 61 (the "*innere Wahrheit*" [inner truth]), without a Moving Line. So another crisis, but at least this one has a direction, with an emphasis on the wound. Having gotten over this, I really believe, in spite of everything, that there's a "germ of life" (in the words of 61) in Cage, and seeing that, all in all, he's a very nice boy (and as I told you before, there's something that really seems to be in his own voice here), I feel I have almost no choice but to tell you yes. If nothing else, it will serve as an antidote to informed hearts.[56] But I think there's more to it than that: and we certainly can't get from one world to the next by goose-stepping.

(to Luciano Foà, Casa editrice Adelphi)

---

56 Allusion to the Bruno Bettelheim book *The Informed Heart*.

BENOÎTE ET FLORA GROULT, *Journal à Quatre Mains*

FIRST OF ALL, there was the matter of figuring out exactly what it is, more precisely if it's an authentic diary or a rewriting/ novel/pastiche stitched together on the pattern of a diary many years after it was written. If you're on good terms with the literary agent, you can figure it out with a phone call.

In that case (the second), it would be a fine book, entertaining, delicate, respectable, with two sympathetic protagonists who aren't easily forgotten—and there's nothing more to say.

In the first case, however, it's really an extraordinary and fascinating "document of civilization" (in Italy, we talk like this), of a high civilization such as no one has even dared to dream about in Italy.

I myself read it as an authentic diary, in part because I got all the way to the final pages without having noticed that on the cover, under the title, it says "A Novel." It had, it's true, particularly in Flora's passages around the age of fifteen and sixteen, something too elaborate and literary about it, something of a lived-through immaturity judged and formulated with excessive maturity, but I didn't suspect anything because, in a world that gave birth to Radiguet among others, anything is possible. And it's possible that the authors have stuck on the word "Novel" to separate themselves from it a little, to create a certain distance between them, today, and their ex–living flesh (to the extent,

302

dear God, that they answer for it, and have reason to answer for it), which is exhibited I wouldn't say with immodesty (they are *extremely pure!*) but let us say with an excess of nonchalance.

The life of two young girls (to begin with, nineteen and fifteen years old) in Paris, from a little before the Occupation to a little after the Liberation, the life of two young girls who know how to be human without forgetting to be women, and to be women without forgetting to be human, bound together by an extraordinary intimacy / friendship / solidarity that is affectionate, detached, and never corny. The older one: the slightly schematic intellectual until proven otherwise; and fortunately there is plenty of proof on offer, of many different kinds. The younger one: the *vamp* (sic!) of the family, seemingly less guarded but with a clear moral intransigence that's truly intimidating.

In the refined and abrupt environment of the good French bourgeois, with no excessive luxury, but with the modesty of genuine comfort, a para-intellectual environment, a haute-couture mother, a master-artisan father, but happily sans *Klatsch* [gossip] or literary anecdotes (the reader is told that the father gave his tobacco ration to Max Jacob; the name Poiret is referenced once or twice; only Marie Laurencin appears on the scene, being part of the family's closest inner circle; not much else). In an Occupied Paris that is depressed but *tout de même* lively, and that comes alive in a hallucinatory way—redeeming the depressed but by no means lively Europe over which the Germans are spreading like an oil stain.

That's the immediate culture, which sets the tone (and also, here and there, accounts for some false notes): Giraudoux who's the God, Cocteau who's his dancer. But the true culture, the life-giving culture, is the true eternal city, with its perfect mixture of charm and seriousness, wild and unbridled vitality and responsibility, elegance intelligence reflection lightness, and genuine and *deep humanity*—which leaps off the page in the purest way possible.

Family life with all the funniest incompatibilities looked back on with bitter, critical, affectionate irony, and with giddily joyful self-irony regarding flirtations, exams, holidays, Germans, more exams, rationing, more flirtations, more exams—and the first girl finally falls in love, then an abortion, a marriage in an environment that's touching, but despised because it's "petit bourgeois"; the death of the husband, who's a member of the Resistance, almost immediately after; real grief, and an extraordinary stand taken against real grief, in favor of not living for grief alone, a stand so successful that, not too many months and only a few pages later, she makes exuberant love to the Americans who've in the meantime liberated her, only to become again, having passed through the whirlwind that's perhaps even over-sated her, a "serious person." The younger girl, who thanks to her uncompromising nature has managed to remain a virgin until the final pages, is married to an ally, too. And the sisters, who almost weren't parted by the older one's marriage, are separated by the marriage of the younger one.

If it's not a novel, it's one of the only modern books of Education I've encountered. Being able to live through all the curlicues and contradictions of the existence of two young girls from '40–'45 without ever falling into chaos, indeed with an unmistakable elegance to the very end, is almost a miracle. If you want an example: on page 320, the cold and uncynical intelligence (and the intelligence of a woman who knows what love is) with which Benoîte decides to have an abortion. And there are dozens of passages such as this. Which compose two extraordinary portraits of two young girls of the race of the masters (not to be confused with *Herrenrasse* [the Master race]) to be set under the nose of the Italians, the race of the dishwashers. To avoid any misunderstanding: masters of their own bodies, their own souls, their own minds, their *own liberty*.

I could go on—but I don't want to try to convince you too much. I'm in love, and love is unreasonable. (But it's not true that love makes you blind. It opens your eyes. And here it has opened my eyes even further—luckily, I already had them open—to what Paris has been and to what it must be even today—the sisters Groult are alive!—and to what shit the rest of Europe is).

I don't want to convince you because I still have enough

clearness of mind to know that I'm in love and that assuming responsibility for its publication would mean me also assuming responsibility for your martyrdom. For Adelphi would be headed straight for accusations of frivolity, snobbism, implicit disqualification, and worse: Montenapoleone.[57]

In Italy, everything that isn't neorealist, provincial, or academic misery is Montenapoleone. And the only permissible way to have suffered under the Germans is to turn yourself into a subject for pity. Now, pitiful cases move me to pity, and I'll always be willing to lend a hand so that there won't be others. But I'm fed up with the confusion of categories that has been created for the purpose of reducing them all to the one common denominator of physical suffering and physical death. The incommensurables of life should not be made commensurate. Between the ordinariness of the lives of poor Anne Frank and poor Simone Weil, and the grandeur of the sisters Groult, there's an abyss. I say grandeur because they have that grandeur that, for whatever reason, you never run into and which is no longer tragic, that grandeur of a standard of life which, *malgré tout* [despite everything], remains almost untouched, and where no one has ever been killed, by history; where you're so alive that you survive *in order to go on being alive*. And that seems like small pottoes to you. (Bear in mind I'm not jotting these words down lightly—and if an analysis could be done, and one day it will be, regarding the reasons for some of the deaths in war, in concentration camps, in highway accidents, etc., you'd see that I'm not completely wrong.)

I must warn you moreover that the book is too long, and however intelligent they may have been, they were still two teenage girls just past puberty, so, it's true, not all their bagels have perfect holes: especially in the early pages there's too much un-childish writing to keep from seeming genuinely childish, there's sometimes too marked a taste for jokes, stunning formulations, and so on—but all that is part of the portrait. And if the great letter writers of the eighteenth century are more "perfect," that's because they're scribbling on a preexisting smooth surface,

57 Montenapoleone is a famous shopping street in Milan.

whereas here, truly and *malgré tout*, and notwithstanding all the discernible conventions, they are living in a created world, but they also create (!!!) a world.

(to Luciano Foà, Casa editrice Adelphi)

June 14, 1963

SPITTELER, *Imago*

WHICH I REREAD after, say, forty years, and was bowled over by
the fact that in these forty years it has lost absolutely nothing
of its value. It continues to be a miracle (and one of the very
few great miracles I know of—it's actually more consistent and
complex than *The Blind Owl*, and of course much more so
than Sartre's *L'enfance d'un chef*, where the intelligence of the
observations is too apparent), combining an extremely lucid,
bone-dry, lab-ready "clinical case study" with the spontaneity
and *Zwangslosigkeit* [nimbleness] that allows the schema to take
on flesh and bone—perhaps the only narrative that hasn't lost
its justification during all these years. The subject you know
well: the young man with many "souls" who projects almost
all of them on a single woman, for whom he makes a big mess
all his own, without her having anything to do with it (but
it's also a miracle of ambiguity, so *almost* without her having
anything to do with it) with all the cold showers and beatings
that, gradually, make him mature.

And then the more I think about it these last few days, the
more new things I discover—in the essentialness of every episode and almost, almost every paragraph. Whether it's a classic
I don't think merits discussion —it's one of the direct determinants (correction: almost direct, a little via Freud / Jung) of our
culture a few years back (today the direct determinants have
aufgelöst [dissolved]: like Marx, like Wilde, like Strindberg, and

307

therefore, as far as I'm concerned, I'd say yes without a second
thought.

[. . .]

The internal nimbleness of the story is weighted down a little by the mode of its telling, which is dated by certain naive-
ties, pedantries, gaucheries, simplifications, rigidities, and little
allegorical things that (to the extent they're taken up by a pure
writer like Spitteler) make too much use of the conventions of
the time, which are too close to us to be tolerated with historical
detachment. And I understand the old-fashioned element can
be a bit annoying. But I think the whole thing is so huge that
considerations of (superficial) "good taste" should take a back
seat here.

GRIAULE, *Dieu d'eau*

After countless hardships in my efforts to get closer to it, I ended up tolerating it rather well. Note that the passing grade I give
it doesn't contain an implicit judgment: it's only the expression
of my own very personal opinion. I remember the shock when,
not longer after the '20s had ended, I came upon documents
like this one for the first time, which really shattered my last
(already quite faltering) Western certainties. Soon there were
too many of them, they lost their explosive force, they entered
into the files of anthropological bureaucracy, and the problem
was absorbed. Now they bore me—or, to be fair, I don't know
if I'm justifiably *désabusé* or senilely obtuse.

I must admit, however, that finding a cosmogonic system
this complete and tight (less complex than it seems, however—in a nutshell, it all comes down to half a dozen extremely
well-intertwined absurdities. And that's already a condemnation—what can a world based on half a dozen anything tell us?
Or on one thing, or on millions and millions and millions!) is

very unusual. Perhaps (I don't know) it's even a unique case. Therefore, of course, nihil obstat.

(to Luciano Foà, Casa editrice Adelphi)

SEIGNOLLE, *Un corbeau de toutes couleurs*

SEIGNOLLE IS AN industrialist (or a big-time businessman, I don't know) who writes, and has one big flaw: his taste, his passion for writing. That's why, in everything he writes, one senses his taste, his passion, the demonic-artisanal pleasure he takes in dominating the sentence and giving birth to life on a blank page, which later (see the exemplary case of Thomas Mann), in the form of dirtied paper, becomes the tombstone of real life. Fortunately, he is not nearly as good as Thomas Mann, and much more ambiguous (a grave offense to the ambition of Thomas Mann, who believed he had a monopoly on ambiguity and only had a monopoly on ambition), so I'm glad to pardon him for beautiful pages.

Beautiful pages put down in the negative column are anyway still to his credit (but note that, apart from this book, I know him only from *La Gueule* and *Le Diable*—and he must have an infinity of books and booklings): a nice, laid-back man who has a full life, a big interest in folklore, especially folklore experienced in subtly ambiguous ways (with an almost eighteenth-century detachment and an almost primitive involvement), and with a feeling (this, too, is ambiguous—half literary, half truly obsessive) for the *uncanny*—and a body of work that lies somewhere between Henry Miller and the *Gothic Tales*,[58] which I find disorienting, which I don't know how to

58 Isak Dinesen, *Seven Gothic Tales*, 1934.

approach, or what to do with, but about which I know, at some point, something has to be done.

(to Luciano Foà, Casa editrice Adelphi)

ROSENBERG, *Durchbruch zur Zukunft*

THIS BOOK IS a very strange kettle of fish—and once in Milan it's required you start talking about fish. —An astrological sketch of the evolution of humanity with fairly detailed predictions covering the next 2,100 years, with a seriousness and zealousness equal to the clumsiness of the writing, and with Christian undertones (and you know the respect I have for Christianity) falling somewhere between the sacristy and base pietism, which I find unbearable. On the other hand, I don't exclude the possibility that in my final stocktaking, a minute before I die, this won't turn out to be one of the books that made the deepest impression on me: seeing that, according to its analysis of the twelve months of the next great solar year (the year of Aquarius) which will end in a fiery catastrophe, I have a directive (intuitively convincing, I'd say almost "logical") toward the future; for better or worse, my life is changed. —The only thing left for us is to talk about fish.

(to Luciano Foà, Casa editrice Adelphi)

BATAILLE, *Sur Nietzsche and La Littérature et le mal*

BATAILLE IS AN aspiring wolf who'd like to run with the hare and hunt with the hounds (which is below the dignity of any real wolf and is even at odds with his only aspiration), who simpers about in the face of the irrational and, what's worse, in the face of the Ur; who invokes cruelty in little post-symbolist phrases that aren't clear but polished to a shine—and who is only a caricature of a little aestheticizing "neurotic" full of self-compassion (we cannot imagine his *solitude*! and his agony!).

(to Luciano Foà, Casa editrice Adelphi)

SYKES, *The Hidden Remnant*

THIS IS A book of unexpectedly high and mature culture, which, despite the subject I'll tell you about and the dedication you'll see, is the first American book of this type that doesn't stink of its college or foundation, written (*very* well) by a *naturaliter* civilized person with the whole of Europe in his blood—and who, despite a few points of departure and a few conclusions aimed more at Americans than Europeans, may be accepted by us almost without reservation and without that implicit *Herablassung* [condescension] that, like it or not, we always feel when dealing with the usual Americans. He's an unusual American: our equal.

The remnants are the "few others"—the rare few who, to use Jung's terms (the book is very "philo"-Jungian, but with no acolytic blindness) are not immersed in the collective banality, but go right straight on along their individual inner paths in spite of all the dangers (including practical ones) of solitude; the only ones who could "save" the world—and according to Sykes perhaps even will save it.

The only ones who, in other words, have come to grips with the psychological problem and will know how to pose the *psycho-political* problem. And the book is, in its most essential and largest part, a review of all the psychological schools (and all the founders of psychological schools) since the new psychology first appeared, and (in the second part) of all the

314

"anti"-psychological positions (in some cases equally justified) in theology, philosophy, literature, etc., etc.

Of course, I am too much a *remnant* myself to be able to subscribe down to the last comma to what the *remnant* Sykes says—but I must say that its *tableau* of psychological schools is the most perfect, equitable, balanced, homogeneous, lively, and broad-minded I've encountered. Seeing psychology purely as a function of psychologists, and creating, with a few well-chosen strokes (and zeroing in on critical points—sympathetic, human, never harsh—that get to the heart of the matter), not portraits, but quite persuasive impressions of individual psychologists, who have never been presented to us this way before. —The second part, about "their natural opponents," on first reading seemed slightly weaker than the "psychopomps" part—but now, leafing through it again at random, I see that almost every page taken in itself is, if nothing else, rather beautiful. —It is always very well written: there is never, anywhere in the book, a superfluous phrase, a gratuitous repetition, a frivolity, a dropping off, an inconsistency. This is what, in my opinion, a writer ought to be: he has something to say; what he has to say comes from life and belongs to him; he says it in words that are his, clearly; with great steadiness and economy. (Sykes trained his hand a bit in the *New Yorker*—or somewhere like that. But because the hand is his, this training strikes me as an advantage: it spared me a great deal of strain and kept me amused.)

The beginning and the end (especially the end) are necessarily a bit journalistic; they aren't representative of the whole book; and beware that the opinion of others may be based chiefly on the framework (although, even in the most forthrightly political pages, toward the end, there are flashes of brilliance, for example the passage on Kennedy, which really filled me with joy).

Too bad we didn't get our hands on it earlier (which anyway wouldn't have been possible—it came out in January): it would have let us avoid Neumann, and Brown (although he may not have anything to do with this), and even McLuhan. —Now I don't know. In any case, also read him yourself, *for your own sake*: it's a book that really offers something. And have others read it—keeping in mind that the two people least well suited to give you an opinion are [. . .] who (this, naturally, shouldn't stay between us, but I beg you to tell them, as I will tell them too) from the summit of their nearly completed mutation have, for good reason, a low tolerance for the poor devils who still need to evolve. I, who am halfway there, am content with goodwill, if the goodwill emanates from a good head of a good human specimen.

(to Luciano Foà, Casa editrice Adelphi)

KUHN, *Structure of Scientific Revolutions*

I'D DISMISSED THE book shortly after opening it when—according to your latest report—I realized you had it under consideration, and then it seemed right for me to start reading it diligently and with good intentions—in order to convince myself that I'd done better than well in chucking it aside posthaste, and not in order to understand the reasons that may have induced someone else not to have immediately done likewise.

This Kuhn, about whom one might say anything, but certainly not that he is a *remnant*, has had the revelation that the history of science (which, moreover, as an end in itself, is a discipline I highly recommend to you) does not progress at the rhythm of a rectilinear Prussian march, from one climactic discovery to the next, but—I'd venture like every other phenomenon in life—by way of hesitations, contrasts, oppositions, incomprehensions, and failures, out of which something crystallizes that is either definitively established or generally accepted, and that forms the starting point for the next non-Prussian march. Now, the fact that an Americunculus tries to divulge this revelation of his to get himself condemned to sterilization by means of grants from some foundation and a teaching position at some college (only to go on to write other books that he'll dedicate to his parents, without whom, as you know, dear Luciano, the books would never have been written) is something I unfortunately can't do anything about and will put up with. But the fact that implicitly there's the almost arrogant pretext of teaching anything to anyone who didn't die before 1914 shows an ingenuousness so offensive that it might be time now, finally, to pick up the whip and drive all these spawn from the temple. If nothing else, it would stave off boredom.

So: the steps from discovery to discovery are taken by way of revolutions, which have an analogy with political revolutions, and concerning this analogy, I beg you to read, I think, page 91, beginning with the second paragraph, where you'll find considerations of a grotesque banality and *redundancy*, almost like every other page (I say almost because—in the lowest current sense of the word—this Kuhn is not an idiot, and given fifty reflections, at least one of them inevitably comes off well) you flip open at random. —And then tell me if Adelphi can publish such a cup of swill! (A bucket is more like it—the first thing that set my teeth on edge was a metallic screeching!)

You probably think I'm going overboard, that my intolerance is exaggerated, and that I don't want to consider certain perspectives from which even Kuhn may have some miserable justification. But put yourself in my place and think of the dirty trick that, at least where I'm concerned, the good Lord played with Kuhn: he made me pick up the book just when I'd finished reading the book on European thought by BRUNSCHVICG. Another book that, to use a plebeian criterion for once, "doesn't say anything new": namely, that Europe is the "only" continent where "intelligence"—and here, too, it's based on "revolutions" (but you'll see with what "European" perspicacity they're defined!)—was delineated, matured, and seeks to defend itself against "myth," which won't go away, and which, no matter how much light intelligence sheds, insinuates itself with more and more insidious cunning where you least expect it.

These are eleven lectures given at the Sorbonne between '39 and '40 (with a single reference to the war on the first page); they do not contain revelations, but they seems to me to be an impressive, authentic, and convincing testimony to the miracle of European thought. Moving in their equity, their poised fervor, their "natural" assimilation of three thousand years of thought down even to the details, the *aisance* of *Übersicht* [overview] and movement, the precision and *Ungezwungenheit* [ease] of their order, authority, and modesty. I'm not saying do the book without a second thought; not only because the nearly mutated will have it filed away for centuries under the heading "disciples of Bergson," but also because it encroaches too much on the territory of Einaudi's Saggi or the essays in ' *Comunità* '59 [. . .] But use it, at least, please, as a point of comparison for the Kuhn.

I didn't take the first page into account, and when at the last line I found myself confronted with the dates (I think *December 1939—March* or *April 1940*), I felt a genuine pang of emotion. Idiot! —We know where the "hole" in Brunschvicg was, *und so mußte es eben kommen* [and that's how it had to be]. But when we consider that after the Brunschvicgs come the Kuhns, instead of pangs of emotion, it's goose bumps.

---

59 An Italian magazine founded by Adriano Olivetti. [AA]

HEYWOOD, *The Sixth Sense* and *The Infinite Hive*

The second is one of the books that I wanted to ask you for and that I still haven't asked you for, and then I found it waiting on the table at Ljuba's. It's the autobiography of Madame Heywood, of a life (a very beautiful life, with a great patrician ease) accompanied by modest and by no means *épatantes* [staggering] "para"-psychological experiences. It made a big impression on me *denn es ist wirklich so* [because that's really how it is]: the most perfect document of the dissolving of the conventional human profile that I know of; a normal life, with a few coincidences "statistically" more impossible than improbable, a few "strange" facts, a few *hints* at more complex relations than those to which rational psychology and physiology have accustomed us, that is to say, no more and no less than what would be the autobiography of any pale face that might see itself living in such ease. But beyond the fact that it's in itself a very charming book, and that it's one of the first to restore the climate in which, whether we like it or not, we all live, it allowed me to confirm the validity, the integrity, of the non-exaltation, the "historical" reliability of *The Sixth Sense*. [. . .] *The Infinite Hive*'s honesty is conspicuous, its objectivity fierce, its good sense unshakable, its diffidence exemplary in the face of every form of mysticism, its exercise of judgment would do honor to any Italianer. Which is why I feel able to answer with even greater certainty than about

The Sixth Sense, and I'd say do it. If the "essays"[60] are supposed to introduce new things, all that's left to us is parapsychology: the new things in mathematics and physics are formulas, which we'll never be able to publish; in the other sciences, they result only from very specialized work. And if starting from these things you want to arrive at general conclusions, you have a choice between the distortions, confusion, and monomania of some cranks and the respectable banalities of Lorenz.

(to Luciano Foà, Casa editrice Adelphi)

---

60 Title of a series published by Adelphi.

GOTTHELF, *Anne Bäbi Jowäger*

2 VOL., I.E. 800 pages written (like everything else by Gotthelf originally, though normally his books circulate in German "translation") in large part, and not only the dialogue, in Bernese dialect, and I had a hell of a time trying to decipher them. However: I found myself confronting (I don't think I'm exaggerating—especially given that the difficulty of reading prevented any easy enthusiasm) the (at least in some respects) GREATEST European novelist of the last century, and confronting an oeuvre that isn't on a level with Stendhal / Dostoevsky, but almost on a level with Cervantes. —It wasn't conceived as a novel but was written at the behest of the Bernese government as a didactic tale to teach the Swiss not to resort to charlatans but to go to real doctors. It has a very simple plot—pure pretext—which is intermixed with long reflections and thesis-driven dialogues: parents who are too enamored of their only son, who gets sick, is treated by charlatans, ends up losing an eye, and is slightly handicapped; they look for a wife for him, are about to marry him off to a bad girl when he falls in love with a good (but poor) girl, whom he finally marries; sickness and death of his child, depression of his mother (i.e., the grandmother), who almost goes mad because she blames herself for not having called in the right doctor and having caused the child's death. Now the real doctor steps in—and an excellent dialogue between this man and the parish priest. —

The handicapped man "wakes up" and makes the farms prosper. —A few episodes and some secondary characters (among them a servant, monumental, constantly offended). —Finale with the death and funeral of the good doctor, who's allowed himself to die because he lacks true faith. —I have recounted it to you very badly because the plot doesn't interest me, I don't have any desire to reconstruct it, and it doesn't matter. What really matters is that, for the first time in the history of literature, Gotthelf created organic characters inserted into an organic life, characters with souls and bodies. For the first time, and perhaps also for the only time—those created after him and that seem to go beyond him are, if you think about it, made not of souls and bodies, but of souls and clinical histories. —Just consider the fact that, even half a century after Gotthelf (who died around 1850), the protagonist, after the crisis, would have an attack of "nerve fever," from which he typically died, or, if he got over it, he came out "another man"; and consider that it wasn't a fever *caused* by nerves but a fever *of* nerves. And consider that Gotthelf was born around fifteen years after Stendhal, and about twenty-five years before Dostoevsky and Flaubert (and a little more than thirty years before Tolstoy). But note that *Anne Bäbi Jowäger* isn't extraordinary only because of its characters—the novel is extraordinary for the whole environment it recreates, for its reflections, for its sermons—which besides being full of great prose, have a *broad* wisdom and an uncritical impartiality such as I don't think you find in any of the other, apparently shrewder and more bitterly experienced writers of the nineteenth century, including the ones who don't write fiction.

(to Luciano Foà, Casa editrice Adelphi)

*[From a letter of May 16, 1963, to Luciano Foà, Adelphi, on the
subject of* STRINDBERG]

[. . .] I draw your attention once again to the fact that it's the
only classic we have, but for a world that will no longer need to
read it (*or to read*).

Bibliography

Georges Bataille, *Sur Nietzsche*, Gallimard, Paris, 1945; *La Littérature et le Mal*, Gallimard, Paris 1957. [*On Nietzsche*, trans. Bruce Boone. London: Continuum, 1992; *Literature and Evil*, trans. Alastair Hamilton. New York: Penguin, 2012.]

Bruno Bettelheim, *The Informed Heart*, The Free Press, Glencoe, 1960.

Maurice Blanchot, *L'Espace Littéraire*, Gallimard, Paris, 1955. [*The Space of Literature*, trans. Ann Smock. Lincoln: University of Nebraska, 1989.]

Ray Bradbury, *Dandelion Wine*, Doubleday, New York, 1957.

Norman O. Brown, *Life Against Death*, Wesleyan University Press, Middletown, 1959.

Léon Brunschvicg, *L'Esprit Européen*, Éditions de la Baconnière, Neuchâtel, 1947.

Christopher Burney, *Solitary Confinement*, Macmillan, London, 1961.

John Cage, *Silence*, Wesleyan University Press, Middletown, 1961.

André Dhôtel, *Le Plateau de Mazagran*, Éditions de Minuit, Paris, 1947.

Heimito von Doderer, *Die Dämonen*, Biederstein Verlag, München, 1957. [*The Demons*, trans. Clara and Richard Winston. New York: Knopf, 1961.

Alexander Dorner, *Überwindung der "Kunst,"* Fackelträger-Verlag, Hanover, 1959. [Translated from *The Way Beyond "Art,"*

New York University Press, New York, 1958.]

Kasimir Edschmied, *Der Marschall und die Gnade*, Kurt Desch Verlag, Munich, 1956.

William Gaddis. *The Recognitions*. New York: Harcourt Brace. 1955.

Witold Gombrowicz. *Ferdydurke*. Warsaw: Panstwowy Institut Wydawniczy, 1938. [*Ferdydurke*, trans. Danuta Borchardt. New Haven: Yale University Press, 2012.]

Paul Goodman. *The Empire City*. Indianapolis: Bobbs-Merrill, 1959.

Jeremias Gotthelf. *Wie Anne Bäbi Jowäger haushaltet*, 1843.

Maurice Griaule. *Dieu d'eau*. Paris: Éditions du Chêne, 1948.

Georg Groddeck. *Das Buch vom Es*. Vienna: Internationaler Psychoanalytischer Verlag, 1923. [*The Book of the It*, trans. Ashley Montagu. New York: New American Library, 1961.]

Benoîte and Flora Groult. *Journal à Quatre Mains*. Paris: Éditions Denoël, 1962.

Knut Hamsun, *Mysterien*, 1894. [*Mysteries*, trans. Sverre Lyngstad. New York: Penguin, 2001.]

H. D. [Hilda Doolittle]. *Bid Me to Live*. New York: Grove Press, 1960.

Sadegh Hedayat. *The Blind Owl*. London: John Calder, 1957.

Rosalind Heywood. *The Sixth Sense*. London: Chatto and Windus, 1959; *The Infinite House*. London: Chatto and Windus, 1964.

Pierre-Jean Jouve. *Le Monde Désert*. Paris: Mercure de France, 1927. [*The Desert World*, trans. Lydia Davis. Marlboro, VT: The Marlboro Press, 1996.]

Thomas S. Kuhn. *The Structure of Scientific Rationalism*. Chicago: University of Chicago Press, 1962.

William March. *The Looking Glass*. New York: Rinehart, 1956.

Marshall McLuhan. *The Gutenberg Galaxy*. Toronto: University of Toronto Press, 1962.

Pierre Minet. *La Défaite*. Paris: Éditions du Sagittaire, 1947.

Robert Musil. *Der Mann ohne Eigenschaften*. Berlin: Ernst Rowohlt Verlag, 1930. [*The Man Without Qualities*, trans. Sophie Wilkins and Burton Pike. New York: Vintage, 1996.]

Erich Neumann. *Krise und Erneuerung*. Zürich: Rhein-Verlag, 1961.

Frank O'Connor. *The Edge of Sadness*. London: Reinhardt, 1961.

José Orabuena. *Gross ist deine Treue*. Zürich: Thomas Verlag, 1959.

Alain Robbe-Grillet. *Le Voyeur*. Paris: Éditions de Minuit, 1955. [*The Voyeur*, trans. Richard Howard. New York: Grove Press, 1958.]

Alfons Rosenberg. *Durchbruch zur Zukunft*. München Planegg: Otto Wilhelm Barth, 1958.

Nelly Sachs. *Eli*. Frankfurt-am-Main: Suhrkamp Verlag, 1962. [*O the Chimneys: Selected Poems, Including the Verse Play, Eli,* trans. Michael Hamburger. New York: Farrar Straus Giroux, 1967.

William Sansom. *The Body*. London: The Hogarth Press, 1949.

Claude Seignolle. *Un Corbeau de Toutes Couleurs*. Paris: Éditions Denoël, 1962.

Roger Shattuck. *The Banquet Years*. New York: Harcourt Brace, 1958.

Fyodor Sologub. *Melkij bes*. 1905. [exact edition unknown; *The Little Demon*, trans. Ronald Wilks. New York: Penguin, 2013.]

Carl Spitteler. *Imago*. 1906. [exact edition unknown]

Gerald Sykes. *The Hidden Remnant*. New York: Harper and Brothers, 1962.

Giuseppe Tomasi di Lampedusa. *Il Gattopardo*. Milano: Feltrinelli, 1958. [*The Leopard: A Novel*, trans. Archibald Colquhoun. New York: Pantheon, 1960.]

Franz Tumler. *Der Mantel*. Frankfurt-am-Main: Suhrkamp, 1959.

Translator's Afterword

"And once and for all, let me tell thee and assure thee, young man, it's better to sail with a moody good captain than a laughing bad one."

Melville, *Moby-Dick; or, the Whale*

The only real danger, as far as I'm concerned, is the right argument or the right word in the wrong mouth. The problem isn't with words, the problem is with mouths.

Roberto Bazlen, *Letter to Luciano Foà*

THERE IS AN extraordinary book by the French poet Henri Lefebvre called *The Missing Pieces,* which consists entirely of a catalogue of creations that have gone missing over the years: "The novel *Theodor* by Robert Walser . . . The letters of Milena Jesenska to Franz Kafka . . . Pierre Guyotat's head of hair." It's an inspired experiment on Lefebvre's part, and, as with all great catalogues, the beauty (and the terror) is that the incantation might go on forever. That the writing of Roberto Bazlen is not one of the missing pieces Lefebvre lists is something of a miracle, or a fluke, or a happy accident. But whatever it is, it is worth our attention.

Bazlen was born in Trieste at a time when that city was still part of the Austro-Hungarian Empire. His father was German, his mother Italian—a double inheritance reflected in his name. It is customary, when Bazlen's name is mentioned, to enumerate famous friends, including Italo Svevo, Umberto Saba (both fellow Triestinos), Italo Calvino, and Eugenio Montale. It is also customary to emphasize the importance of Bazlen's background. *The Oxford Companion to Italian Literature*, for example, describes him as: an "eccentric Triestine intellectual of Jewish origins with a wide range of recondite interests." The trouble with such a description isn't that it's entirely inaccurate. The trouble is with the way it's phrased. By "eccentric," are we to understand that Bazlen is slightly trivial—like one of those intellectual oddities who devote themselves to comparative studies of the language of cats and dogs? Do Freud, Jung, and modern physics really count as "recondite interests"? And what, exactly, are these plural "Jewish origins" meant to signify?

It's true that the publicly known facts of Bazlen's adult life are few. Most of them can be gathered from the short text on the back cover flap of the Adelphi edition of his *Scritti* (1984), a short text composed by Bazlen's friend Roberto Calasso:

Very early on, [Bazlen] invented a mode of life that he would never abandon: spending a certain number of hours every day reading, stretched out on a bed with some pillows. [. . .] After some vain attempts to dedicate himself to a practical activity, in Trieste, Genoa, and Milan (where he lived for some years), Bazlen landed in Rome at the beginning of 1939, having meanwhile, deliberately, blown through the family inheritance. He would live in Rome, in a furnished room on the Via Margutta, for twenty-six years, until two months before he died, in 1965, in Milan.

Bazlen made ends meet during those twenty-six years in Rome by translating from German (Freud, among others) and serving as a consultant to various Italian publishing houses (Einaudi, above all). In the 1940s, during the last years of the war, Adriano Olivetti had enlisted him to help develop an ambitious plan for his Edizioni di Comunità; but when Olivetti put the plan into action after the fall of fascism, very few of the titles Bazlen had proposed appeared. Only with the founding of Adelphi Edizioni in the early 1960s was he able to draw up a program that more fully reflected his curiosity and taste.

Without Calasso (who began working at Adelphi in 1962 and continues to oversee it today), the present volume would not exist. I say this not only because I was introduced to Bazlen's writings through Lila Azam Zanganeh's *Paris Review* interview with Calasso—and not only because Calasso was the first to edit and publish these writings—but because, except for the editorial letters that Bazlen composed in Italian, my translation is of Calasso's own translation of the largely German originals. The state of Bazlen's notebooks and papers, which were found in a suitcase after his death and have never been published in a definitive German edition, makes this double translation necessary.

Though I sympathize with those readers educated to distrust translations of translations, I'd also say that Bazlen is peculiarly well suited to a two-leg journey into English. His writings, especially the novel and the notes, gesture beyond language. He was no cultist of the *mot juste*. As a reader, he cared much more for literature that handled what he called "the great themes" than for "Bovaryist" fetishists of style. Bazlen's language is rather pure energy, and as such designed for travel.

The Sea Captain, which Bazlen began early and worked on until late in his life, is a brilliant but unquestionably unfinished work of fiction. Following the multiple accounts of the captain's shipwreck, the novel, qua novel, founders. However, it founders to a depth that's far more interesting than the superficially smooth sailing that takes many novels to their destinations. Despite its title, *The Sea Captain* does not owe very much to Conrad or Melville (even if there are shades of Ahab in Bazlen's moody Captain). Its relations are Walser, Kafka, Beckett. Its descendants (even if they don't know their father) are Thomas Bernhard, Jon Fosse, Markus Werner. But I only indulge in these comparisons to evoke the novel's outward inwardness, its quickness, its significant repetitions. In fact, *The Sea Captain* is like nothing else I've read. More than most books, its sensibility belongs uniquely to its author.[61]

If *The Sea Captain* is one of the great unread twentieth-century novels, "Notes Without a Text" is surely one of the great unread documents of twentieth-century thought. The only predecessors I can think of might be Lichtenberg's *Waste Books* and Joseph Joubert's *Carnets*. In entries that telegraph enough material for a lengthy essay into a few incisive lines, Bazlen examines religion, animals, noise pollution, numbers, European politics, prejudices, mythology, and literature. But unlike the typical self-conscious litterateur's diary, these notes are truly notes, not written for publication but out of personal necessity—and, for that reason among others, they reward rereading.

Probably the most public compositions included in this volume are the editorial letters, which need no comment. Nevertheless, I would point out that they are not merely a record of Bazlen's reading habits and editorial alertness, but also shed light on certain passages in his fiction and notes.

Bazlen was that rarest of beings: a private intellectual. The texts collected in this book are not the contents of other books;

---

61 When several years ago I learned of the existence of a German edition of the novel (*Der Kapitän*) illustrated by the painter Norbert Schwontkowski, I was pleased and, for purely personal reasons, surprised: there is no contemporary painter whose work affects me more. To think that Schwontkowski himself was moved by Bazlen's fiction still seems to me wonderful, but on reflection not so surprising at all. What distinguishes Schwontkowski among his contemporaries is also what distinguishes Bazlen: a concentration on themes (rather than subject matter), on "figures" (rather than naturalistic characters), on life experienced through thought and feeling (rather than life observed by a camera-trained eye). The captain's cabin; the tavern, the One-Eyed Man, the Craterface, and the Peg-leg; the coral atoll; the gray city; the Sirens and their songs; the Girl of the Woods; the burn-marked sewing machine and the blue marks on the captain's wife's body—all of these things are seen, to borrow one of Bazlen's words, "visionarily," as though a spotlight were thrown on what were being depicted.

they are the contents of a suitcase. Like the papers in Pessoa's trunk, they form a living creation in which every part relates to and depends upon the others. This creation remains, not to be dissected, but to be discovered.

—Alex Andriesse

Notes on the Manuscripts

The Sea Captain

IT IS IMPOSSIBLE to establish in exactly what years these texts were written. The only firm point of reference is the date inscribed at the end of an early, cursory draft of the story, consisting of eight typescript pages: October 3–4, 1944. According to the testimonies of Ljuba Blumenthal, Luciano Foà, and Sergio Solmi, it appears that Bazlen devoted himself to this novel in the years immediately following the Second World War: on occasion he read a few pages to friends. During this period the manuscript was voluminous, running to at least four hundred pages. It may be supposed that Bazlen eventually destroyed this draft of the novel and cut it down to some more linear form, as it stands today. In any case, he returned to the book many times, even in the last years of his life. The text published here is made up of the following parts:

(a) a "fair copy" typescript, where one finds, successively, the story of the Captain up to the moment when he is shipwrecked and swallowed by the whale;
(b) several pages, some typed and some handwritten, more fragmentary and more thoroughly corrected, comprising an obviously unfinished draft of the part entitled "Shipwreck," which were found in the same suitcase that contained the "fair copy" typescript;
(c) notebook B, handwritten, in which the story of the

333

Captain is picked up, beginning with the shipwreck and proceeding to the end.

These three parts give us a complete sketch of the Captain's story, told in what is probably a finished form in part (a), and more fragmentarily in parts (b) and (c). The reader will immediately notice a few vacillations and variations in the development of the story: for example, there are two versions of what transpired after the shipwreck. According to the first, contained in the "fair copy" typescript, the Captain is swallowed by the whale and later spit out. According to the second, which is found in the section "Shipwreck" at the beginning of Notebook B, the Captain washes up on a coral island and is eventually saved by a naturalist who lands there to conduct research. But the relationship between the two versions will become clearer if one reads the rest of the fragments, in which, more than once, reference is made to the fact that the Captain's forebear had been swallowed by a whale—though he didn't succeed in getting out, as the Captain, for his part, did. And somewhere in the Appendix there is a reference to the symbolic equivalence between whale and island.

In the Appendix, the reader will find Bazlen's notes on *The Sea Captain*. This appendix is made up of:

(a) Some verso pages of Notebook B, running to the end of the section "Wine," where Bazlen had collected a few notes and sketched the variant of the "Castle of the Grail," which is specularly linked to the "Gray City" of the fragments. These are two necessary wrong solutions on the Captain's road: the modern and the ancient.
(b) Some notes drawn from Notebook D, which make reference to various episodes recounted in typescript (a), often accompanied by annotations pertaining to research to be done, books to read, episodes to develop.

Regarding the book as a whole, it will readily be recognized that Bazlen constantly bore in mind, as a reference, the schema of the *Odyssey*. The reader will find explicit comments on the *Odyssey* in the section "Anti-Odysseus," from Notebook E, in "Notes Without a Text."

Typescript (a) is translated in full. A few doggedly indecipherable passage were excluded from the text, as well as some work notes and a few strictly personal references.

The punctuation of the original has almost always been retained.

Notes Without a Text

Handwritten notes selected from notebooks left behind by Bazlen, and more precisely from those labeled, after his death, with the initials C, E, N, and P.

Notebook E, which has been reproduced almost in full, is the only one that Bazlen organized by theme. A few strictly personal notes have been omitted, along with passages difficult to decipher.

The vintage of these notes is uncertain. Bazlen wrote in Notebook E on many occasions over the course of many years, as is apparent from various references. But notebooks C, N, and P were presumably written in sequence, over a shorter period. In any case, everything published here, with very few exceptions, can be understood as having been written between 1945 and 1965.

Editorial Letters

This selection of opinions on works and authors has been taken from the letters written by Bazlen in his capacity as consultant to the publishing house Einaudi, from 1951 until the summer of 1962, and thereafter to Adelphi, founded that year with a program on which he left, in a determining sense, his mark.

To these opinions are added some letters written directly to Sergio Solmi in this same period regarding books and themes that are also mentioned in those sent to the two publishers.

In the texts as presented here, certain passages that deal with practical matters or that are of a strictly personal and private nature have been omitted. The titles that precede each report are almost always reproduced here exactly as they appeared in the letter.

—RC